CONSEQUENCES

Gillian Wells

Printed in Australia
Cover design by Shawline Publishing Group Pty Ltd
First Printing: November 2021

Shawline Publishing Group Pty Ltd
www.shawlinepublishing.com.au

Paperback ISBN- 9781922594587
Ebook ISBN- 9781922594570

A catalogue record for this book is available from the National Library of Australia

To all the foster parents and carers of abused children and to those people who nurture and heal them.

Chapter 1

'RACHEL! DADDY! WHERE ARE YOU? COME QUICK!'

Ben was shouting, then Emma joined in. Rachel, who was out the front tending to her roses, heard them and, putting down her secateurs, started to run in their direction. 'Whatever's the matter?'

'It's Ruby. There's a brown snake in the chooks run, and she is trying to kill it! Quick, before it gets her.' Both children were getting very tearful and upset. Then there was a loud bang, and the three of them ran around the house and up the path to the chooks' pen. Mike was standing there holding the dead snake up by its tail, and Ruby, the lovely red cattle dog, was running about. She looked pleased with herself. Under his other arm, Mike had the gun with which he had despatched the snake.

The children immediately made a fuss of Ruby and also fired questions at their father. How come he'd known about the snake? How easy was it to shoot it and not hurt Ruby? It was a few minutes before Rachel could get a word in edgeways.

'Time for a nice cool drink, and maybe calm down, then we'll go out to the swimming hole. What do you think?'

Both children nodded enthusiastically and rushed off into the house. Mike dumped the dead snake by the door into the chooks' run and grinned at Rachel. 'Never a dull moment with these two around, is there, sweetheart?'

Rachel laughed, 'Not on your life. But it's so good to have them here. I just hope when their mother and Keith come, it will be alright.'

'Course it will, darlin' don't worry.'

But Rachel was rather worried. Since she and Mike had married almost five years before, they had worked hard to make their Braham Cattle stud a success. Mike had been left quite a substantial amount of money by a bachelor uncle, and they had poured most of it into their property. One of their projects had been to restore the old homestead, which had been the original house and turn it into a self-catering but plush holiday let. It was advertised in Brisbane to start with, and they had been amazed how popular it already had become as it was still in its infancy.

Mike's children, who lived with their mother Clarissa and stepfather Keith Smith, in Brisbane, had persuaded their mother and Keith to hire the homestead and stay for a week while they were out at the farm staying with their father and Rachel. They were due in two days' time, and Rachel had never met them. Hadn't even spoken to them on the phone.

Before she followed them into the house, Rachel paused a moment and took stock of her surroundings and the people that meant so much to her. Mike and herself hadn't had the easiest start to their relationship. He was five years younger than Rachel and had been a career policeman, though a frustrated cattle breeder too. Rachel's first husband had died of cancer, and they had a child who became a drug dealer and leader of a bikie gang. Rachel had been scared of him. He had threatened to kill her, but it was him who had died in the end. Then there were Mike's children, whom Rachel adored. Emma was thirteen and Ben eleven, and whenever they came to stay, the four of them had a ball as Rachel and Mike spent as much time as they could giving the children the time of their lives. Both had learnt to ride and helped with the cattle. They learnt about straining fences, training dogs, looking after the odd poddy calf. They each had their own horse, and the four of them liked nothing better than riding out to the swimming hole with a picnic and the dogs in tow. Ben had a buckskin called Dusty, Emma had a palomino named Danny.

Mike had bought Rachel's horse, Smokey, as a surprise present a couple of years ago. She was a beautiful dark grey and had been a racehorse but was retired early through injury. She was very well-bred, and the owners had thought to put her in foal as it was felt her foal would be very valuable. However, they hadn't managed it as it seemed as if she was barren, so they gave up, disenchanted with the whole business. Mike had got her for a very reasonable price. She looked what she was, a creature of class.

The house looked beautiful. It had been freshly painted last year when they did the old house up, and both were white, with green trim. Rachel's veggie patch at the back and rose garden at the front were at the moment thriving as the rain had been plentiful lately. The paddocks were green, with the cattle dotted about, horses too. The tall gums, the deep blue sky and in the distance the hills that looked to be shimmering in the heat haze. *I'm so lucky,* Rachel thought.

Later, as she clambered into bed, Mike reached for her as he always did. Sometimes to make love, sometimes just to cuddle. He said, 'Rach, if are you really worried about Clarrie and Keith coming, I can try to put them off.'

'No way, they are paying like everyone else. Perhaps I'm just getting old.

'Old!' he clicked his tongue, and his words were slightly muffled as he pressed his lips to her neck. 'Listen here, woman, I won't have that sort of talk. You'll never be old to me. I'll show you just how young you make me feel!' With that, Mike started to caress her, and Rachel forgot all her misgivings. Their lovemaking hadn't diminished at all in the five years they had been together; it was as fulfilling as ever.

Two days, later the misgivings returned as the time of arrival neared. Keith was a barrister. Clarrie didn't work. She had started out as a law student when Mike had met her, though she had been a mature student, having been unable to make up her mind exactly what she wanted to do. Perhaps she had thought it would be glamorous being a policeman's wife, especially as Mike seemed to be climbing the career ladder with alacrity. But even before Emma had been born, the cracks had been appearing. Mike realised he didn't really love her. They were poles apart. The same went for Clarissa; however, they had remained friends, not close friends, but there was no bitterness or recriminations in their dealings with each other.

Mike had found it hard to accept Keith as his children's stepfather but had come to terms with it over the years. More so since he and Rachel had found each other. He loved her with a passion that had taken him entirely by surprise. It was a deeper emotion than he had ever felt about anyone or anything before. Sometimes his feelings almost made him afraid they were so deep and strong.

The children, too, were like cats on a hot tin roof and couldn't settle to anything even though they knew it would be late afternoon until their mother and stepfather arrived.

Chapter 2

It was nearly sunset before they heard a car coming slowly down the drive towards the house. The children rushed out of the house at top speed. Mike followed them out, but Rachel took her time. She had brushed her hair and put on a dab of lipstick. She was wearing a new pair of shorts and a pretty blue top, but as soon as she saw Clarrie, she felt dowdy. She wasn't quite as tall as Rachel, but she was groomed to perfection. Her platinum blonde hair was immaculate, as were her clothes, shorts and shirt, makeup and blood-red nails. She looked like something out of a fashion magazine. Keith was well dressed, too, but was quite short and bald. He hardly looked like the sort of man to escort Clarissa. He was also rather on the plump side.

The children were dancing around, both speaking at once and wanting to show their mother their horses, the chooks, the dogs, everything they could think of. Mike kissed Clarrie on the cheek, shook hands with Keith, then turned to Rachel, who was still hanging back. It was out of character, but Rachel felt out of her comfort zone and wasn't sure if she should kiss Clarrie or shake hands. Still, it seemed Clarrie was feeling the same, and she held out her hand, then changed her mind and leant toward Rachel as though to kiss her. This gave Rachel the signal she needed, realising Clarrie was as uncomfortable as she was. So she gave Clarrie a small hug and a peck on the cheek before turning to Keith and shaking hands with him.

'Do you prefer to be called Clarrie or Clarissa?' she asked.

Clarrie laughed, 'What does Mike call me when he's talking to you? Apart from a pain, that is.' To some, that might have sounded bitter or nasty, but Clarrie said it with such mirth dancing in her eyes it made Rachel laugh. 'Clarrie.'

'No-one except for Keith here calls me Clarissa. He has this thing about shortening names.'

Keith shrugged and didn't respond.

'Now, would you like a drink of some sort or go straight to the house? 'said Mike, who had stood watching this exchange with a bemused expression on his face.

'But we want to show mummy round, and Keith too' Emma looked mutinous.

'Yes, yes, please' Ben joined in.

Clarrie bent down to pat Ruby, who, after being told that their visitors were acceptable, had been sitting quietly watching the proceedings. 'Darlings, we are exhausted, and it's getting dark or will be soon. We'll save it all for tomorrow, okay?'

'No, it's not fair. We want to show you now!' Ben wailed.

'NO. You heard what your mother said.' Keith sounded very authoritative.

Mike opened his mouth to speak, then shut it again and turned towards the house. The children looked as if they would make a fuss, but having snuck a look at Rachel, who shook her head slightly, followed on behind. Rachel fell into step beside Clarrie, and that left Keith to bring up the rear.

'Have you ever been out this way before?' Rachel asked Clarrie.

'No, I've never been this far west before. We tend to go to the coast or abroad when we travel. I'm sure the kids have told you.'

'Yes, but I wasn't sure if you had been this way when you were younger.'

'No, I'm essentially a city girl. This will be a new experience!'

Rachel wondered for the umpteenth time what Carrie and Keith would make of their home. She was confident they would like the old homestead as it was done to a high standard. Their house wasn't grand but clean, fresh and comfortable. As they had entered through the front door, they had the passageway to walk down to the kitchen, where Mike and Rachel spent most of their time when indoors. It had an old but reliable range, a large table in the middle of the room, and a big cosy sofa. Rachel used to have an armchair by the range, but when Mike came to live there, they decided a sofa was more companionable. With large windows and a door leading out onto the back verandah, it was light and airy. Clarrie turned to Rachel, 'What a lovely country kitchen,' she said.

Rachel was pleased. She decided there and then she quite liked Clarrie even though she had been prepared to dislike her. Keith was another matter and looked like a fish out of water. He stood in the doorway looking as if he would like to make a run for it.

'It's late enough in the day, I think,' said Mike brandishing a bottle of wine he got from the fridge.

Minutes later, they were all sitting around the table, the children with homemade lemonade. Rachel watched Keith out of the corner of her eye. He took a sip of wine and all but screwed up his nose, then proceeded to look hard at the bottle. Clarrie, who was sitting beside him, put her hand on his arm as he seemed about to speak. She talked to the children mostly as they were feeling very important and dying to show their mother around. Rachel sat watching as Mike tried to engage Keith in conversation but soon gave up. Finally, after only having a few sips of his wine, Keith stood up. 'I think we should go to our cottage or whatever you call it before it gets too dark.'

Clarrie looked up and, seeing his expression agreed, Mike said he would show them the way. Of course, the children wanted to go too, so soon after, Rachel found herself alone.

Going out to feed the dogs and shut the chooks in their coop, she thought about the Smith family. She instinctively didn't like Keith. She knew the children didn't really like him though they seemed to tolerate him. Clarrie, whom she hadn't expected to like she did, *how surprising things are sometimes*, she thought.

When Mike and the children returned, they were full of Clarrie and Keith's reactions; and what they had said. Rachel only half-listened as she was occupied readying their evening meal and worrying about Mike's horse, who had gone very lame earlier that day for no apparent reason.

However, finally getting into bed that night, she suddenly said, 'I gather from what you said Clarrie was pleased but Keith not so much with the accommodation?'

'I always thought he was a grumpy bastard, partly by what the kids have said. I suppose he gives Clarrie everything she wants, and the kids don't want for anything. '

'Material things are okay, but children need love and understanding as well. By the way, I'm worried about Jock. That lameness seems to have come out of nowhere. There seems no reason for it' Mike's horse had been seen by the children earlier that day hobbling around the paddock.

'Mmmmm, I need some love and understanding too,' said Mike, ignoring her comment about Jock, in favour of brushing his lips against her neck.

Chapter 3

Mike was true to his promise and, with the children, gave Clarrie and Keith a conducted tour of the farm the next day. He could tell Keith was bored out of his brain within ten minutes, but Clarrie was more interested. However, the children were disappointed she didn't want to be driven out to the swimming hole. Rachel and Mike had put a spa in at the old homestead, and she stated she would be using that. Mike drove her back, Keith having walked back earlier. The children opted to stay and have morning tea with their mother and would walk to the main house when they were ready.

Mike and Rachel then got on with tending to Jock. His hoof was hot, so Mike pulled his shoe off, and after paring the hoof back, a bit of black pus shot out of a tiny hole. 'At least we know now. Must have got a small piece of grit or something under the shoe which worked its way in,' said Rachel. 'We'll poultice that, and he'll soon come good.'

Over the next few days, the children divided their time between the two houses, though they spent more time with Rachel and Mike. 'Keith is so boring Daddy, he's either on his computer or reading. He doesn't want to come and see the horses or anything. At least mummy has been for a walk and things.' Ben sounded frustrated.

'He's a busy man, mate; I expect he has work to do.' Mike found himself sticking up for Keith. 'Internet is pretty patchy out here, which must be frustrating.' Rachel commented.

The week seemed to fly by. Rachel and Mike had Jock to attend to, and the cows with young calves had to be moved to a fresh paddock. The children wanted to help as usual, but in the end, it was only Emma who helped. Clarrie and Keith went into town to explore, and Ben wanted to go too. Then there were all the other jobs they had to see to. As the week was drawing to a close, Mike asked, 'do you think you could stand it if we gave a barbeque and invite them down on their last night?'

Rachel smiled at him, then put her arms around his neck and gave him a quick kiss, 'yes, of course, why not, it hasn't been so bad.'

Mike hugged her to him, then they heard a small cough behind them and, turning, saw Clarrie standing just inside the kitchen doorway. 'Sorry to interrupt, I was wondering if you'd like to come and eat with us on our last night?'

'We were thinking along the same lines,' Rachel said, 'Would you like a coffee or tea? We were about to have one.'

Clarrie came into the room and sat down. Rachel was slightly amused as she noticed Clarrie wasn't wearing so much makeup, nor was her hair quite so well-groomed. 'It's been very restful out here for us, but I have to say I'll be glad to go home. Nothing against this place or you, but it's too quiet for me and so lonely! How did you manage Rachel after your first husband died?'

A shadow passed over Rachel's face. She didn't want to remember how frightened she'd been of Johnny after her husband had died. Or her son's threats, Mike's involvement, her anger at Mike and at Johnny. Though fear had been the main emotion when dealing with her son. He had come close to killing her but had lost his life instead. She'd never know if he would have taken her life, and she didn't dwell on it. She lived for the now, her happiness with Mike exceeded anything she had ever known before, and she firmly believed that looking back was a waste of time.

'I managed Clarrie. There are things that need doing out here that require two people or a bit of brawn, but Sid and Norma next door were always ready to lend a hand if I wanted help.'

'And you've got me now, haven't you, sweetheart?' Mike gave her another quick hug.

Clarrie felt a frisson of jealously. Mike had never behaved like that with her, nor did Keith. She recognised that Mike and Rachel were as close as any couple she'd ever seen and wondered if they knew how lucky they were.

Over coffee, they decided that Mike would cook a barbeque and Clarrie would contribute a salad. The rest was up to Rachel. She was happy with that and told Clarrie she would get Emma to help her.

'Emma, help? How do you get her to do that? She never wants to help me!'

'I expect she will. It's just so different out here. Everyone helps with jobs all the time. Anyway, she is growing up fast.'

'Yes, we always called her Em, but she gets very cranky if you do that now.'

Rachel smiled, 'We noticed.'

The barbeque was a success. Even Keith seemed more relaxed, though Rachel thought it was because he was going home tomorrow. The children were going back with them as the long summer holidays were just about over. The following day was Australia Day, but Mike pointed out they didn't do much out of the ordinary on the farm. Often there were important jobs to see to, anyway.

The next morning the children were subdued as they always were when they had to go back to the city; they both loved the outdoor lifestyle they had out at the farm. Life in the city seemed so dull to them. So they tried to spin out breakfast, packing, everything they could for just a little longer. When Keith and Clarrie drove to the house, they weren't even half ready, much to Keith's annoyance.

When finally they had disappeared down the drive, Mike put his arm around Rachel, 'How about a coffee and a few minutes to ourselves? It always seems so full-on when the kids are here and with Clarrie and Keith in the mix… well, not sure I could have hung in there much longer.'

Rachel laughed at him and gave him a little shove, 'They're your kids and ex and partner; how do you think I feel? Actually, I love the children to bits, but it is nice to have the place to ourselves again.'

'Ummm, I'm thinking maybe I need a little lie-down, how about you?'

'In your dreams, lover boy, there's work to be done. But I'm up for the coffee part.'

Mike grinned, 'It was worth a try. After all, it is a Bank Holiday. '

'I suppose, but we didn't check the two bores yesterday out towards the forestry, and then there's Jock to see to, and the fence down by the gully wants fixing and—'Mike stopped her with a kiss.

'I get the message, darlin'. We also need to ring my folks and let them know we are planning a visit soon.'

Chapter 4

A couple of weeks later, Mike and Rachel set off to visit Mike's parents and family. Rachel hadn't had any other help, but once Mike and herself were settled, they had hired a couple to live in a little cottage that was at the far end of the main buildings. They were of retirement age, but the man, Ted, was still up for doing odd jobs, and it meant there was always someone on hand when Rachel and Mike went away.

Mike's family lived not far from Blackhall, between there and Barcaldine, off the Matilda Highway. It was a big property, and just as well, as Mike had three brothers as well as his parents, all living there. Of course, they all had their own houses except for Tommy, Mikes eldest brother, who, with his wife Nancy and two children, lived with Mike's parents. Rachel had been very nervous the first time she had been to see them. Partly because of her history with Mike, but she need not have worried. Catherine, Mike's mother, had been very welcoming and kind. They all had, and Rachel had soon become part of the family. They all admired her strength of character and determination and were all happy to welcome her into their lives.

Nancy came out of the house to meet them as they drove up. They had brought Ruby with them; she had been one of a litter of pups born there and always seemed as if she knew this had been her first home.

Nancy and Tommy's children were both grown up now. Their son,

Shawn, had gone to college to train as a vet, and Julia, their daughter, was also away. She was a ranger in a National Park in the Northern Territory.

Nancy gave them both a big hug. 'You both look wonderfully well. I am so pleased to see you, ' she said as she led the way indoors.

'How're the oldies?' Mike asked as he followed the women, heaving their bags with him.

'Not so much of the old, young Michael,' a voice said behind them. They all turned around, and Mike's father gave him a big hug and pat on the back before enveloping Rachel in a bear hug too. Henry Grimshaw was a big man in every sense of the word. Tall, broad, with a booming voice and generous nature, Rachel was very fond of him and gave him an equally big hug back. 'Mike's just being cheeky as usual,' she said.

Mike's mother, Catherine, appeared from the large open plan living area.

'Cheeky? Mike? I can't believe that!' she said, hugging her son, then Rachel. She was as small as her husband was large, and as she got older, she seemed to get tinier and tinier. She was an identical twin, though her twin brother had died six years before, and Catherine had been taken ill at the same time. The doctors had never really been able to put their fingers on what was wrong with her, but she had recovered. Though perhaps with less vigour than before.

Now she threaded her arm through Rachel's. 'My dear, you look well. How are you? It's so good to see you.' All this was said in a rush. It was the same way Mike spoke sometimes. When Rachel first got to know him, she was surprised to find that, unlike in person, on the telephone, he was always brief. Catherine tended to be the same, but face to face, she was very chatty. 'How are my two beautiful Grandchildren?' she now asked, looking over her shoulder at Mike, who was already talking cattle with his father. Before Rachel and Mike had got together, Catherine and Henry had only seen the children a couple of times. They had only met Clarrie when Mike and her married. Mike had always come out alone to see his parents after the wedding. Consequently, Mike had only managed to take the children out to his parents for a couple of brief visits when they were smaller. Now, when they were staying with Mike and Rachel, they came at least twice a year. Clarrie liked the children to be with her at Christmas, so they hadn't come out to see the Grimshaw's lately.

Though it was only three months, somehow it felt longer since they had last visited. Now Rachel looked at her mother-in-law with concern. She seemed smaller than ever. Leaving her concerns aside, Rachel began by relating all the latest news of the children and also her first meeting with Clarrie.

'What about—what's his name? Her husband—Kevin? What's he like?'

'It's Keith. I didn't see much of him; none of us did, really. The kids got fed up with him as he just wasn't interested in anything, just sat indoors most of the time.'

'Hmmph. What about Clarissa? Did you see much of her?'

'She looked at the animals and went for a few walks. The kids spent some time with her too, which was good. I didn't see much of her, but she was alright; not disagreeable or anything.'

'I should think not!'

Mike touched Rachel's arm, 'I'm just going out with Dad to see this new bull. Do you want to come, sweetheart?'

Rachel shook her head, 'It'll be dark soon. I can wait till tomorrow. I'm off to have a shower in any case in a minute.'

Later, as Mike got into bed beside her, Rachel said, 'I don't think your Mum looks that well. What do you think?'

Gathering Rachel into his arms, he said, 'I am sorry to say I didn't really notice, darlin'. Mike frowned. 'Maybe she's been doing too much. She sometimes forgets she isn't as young as she was'.

Rachel had difficulty getting to sleep that night as Catherine had worried her. She had looked so tired and pale. Rachel resolved to get to the bottom of it in the morning if she could.

Chapter 5

The next morning was very busy. Mike wanted Rachel to see the new bull, then Henry wanted them both to look at some young heifers, and Nancy wanted Rachel to go shopping in Barcaldine with her. Rachel tried to do everything that was asked of her, but it made them late leaving for their shopping trip. Then, to Nancy and Rachel's surprise, Catherine announced she would like to come with them. She had been asked many times in the past but always said, 'No, you young things go on your own.' Rachel and Nancy were always amused by this, as Rachel was now in her mid-fifties, and Nancy was fast approaching her sixties. Catherine, of course, was in her eighties but until recently had always seemed younger.

It was lunchtime by the time they got there, and as they were all hungry, they decided to have lunch first. Once they were settled at a table and had ordered their food, Catherine cleared her throat and said she had something very important to say.

'Please hear me out, my dears and don't interrupt. This is hard enough without you saying anything until the end.' Nancy and Rachel braced themselves mentally, almost half guessing what Catherine was about to say.

'A few weeks ago, having felt very tired for some time, I finally went to the doctor. Henry didn't come with me, and so far, I haven't told him exactly what was said. Anyway, I had to have a blood test, then other tests, and it seems as if my number will be up soon. I have cancer.' Catherine held up a hand as Rachel opened her mouth to speak. The older woman's eyes were flinty, and her shoulders squared as she continued. 'I told Henry a fib. He knows nothing about me seeing a specialist or how bad it is. They tell me it has spread too far, and an operation is unlikely to help. I have managed to keep it to myself because I don't want anyone fussing around me.' Her eyes twinkled as she laid her hand over Nancy's, where it rested on the table. 'You two are my favourite daughters-in-law. I love the others, of course, but feel closer to the two of you. I wanted to tell you first and get you to make everyone else understand my position. I do not want any fuss nor hospital. I want to die at home. Now, will you back me when I tell everyone?'

By now, Nancy had tears running down her face, and Rachel was fighting hard to keep her tears in check, too. Rachel had a feeling of déjà vu. It brought back all the memories of her first husband, Sam, who had died of cancer seven years before.

Both women clasped Catherine's hands, 'Oh no, can't they do something? Surely they can.' said Nancy.

'No, my dear, I don't want to go through an operation at my age. I'm not at all sure I could cope, and the doctors' feel the same. My heart isn't so strong now, and the whole thing....' Catherine trailed off and shook her head. 'This is why I've told you two I want you to back me up. I know I will get a lot of pressure from everyone else, mostly Henry, but the others too.'

Just then, their food arrived, but all they did was pick at it; none of them had an appetite.

Catherine laid down the fork that she had been poking her food with. She put her hand on Rachel's arm. 'Rachel, you above all the others must know what it's like; for the family, I mean, not me.'

Rachel was fighting hard to keep her emotions in check. It was bringing the terrible time of Sam's illness, death, and everything else that followed back.

'Catherine, this is so sad. Are you sure?' She finally croaked, her mouth was dry, and her throat was closed up.

'Yes dear, there is no doubt.' Her eyes fixed on Rachels' as she repeated her question, 'Will you back me? I don't want to go through an operation and chemo then die anyway. I want to enjoy what time I have left.'

Rachel nodded. 'If you are sure that is what you want, of course, I will be as supportive as I can. Sam's illness took us both by surprise, and he actually died much quicker than the Doctors predicted.' Rachel's eyes were swimming in tears as she said this.

Nancy had sat with the tears hardly in check, looking from one to the other, now she spoke up. 'If this is what you want, Catherine, I will try to make the family understand though it will be hard. You are so important to us all.'

'Henry will be the hardest to convince. He is so remarkably fit for his age and never seems to be ill, though he gets the odd aches and pains.'

They finished their meal, that is to say, as well as they could. Then Catherine announced she had a couple of errands to run and she would meet them at the car in an hour.

Nancy and Rachel looked at each other. 'What do you want to do now, shop?' Rachel asked.

Nancy shook her head, 'I feel as if I've had the ground taken out from under my feet. The last thing I feel like doing is going shopping.'

'Let's go and sit under the Tree of Knowledge shelter and talk then, shall we? I don't feel like shopping either.'

So, having made their way there, the two of them sat down. For some minutes, they sat quietly, then Nancy said. 'How was it, Rachel, with your husband? We've never talked about it. I just know he died of cancer and that your son was a bad lot. Sorry, I—'

'Tsk,' Rachel cut her off, 'I have always tried to move forward as I am a firm believer there is no point in dwelling on the past. You can't change it. Sam was in denial there was anything wrong and typically wouldn't do anything about it until it was advanced. He had a spell in hospital then came home for Christmas. The family were all there, and he died Boxing Day. It was almost as if he had planned it that way. Even the doctors were surprised at how quickly he went. The good thing was that he didn't suffer too much. It was over so quickly.'

'How did you manage though, Rachel? It must have been awful.'

'Yes, it was desperately sad. Sam thought he had time to sort all our affairs out, but it all landed on my shoulders as he ran out of time. I thought I would have to sell and then, of course, there was Johnny. '

They sat in silence then for a time. Nancy didn't know the full story of how Johnny terrorised his mother, and she wasn't sure what to say now. It was the most Rachel had ever said about her first husband. Mike had always been protective when any of them had asked questions and said it was Rachel's business.

Rachel now spoke again. 'Silly, I know, but one of the times I was at the lowest was after Johnny had paid a late-night visit and my old dog had gone ballistic. I thought Jonny would hurt her, so I shut her up. When I finally went to let her out, she was very distressed and died. I sat nursing her, and for a time there, I gave up. I was just so tired of everything. Then Mike turned up. We hadn't known each other long, but I think that is when I fell in love with him; he was so kind and gentle.'

'Mike told Tommy he fell in love with you when he first saw you, but he reckoned you were a formidable woman!'

Rachel smiled then and put her arm across Nancy's shoulders. 'Come on, we'll get through this. Catherine is the formidable one, I think.'

Chapter 6

That evening, the whole family gathered as had been arranged. As always, when Mike and Rachel came to visit, they had a good get-together. Rachel had avoided Mike as much as she could since they returned from town; she didn't want to say anything, feeling it was Catherine's place to tell them her sad news. Mike had looked at her intently a few times. He had picked up there was something but knew he would know soon enough.

They had a barbeque and were all sitting around with drinks. Some soft, some alcoholic when Catherine got to her feet and banged on the big wooden table they were seated at.

'I have something to say. Henry, can you come and stand with me, please? This isn't easy.'

Henry got to his feet, looking alarmed, 'What is it, Cath?'

'Henry, forgive me for not telling you before everyone else, but the truth is I had to give myself time to come to terms with this, and it was easier for me to do that alone.'

'Christ woman, get to the point, will you.'

Catherine took his big hand in hers and, with a wobbly voice, said, 'I have cancer and can only expect another six months or so.' With that, she buried her head against Henry and started to cry.

Everyone sat in stunned silence, then all started to speak at once. For a few minutes, there was quite a hubbub until Henry raised his hand. 'Quiet! If you want to say something, then please, everyone take it in turns. Let us hear your view. I am actually going to say that Cath is, of course, looking on the black side. She will have the best treatment money can buy.'

Cath pulled away from him, tears flowing but a determined expression on her face. 'No, Henry, you don't understand. I'm not having any kind of operation or treatment. It's too far advanced. Anyway, I want to enjoy what time I have left, not spend it feeling ill and miserable.'

Again silence, then Jacob spoke up. He was the second eldest. 'I reckon if that is what Mum wants to do, then it's her life' he shrugged, looking very emotional. Trish, his wife, put her arms around him and hugged him, saying nothing. Their two boys Ian and Bob, just sat there looking bewildered. They were in their early teens and didn't know what to think.

Then the third son, David's wife Wendy, spoke up. 'Don't be silly Catherine, there must be something they can do. You are just being selfish.'

Nancy and Mike both spoke at once. 'Selfish?!'

'How do you make that out, Wendy? What do you mean by that?' Mike sounded furious.

Wendy had the grace to look uncomfortable, 'Well, perhaps selfish wasn't quite the right word, but we all will have to look after Catherine and Henry and…' her words trailed away, as she looked around and saw that no one was agreeing with her.

Rachel stood, 'I know I haven't been part of this family that long, but I do know a little of what you are all going through. I kind of know what you will experience in the coming weeks and months. It won't be easy for anyone, but from what I can gather, I think Catherine is being very brave and, in some ways, positive. It's her life, as Jacob said, and I think we should all respect her decision.'

When she sat down again beside Mike, he put his arm around her and gave her a quick kiss, saying quietly, 'Well done, darlin'."

They all sat on for a time, but it was quieter now. Her sons and their wives all gathered around Catherine and Henry and talked quietly. Rachel sat apart a little. She felt slightly like an outsider. Not because she was the newest member of the family, but because she had been through a similar situation with Sam and knew more of what to expect.

It was some time later that Mike and she had a chance to speak together. The gathering had gone on well past bedtime, and everyone went their separate ways, feeling sad and unsettled. Rachel was just getting undressed when Mike came into their bedroom, and without a word, he gathered her into his arms. Rachel realised he was crying. She hitched them across to the bed and sat Mike down, still with his head buried into her breast.

For a time, they sat thus until finally, Mike got himself under control.

'Oh, Rach, this is terrible.' I can't imagine how we'll all cope without Mum. Don't you get ill too.'

Rachel smiled at him gently, 'not if I can help it, mate.' she said.

Chapter 7

The rest of their stay passed quite swiftly. Rachel spent a lot of time talking with Catherine and Henry as they were trying to come to terms with what was happening. Catherine was very upbeat and positive, though Henry was struggling, as were other members of the family.

Wendy, however, seemed quite hostile and almost accused Rachel of planting the idea of no treatment in Catherine's head. This happened two days before they were due to go home when Jacob and Trish had invited Mike and Rachel, David and Wendy over for dinner. Craig, Wendy and David's youngest had come too. He was very different from his siblings. Christine and John were dark like the rest of the Grimshaw family, whereas Craig was very blonde and slight. He was like his mother with gingery blonde hair and a pale complexion. He was now twelve years old but seemed much younger, and in Wendy's eyes, he could do no wrong.

The evening started off all right, and the conversation flowed easily enough. Although Catherine was at the back of everyone's mind. Then in a lull, Wendy suddenly said, 'I take it you'll be on hand Rachel when Catherine is confined to bed. Goodness knows the rest of us have enough to do.'

There was silence around the room until gathering himself, David said, 'Wendy, this isn't the time or place.'

But she said, 'Well, Rachel seems to think she's the expert, so I took it as she had given Catherine the idea, she could do the nursing.'

Mike pushed his chair back, but Rachel forestalled him, putting her hand on his arm.

'I will do anything that Catherine requires of me certainly, as I am sure *all* members of the family will. As for putting the idea in her head, Catherine is very much her own woman, and she had made up her mind before we all knew.'

'Really!' But Wendy got no further, David stood up.

'Time we went, I think Craig is falling asleep by the looks of things'

They all stood, and Rachel noted Wendy was the same height as David though twice as broad. She had put on weight lately. Rachel didn't remember her being so belligerent before, though she didn't know her that well. She felt sorry for David, who was obviously embarrassed.

Craig, however, had other ideas. 'I want more ice cream, ' he said peevishly, looking around.

'Sorry mate, we're going home.' said David.

'He can have some more if he wants it, can't he?' Wendy still sounded angry, but she sat down again and patted her son's back.

For a moment or two, David looked as if he would follow through with going home, then having visibly wavered, he sat down again too. 'You'd better ask Auntie Trish if you would like some more then, Craig.'

Craig held his bowl out towards Trish, 'I'd like more ice cream, Auntie Trish.'

Trish was looking annoyed by now 'there is a word that goes with that Craig, what is it?'

'Please.'

'Ok, you can have more since your mother said you could.' Trish looked at Wendy with a slight frown on her face.

Wendy just glanced at Trish but said nothing. Watching this exchange, Rachel realised that the two women didn't like each other at all. It was a pity, she reflected as the three brothers got on really well, and everyone loved Henry and Catherine. Or did they? Rachel thought she sensed undercurrents she hadn't noticed before. She looked at Mike, who winked at her, everyone quiet now, all feeling embarrassed at the exchange. The silence continued, all busy with their own thoughts, Craig noisily spooning the ice cream up.

Jacob asked Mike about the newest bull that they had. He knew the answer to the question already, but it was the best he could come up with to break the tension around the table.

The conversation got back onto safer ground, but the tension simmered below the surface, and after another twenty minutes or so, Craig had finished his ice cream, and David stood once more saying, 'come on, time to go.'

Again, everyone stood, and Mike said, 'Rachel and I will head off now too, won't we darlin'

Rachel nodded in agreement. The evening had gone sour, and she just wanted to go back to the main house and go to bed.

They had walked as it wasn't that far, and it was a beautiful, warm night. Rachel thought it would have been romantic if her thoughts, and she suspected Mike's, weren't busy with the events of the evening.

'Wendy seems to be David's boss.' Rachel finally broke the silence.

'Like all women, I reckon,' but as he said this, Mike sidestepped, knowing Rachel would take a friendly swipe at him. It was a subject they had talked about before, though not seriously.

'Actually, sweetheart Dad is worried about David and Wendy. He thinks she gives David a really hard time. He's noticed how she spoils Craig and is turning him into a horrible little kid.'

'I agree.' By this time, they had reached the main house. Nancy was still up, mending a pair of Tommy's jeans, though everyone else had gone to bed.

'You're back in good time. Look at this; they are practically brand new. Honestly, that man!'

'Wendy was feeling very unpleasant. So yes, the evening broke up quite early,' said Mike.

'Oh, how's that then? What did she say?'

Rachel and Mike filled her in on Wendy's comments. Rachel ended by saying that on reflection, it wasn't that bad. 'Sweetheart, she had an unnecessary go at you. I won't have it' Mike sounded angry again.

'For what it's worth,' Nancy interjected, 'I think her problem is that she is jealous of you and perhaps you too, Mike.'

'But why?' Mike and Rachel spoke at once.

'The list, as I see it, is long.' She set the now mended pair of jeans aside and steepled her fingers under her chin. 'First of all, Rachel, you are a very attractive woman, and you, Mike, are far more dynamic than poor old David. You were left your Uncle's entire estate, so you have money that maybe Wendy thought David should have had a share of. Also, you have a wonderful relationship. Anyone can see that you are totally besotted with each other, and it hasn't diminished even after five years or so; it's as if you're still on your honeymoon.'

Both Rachel and Mike looked sheepish at this, 'Sorry, are we that bad?' Rachel was blushing.

'Don't be silly. It's wonderful to see, especially after your rocky start. You are very lucky people; not everyone has such a close bond.'

Mike gave one of his rare smiles, 'on that note, it's bedtime, I think.' Taking hold of Rachel's hand, he winked at his sister-in-law and together, they disappeared. Nancy watching them go and gave a little sigh. They seemed to be made for each other.

Chapter 8

Two days later, Mike and Rachel were heading home. The goodbyes with Catherine were the hardest, even though she and Henry were planning on coming down to stay with them for a few days soon. They hadn't seen Wendy again, but David had come over, saying Wendy had a bad headache and was lying down. Trish audibly huffed. She had gone out of her way to be friendly with Rachel, as had Nancy and, of course, Catherine, when Rachel had first met the family. Now looking back, Rachel realised Wendy had always been distant and not that welcoming.

'I don't think Trish is that keen on Wendy, is she?' she asked Mike soon after they set off.

'If I am perfectly honest, no one was keen on Wendy when David first brought her to meet the family. She lived in inner-city Sydney when David met her. He went to some big beef promotion thing down there. Tom and Dad went too. Jacob was due to go, and David was supposed to be staying home to look after everything. I was in Brisbane then, enjoying the novelty of being a copper. Anyway, Jacob had a crashing fall off a horse and broke his leg, so he couldn't go. I think Wendy was serving in some bar or another. She had a part-time job and was training to be a beautician. Somehow or other, David and her ended up staying the night together. David was very shy around girls, and I think she was the first he'd had. Dad and Jacob had gone back to the hotel early. Dad always said he wished he hadn't! Anyway, it wasn't long before she turned up here; she said she wanted to help out. Nancy was struggling with Julia and Shawn at the time, and well, you kind of know the rest.'

Rachel sat mulling this over for a time. 'Doesn't sound as if poor old David had much chance once she rocked up here.'

'No, I don't think Nancy was even that keen either, but both the children were going through a difficult time. They were only toddlers, close in age, and Mum was very busy as ever. Trish and Jacob had just got married. Their house was being built, but they were living at the main house too, which was overcrowded, and there was Wendy being so helpful!

Rachel smiled at Mike, 'Funny how things happen. I'm so glad you were sent to investigate Johnny's gang.'

It was the first time Rachel had ever said anything like that, and Mike pulled the car onto the side of the road. 'What's the matter?' Rachel looked alarmed. Mike leant across and kissed her long and hard before she had a chance to say more.

When he came up for air, he said, 'God Woman, I do love you. What you said just now, well it was good to hear it.'

Rachel smiled. 'Oh, Mike, that is silly, of course, I'm glad. What made you think I wasn't? We've been together long enough now surely for you to know I am happy the way things turned out.'

'I know, but we don't really talk about those times, do we? We always skirt 'round it.'

Rachel looked down at her hands and the beautiful sapphire ring and gold band on her left hand. 'You're right, but I don't want to be reminded about what a fool I was to turn against you, even if it was very short-lived. I don't really want to think about Johnny either. It's passed and gone like he has. Mike, I don't regret any of it, only how stupid I was to nearly lose you.'

After another long kiss, they resumed their journey home. Although they were sad about Catherine, there was so much they were happy about it made her illness easier to cope with.

All was well on their return. Ruby was pleased to be home and raced across the paddock to inspect the horses as she always did. It made Mike and Rachel laugh, and as they stood on the verandah watching her, the telephone rang. It was Norma from the property next door.

'Good, I'm glad you're back. We wondered if you and Mike would like to come for dinner tomorrow night?' she said to Rachel after the greetings were over.

'Yes, that would be good, thanks. Any special reason? We only came over just before we went to Mike's parents.'

'Yes, but we'll talk tomorrow night. Good to know you are home safe and sound, must go, bye.'

'See you.' Rachel was frowning as she replaced the receiver, and Mike, who was still watching Ruby, turned and saw her expression. 'Something up?'

'Not sure. Norma asked us for dinner and said they had something to talk about, but she wouldn't say what. It was just a strange conversation. She hurried off the phone too, not like Norma.'

'Well, we'll find out tomorrow. Now, what's for dinner? I'm hungry.'

Chapter 9

The next evening, Rachel and Mike set out for the Newberry's place next door. It was further by road, but they went the more direct route across their property and through a gate in the fence line.

Now they were into autumn, the days were getting shorter, and the sun had almost set as they started out. The trees and distant hills were tinted pink and gold, and it was so still it was almost as if they were driving through an enormous painting.

'You know what?' Mike said quietly, 'I never, never want to leave this place. I want to die here peacefully one day when I'm old and grey. It's just so beautiful. I think even then, I will be sad to leave.'

Rachel felt tears pricking her eyes. She knew exactly what Mike meant. She just patted his arm but said nothing. They were so in tune she didn't need to speak.

Sid and Norma Newberry were excellent hosts, and soon after they arrived, they sat down to a great spread. Norma always over catered, so she would send her guests home with leftovers. Over the years, Rachel had learnt not to protest. Even now she had Mike, Norma couldn't resist sending her home with goodies. When Rachel had lived alone, she had been very pleased with this generosity so felt it would be churlish to refuse it now.

'Now, I rather think you have something important to tell us?' Mike said.

When they got there, Rachel had thought Sid looked worried. There was something really bugging him. She had known him ever since she had married Sam over thirty years before, and Norma and Sid had been wonderful neighbours.

'Two things really,' said Sid, 'the first being that I have been diagnosed with Prostate Cancer. It's in the early stages, so I should be right, but it's been rather a shock. I have always been so fit, hardly ever ill, now this, it's a bugger.'

Mike and Rachel both went to speak, but Sid continued, 'there's more. The other day, young Jim was checking the boundary fences and found a place where the fence had been cut and peeled back. Large enough to get a truck through. Checking further along the fence where it joins your place, he found another section where the fence had been cut. In both spots, the fence was put back roughly but can be undone very quickly. We reckon cattle duffers, have you got many clean skins, that's what they will be after?'

Rachel had a memory of her and Mike talking or rather joking about cattle duffers years ago, but this was serious.

'We have a few, but they are up nearer the house. Being away and with the children staying, we've got a bit behind branding them… I'll take a look tomorrow. You will have spoken to Josh?' Mike said.

Josh was the local police sergeant and married to Sid and Norma's daughter, Annie.

'Yes, Josh is coming out tomorrow. He was coming before, but little Karen, his youngest was sick all night, then Mandy took sick. In the end, they all did, including Josh, and I said we didn't really want his bug or whatever it is.'

'No, none of us want one of those horrible stomach bugs. I'll have a good look 'round. I think Ted would have noticed if anything was amiss; he hasn't said. Can you hazard a guess how big the truck is?' Mike had his policeman's hat on, even though it was six years or so since he had left the force.

Sid shook his head, 'Nope, no tracks or anything, but then it's too dry now for there to be any. I was going on the size of the fence opening.'

They talked some more and speculated about who might be involved but couldn't actually think it was anyone local. What surprised them was where the duffers had made the first hole; although it came off a public track, it was one which was hardly ever used and had become fairly overgrown in recent years. It led off the back road, which again wasn't used that much. 'Someone who has a good handle of the layout about here', Mike commented. They talked a bit more about all this, then returned to Sid's diagnoses.

'What are your options Sid?' asked Rachel, who had just sat listening for the most part about the fence cutting and what it might mean. She felt shocked. This was the second person she was close to that had been diagnosed with cancer recently.

'I told them to cut it out, get rid of the damn thing. They said as it was early stage, I didn't need surgery, but I just want to get rid of the bugger, so I am going into hospital next week.'

'How did you find out, Sid? Did you have symptoms?'

'Nah. My brother down in Victoria wasn't well. Turns out he has it bad, so he told me to have a blood test, and you know the rest.'

'Oh, Sid!' Rachel's eyes filled with tears. First Catherine, now Sid. Before that, Sam, but that was getting on for eight years ago.

Norma patted her hand, 'It's okay, Rach, I'm sure we'll be fine.'

'It's just that Catherine has been told she has cancer, it's advanced, and she doesn't want treatment, and there was Sam, a while ago, it's just unfair!'

Rachel was seated between Norma and Sid. They both put their arms across her shoulders which ended in rather an uncomfortable moment. But also lightened the mood, and Mike burst out laughing; it looked so comical.

Soon after, they set off across the paddocks home. Mike asked Rachel if they should make a detour to see if they could see any evidence, but Rachel pointed out it was very dark and best to look in the morning.

Chapter 10

The next morning, Mike was up bright and early, ready to investigate the fences and to see if he could find any other evidence that might be out there. Rachel got into the ute beside him, still eating her toast. 'God, Mike, you might let a girl have her breakfast in peace!'

Mike flashed her a quick smile, 'Sorry darlin' places to go, things to see!'

After a bumpy ride, they got to the further paddock where Sid had indicated the fence had been tampered with. Rachel didn't like the part they were going to, as some time before, she had found a dead man there, and it always reminded her of things she would rather forget. That was also the day she had met Mike; he had come out in his capacity as sergeant at the time. To cross to the fence line, they had to cross the creek, and that was the best place to do it. It always depended on how high the water level was; today, it meant going to almost the exact spot. Rachel gave an involuntary shudder.

'You okay, honey?' Mike glanced across at her.

'Yep, fine, a goose walked over my grave, that's all.'

'I always thought it was a ghost, not a goose.'

Rachel gave a little snort, 'I dunno, I'd rather a goose than a ghost, but it was a shiver of some sort.'

Just as they got to the fence line, a police-issued four-wheel-drive appeared coming down the slope from the Newberry's place. Josh was driving, and a young constable that Rachel didn't know sat beside him.

They all got out of their respective cars, and introductions were made with the new policeman.

He looked quite young and was tall and thin with a rather arrogant air about him. When Josh said Mike had been the sergeant before him, he said, 'oh yes, I've heard about you. Got involved with a woman and lost your job. No longer a copper.'

The other three stood rooted to the spot, then Josh cleared his throat and said, 'This is Rachel, she is Mike's wife and….' He didn't know what to say.

Rachel had no such qualms, 'I'm Mrs Grimshaw, and it's thanks to Mike that a desperate drug gang got their just desserts. If he hadn't looked out for me, I might well be dead. Your precious police force would be pretty useless if it wasn't for men like my husband!'

Mike turned away. Rachel could see he was both angry and humiliated, 'Let's see what we can see, shall we? Josh, Rachel.'

Mike, flanked on each side by Josh and Rachel, walked a little further along until they came to the spot where the wire had been cut. It was only roughly twisted together again, and it would take only a minute to undo it and gain access to either property, depending on which way they were going. It was also big enough to drive quite a large truck through or a biggish mob of cattle.

However, apart from the cut fence, there was nothing else to see. It looked as if it had been done some weeks ago though even that was difficult to be sure of.

The new young policeman they had largely ignored since his remarks had trailed along behind, still looking as if it was all beneath him.

'Have you looked at the place they cut in the other fence yet, Josh?' Mike asked.

'No, I was hoping you'd come too. Sid said I might meet you here, so I thought you'd like to look as well.' Josh almost sounded pleading.

'I'll come too if that's okay?' Rachel didn't want to miss out, although being in the same vehicle as the new constable didn't fill her with joy either. It was even worse than she thought. Having scrambled through the fence, which they partly undid, she found herself in the back as Josh invited Mike to sit in the front with him. Rachel stole a sideways glance at PC Jem Jones. He looked extremely displeased but said nothing. Rachel first thought she would just ignore him but then decided to find out more. Mike and Josh were chatting away companionably in the front.

'So, Jem, where do you call home?'

This took him by surprise. 'Gold Coast,' he muttered.

'Rather a shock to the system coming out here then, I imagine.'

'You can say that again. I don't understand why anyone would want to live in this godforsaken place. Look at it; nothing by scrubby trees, cattle and a few rocks!'

'You poor thing,' Rachel couldn't resist the mocking tone. 'There is so much more to it than that. But if you can't see it, then it's your loss' she turned and looked out of the window. Josh was driving slowly with the window down, watching the ground, as was Mike, in case they saw anything.

Turning back, she said, 'Why in the world did you come out here then?'

Jem looked slightly uncomfortable. 'My Uncle's in the force. He wanted me to experience policing out here.'

'I see!'

'Yes, my uncle has done well, and he is hoping I will follow in his footsteps and—'

'JEM, I WAS TALKING TO YOU!' Josh sounded exasperated. 'I might want to take some photographs if there is anything to see that might be useful. You brought the camera, didn't you? I told you to.'

Jem coloured up, 'Er no sergeant—er I forgot—er sorry.'

Josh looked ready to explode but gritting his teeth, he said. 'Well, let's just hope for your sake there is nothing to photograph.'

By this time, they had reached the fence line, and Josh drove slowly, looking for the place where the fence had been cut. They found it quickly, as it was pretty much in direct line to the other place they had just come from.

Josh stopped the car and, before they got out, said, 'be careful where you put your feet, folks, just in case there is anything to see on the ground.'

So carefully looking where they put their feet, they all got out. There were no tracks that they could see, but they approached the fence line carefully. It had been cut the same as the other one. It was well done and not very obvious unless looked at closely. Having looked all around, Josh clambered through and walked towards the gravel road that ran parallel with the fence for about half a kilometre. It was about 100 metres to the edge of the road, and as Mike joined him, they could see where a large vehicle had mounted the verge and crushed the bushes down to get to the fence line. There were many bushes, however, and unless one was looking, it would have been easy to miss. Josh muttering to himself, got out his mobile and took some pictures with it before they returned to Rachel and Jem. They had stayed on the other side of the fence.

'See anything?' Jem spoke first.

'Nothing that helpful.' Josh rubbed his chin thoughtfully, and they all got back into the car.

'What I don't get is why go to all this bother then? As far as we are aware, they have taken nothing.'

'Maybe they couldn't find any cleanskins to take. Our few were up near home, and Sid said he hadn't really got any just now.' Rachel said.

'Hmmm, well, ours were in the creek paddock. We only moved them a day or so before we went to see Mum and Dad. But how would they know they were there? It's not like anyone can see that paddock, even with binoculars. Unless, of course, you sat up on Mount Bluff. Even then, it's a long way. You'd need powerful ones.' Mike had his policeman's hat on, speculating what was going on.

'Mike' Rachel touched him gently on the shoulder as she was once again sitting behind him. 'I'm sure Josh will sort it out.'

Josh looked at her in the mirror. 'Always happy to have Mike's opinion.'

'I thought he had to resign. Is his judgement any good?' Jem piped up.

Josh clenched his jaw. This young upstart was really getting on his nerves. How dare he be so rude? He was speaking as if Mike wasn't there.

'I'd stake my life on it. Which is considerably more than I'd trust you with. Just so as you know, Rachel and Mike are friends, and I don't appreciate you being so rude.'

'Sorry.' But Jem sounded far from it.

They drove back to the fence line in silence, each busy with their own thoughts. Rachel was seething about Jem, and when she got out of the car, she thanked Josh and ignored Jem, who also got out so he could sit in the front with Josh.

Mike and Josh exchanged a few more words, then Josh drove off almost before Jem had got in the car.

Rachel and Mike watched them go before wriggling back through the fence and driving off home.

'What an obnoxious young man!' Rachel burst out.

'What? Oh. Yes, he sure was.' Mike was deep in thought and hadn't really taken in what Jem had said anyway. Rachel left it alone, knowing Mike had the possible duffing on his mind rather than a very rude young copper.

Chapter 11

Mike asked Ted and his wife if they had seen or heard anything, but of course, they hadn't. He went and sat in the office for a long time, going through all the comings and goings of people who had been out their way, but that wasn't any help either.

In the end, he gave up. He was getting nowhere fast, and there was work to be done.

So life returned to normal, though Rachel or Mike had taken to ringing Catherine or Henry every few days to see how things were. Then, a few weeks later, Catherine announced that they were coming down to see them. She didn't want them to make a fuss, but as the school holidays were coming up, they had wondered if Ben and Emma would be coming as they would love to see them.

Mike said, of course, he would arrange it. Though there had been no plans for this holiday: it was a short one, and as the children grew older, they had more things going on in Brisbane that they didn't like to miss. Mike and Rachel were both concerned as to what the reaction in Brisbane may be. Clarrie had, on occasion, been difficult about the children coming to the farm. Partly because she was jealous as the children adored Rachel, and deep down, she envied Rachel and her relationship with her children. Also, since she had seen Mike and Rachel together, she also envied their closeness.

When she had first met Keith, he had seemed her ideal husband. Now she wasn't so sure. Money wasn't everything.

So, to start with, she said no, but when in the end, Mike said his mother was very ill, and it may be the last time the children would see her, she relented. 'Emma is being very difficult just now, so I'll be glad, really. It will be nice to have some peace.'

Rachel grinned when Mike told her what Clarrie had said. 'Well, I haven't had a teenage daughter, but I'm guessing that's what is the matter with Emma. Fourteen next birthday and I noticed when they were here last how she is developing.'

It was arranged that Clarrie and Mike would meet in Roma, and Mike would bring the children back with him. Catherine and Henry would already be staying, so Rachel said she would stay at home with them. They didn't all need to go. When the time came to go, though, Catherine announced she would like to go with Mike. She had only met Clarrie the once and quite thought she would like to see the mother of Mike's children again. Mike wasn't too happy, but off they went.

Rachel was quite pleased she didn't have to go as she had no inclination to see Clarrie again. Though their exchanges had been cordial enough, she hadn't been that comfortable with her.

Henry was happy enough too and asked Rachel to take him on a tour of the farm as they hadn't got around to it yet.

Taking time, Rachel drove Henry through the different paddocks, looking at the animals in various stages of development. The cows with calves at foot were her favourites, and they lingered a long time in this paddock, looking at them and talking about the merits of different animals and bloodlines. Then Henry asked could he see where the fence had been cut.

'Yes, if you really want to, but there are no animals in that paddock.'

'I know, Mike said. It was lucky, but I'd just like to see. We had a similar thing happen many years ago when Mike was a little 'un. I'd just like to see if it's the same kind of fence tampering we had. Besides, I don't think I've ever been that way.'

'You have. The first time you and Catherine came, we had a picnic by the swimming hole, you remember?'

'Ha yes, it's the same place as you found a dead man and met Mike'

'Yep, that's it.'

When they got there, they found the fence was down. Someone had opened it again, and there were fresh tyre tracks as it had rained a couple of nights before. These tracks were very fresh, but not big enough for a truck nor a ute, but a quad bike or something similar.

The tracks led to the creek, but having followed them, they didn't appear to be the other side. It was very strange. On the Newberry's side, they looked as if they led straight towards the other place in the fence and having driven through that is where they went. It was a bigger vehicle then that had met the smaller one. Instead of driving home, Rachel drove straight to the Newberry's house. No one there; then Rachel remembered yesterday Sid had told her he had to go back to the hospital for a follow-up appointment. Norma was going with him. She drove across to the other house where Sid's son Barry lived. Barry had been born with a serious heart defect and had never managed to do much physical work as a result. He was small and weak looking, so unlike Sid, it seemed impossible they were even related, let alone father and son.

However, he did what he could and had a good brain. He did most of the paperwork and kept the books up to date. He had done a course and now helped people who were feeling desperate and alone, all done online in spite of the vulgarities of the internet. Living by himself, not wanting to be anything other than independent, and to that end had earned a lot of respect from the broader community. He was always friendly, and now, as they drew up, he gave them a cheery wave. He had been sitting on the front verandah and now got to his feet as they approached him, not coming down the steps but waiting at the top. Rachel introduced Henry.

'Pleased to meet you. Can I get you a cold drink or anything?' Barry asked.

'Thanks, but no thanks, this is a brief visit. It's your Dad I really wanted to see.'

'Anything to do with the suspected cattle duffers or whatever they are?'

'Yep, they have been through again. Only this time haven't put the fence back. Lucky neither of us have cattle in those paddocks.'

'I'll tell Dad when he gets back, or you can go and find Allen or one of the others.'

'Nah, don't worry, we'll sort the fence. No worries. Better get back, Barry.' Rachel paused.

'How is your Dad *really,* Barry? He just shrugs when I ask him, and your Mum doesn't say much either.'

'No, Dad plays it close to his chest. Fair dinkum though, I think he's doing okay.'

'Good, better get back. Catch you later.'

Rachel and Henry returned and mended the fence as best they could, then drove back home to wait for the others to return. Rachel was preoccupied trying to work out why the thieves or whatever they were had come back when there was nothing for them. It didn't make sense.

It was getting late when finally Mike got back and taking one look at Catherine; Rachel could see she was exhausted. Needless to say, the children were tired and a bit cranky too.

It wasn't until they were getting into bed that Rachel finally managed to tell Mike about the fences and speculate about what was going on.

Chapter 12

The next morning everyone was up bright and early as usual except Catherine, who didn't put in an appearance until midmorning. Henry had explained that she hadn't slept well and only got into a proper sleep as dawn was breaking. Henry explained this to the children. Emma, who had been the most upset to hear of Catherine's illness, just said she was going out to ride. Ben, on the other hand, was quite grumpy that his grandmother wouldn't be coming out to help collect the eggs and see him help Mike do some repair jobs that he wanted help with. He had been waiting to show Catherine, and now it was spoiled. He eventually went off outside with a very gloomy face and refused to help his father when he got there.

Rachel felt the need to apologise to Henry about the children's behaviour.

Henry snorted a laugh. 'My dear girl, don't forget I've seven other Grandchildren. Not all boys, I know how these things work.'

A small frisson of sadness passed over Rachel. She would have loved to have had at least a grandchild, but that was an impossibility. Pulling herself up mentally, Rachel reflected on how lucky she was to be a stepmum to Emma and Ben. Maybe one day they would have children too, then she would be a granny.

The rest of the children's stay went reasonably well though watching Emma, Rachel felt there was something which wasn't quite right, though what she couldn't guess. Maybe it was just her hormones all over the place. When it came to saying goodbye, though, Emma clung to Rachel, tears threatening.

'I wish I didn't have to go back to Brisbane. I wish you were my real Mum,' she whispered in Rachels's ear.

'Come on, sweetie, this isn't like you. You can come anytime you like in the holidays, and there will soon be some more.' Rachel was so surprised by Emma's words, she felt she wasn't saying the right things, but words failed her.

Emma shook her head, 'You don't understand, ' she said and got into the car.

'What was all that about?' asked Catherine, who had stayed behind this time.

'I'm not sure, really. Emma didn't want to go home and said she wished I was her real Mum.'

Rachel stood watching the car disappear, feeling unsettled. Catherine touched her arm.

'Sounds like a large dose of teenage melodrama, dear. I don't think you should worry too much. She will be right as rain when she gets back.'

'I hope so.'

'Course she will, dear. You worry too much. Now I would love a walk around your garden. You were going to show me the other day, but we didn't do it. You have some new natives you've planted since we were last here.'

'Yes. They're just 'round this side of the house.'

Henry appeared just then, and the three of them wandered around the flower garden, then the veggie patch. Rachel had expanded both in recent years, and the seasons had been kind with rain, so everything was looking good. All this distracted Rachel from worrying about Emma, but that night when she was lying beside a peacefully slumbering Mike, the worry Rachel had felt resurfaced. There was more to it than teenage melodrama she instinctively felt.

A few days later, Mike's parents returned home. They had devoted as much time as they could to just being with them, conscious of Catherine's illness and the time spent was precious. It was a rather emotional goodbye, but Catherine was very business-like, which somehow made it easier.

'We will see you again before too long,' Catherine said firmly.

Chapter 13

Two weeks later, Clarrie phoned in the middle of the day, much to Rachel's surprise. As she answered the phone, she could hear Clarrie was very upset. For a start, Rachel couldn't comprehend what Clarrie was saying.

'Clarrie, please slow down; you're too garbled.'

'FOR GOD'S SAKE, EMMA IS MISSING.'

Rachel felt her veins turn to water, 'Oh my God, how long? Where? What happened?'

'Where's Mike? I want to speak to Mike.'

'He's checking fences. He won't have reception on his phone. I'll have to go and tell him. Tell me all then I can fill him in when I find him.'

Clarrie took a few breaths then, gulping, said, 'The school rang me and asked after Emma. They wanted to know why she wasn't at school. Apparently, she didn't go to school yesterday either, though she came home as normal. I have driven around the parks and looked anywhere I can think of, but she isn't anywhere. I'm so scared something bad has happened. Maybe it's drugs or something. She has been so difficult and rude lately. Says she hates Keith and me. Especially Keith. They always got on so well too. I'm so scared, Rachel, please go tell Mike.'

'I will don't worry. I'll go now, and Mike will ring you soon. Has Emma got her mobile with her?'

'Yes, but it's switched off. Please hurry' Clarrie rang off, and Rachel hurried outside. Going to the home paddock fence, she called Smokey, who fortunately usually came when Rachel called her, hoping for treats. Not today, though Smokey and the others were standing the far side and looking very alert. They seemed to be watching something in the distance. Rachel, however, was in no mood to wonder why and grumbling, threw a rope around Smokey's neck and led her back to the gate, where Ruby had waited as Rachel had told her to.

Minutes later, Rachel was galloping across the property as fast as she dared, Ruby trailing along behind.

Mike was checking the boundary fences for the third time in recent weeks as they were worried the duffers, or whatever they were, would try another spot.

Rachel knew Mike intended to start in the paddock where the fence had been cut, and thinking he would have moved further on, she rode that way. Smokey, who was normally laid back and sensible, appeared to be in a silly mood and kept shying at imagined things and being generally difficult. She was going to cut across to the fence line in the next paddock, but to her surprise, she caught sight of Mike's ute just approaching the gate, so turning to her right, she cantered across to him just as he got out to open it.

Frowning when he saw her and her expression, he said, 'Rach. What's up, sweetheart?'

Sliding off Smokey, Rachel told him about Clarrie's phone call, by now tears running down her face. Rather to her surprise, he put his arms around her and hugged her tight. 'I'll go back and speak to Clarrie, but I am sure Emma will be okay. This sort of thing happens all the time, especially with teenage girls. I expect she's just playing hooky because something has upset her. Come on, darlin', this isn't like you to be so upset and looking on the black side.'

Rachel gave a big sniff, and Mike handed her a hankie. 'Don't tear that one like you did the first time', he observed.

Rachel smiled weakly through her tears. 'Clarrie is in a state. You better go and speak to her.'

'Yes, I suppose so. Will you be okay?'

'I'm fine now. Sorry, I expect you are right. We are overreacting; off you go, I'll walk back; poor Smokey is hot and bothered like me.'

Giving Rachel a quick kiss, Mike jumped in the ute and drove off, leaving Rachel to get back on Smokey and walk home. Smokey still seemed rather jumpy though as they got nearer to home, she settled more. Rachel patted her neck that was glinting silver in the sunlight. 'What's got into you today, then, Smokes? You feeling silly, are you?'

Smokey relaxed under Rachel's hand, and by the time they got home, she seemed to be her normal self.

Having seen to Smokey, Rachel hurried to the house, she was half expecting Mike to say he had to go to Brisbane to help search for Emma, but he was busy making coffee when she entered the kitchen.

'There you are. Fancy an early lunch? Thought I may as well eat before I go out again.'

'What about Emma?'

'Well, yesterday, it seems she did the same thing. Clarrie didn't know because the school didn't chase it up, so presumably, she will turn up as usual, as if she has been to school.'

Rachel sat down at the table and absently took the mug of coffee Mike held out to her. 'I hope you're right.'

'Trust me, darlin', it'll be okay. She will have to have a talking to, that's for sure, but she's not silly. I'm sure we can sort it.'

Rachel, though, wasn't so sure and only picked at her food. Mike had no such hang-ups, and having eaten his lunch, was gone again, though before he left, he promised to be back in time for an update from Clarrie. Emma usually got home about four fifteen that day of the week, so they had a little time to wait.

Rachel found it impossible to settle to anything and mooched around the house and garden, looking at the time every few minutes. The phone ringing made her jump; it was too early for Clarrie but hoping against hope that all was well, she answered it.

'Hello, Clarrie?'

'No, were you expecting to speak to her?' it was Catherine.

'Er, no, yes, no.' Rachel felt thrown. It was an unusual time for Catherine to ring, and Rachel didn't want to tell her about Emma in case it was just a storm in a teacup.

There was silence for a moment as both gathered their thoughts, then they both spoke at once. Finally, Catherine said, 'What *is* going on, Rachel? You aren't like this normally.'

'Clarrie phoned this morning. Emma didn't go to school today or yesterday, and we don't know where she is.'

Catherine was quiet for a moment then said, 'Does Mike know? What does he think?'

'Well, as she turned up yesterday as if she had been to school, that's what we are hoping happens again today.'

'Hmmm, I think Mike is right to wait and see. She is a sensible child. This is out of character. Let's wait and see. I'll ring off now, then Clarrie can phone in. Alright?' Catherine hung up before Rachel could reply. Rachel then started to worry why Catherine had phoned when she did and felt bad for not asking.

She sat down with a cup of tea to wait again. The time dragged, then Mike came in and simultaneously, the phone rang. Mike was nearest and picked it up. Though she couldn't hear what Clarrie said, Rachel could hear her voice almost screaming into the phone. Mike looked grim but spoke quietly once Clarrie had run out of words.

'Stay calm, Clarrie. There is nothing to say she isn't just playing hooky. Phone the local police station, and I will talk to some of my contacts I still have. We will find her, okay?'

Rachel sat with a pounding heart and watched as Mike hung up and immediately flicked through the phone book sitting by the phone. He gave a sigh and disappeared, returning moments later with an old worn pocketbook from the office. Rachel recognised it as one he used to have in the top pocket of his uniform when he was a servicing police officer.

Not wanting to interrupt him, she stayed sitting quietly as he rang a couple of numbers and tersely spoke into the phone, explaining his reason for ringing. After this, he came and sat at the table beside her.

Putting his arm around her shoulders, he gave her a brief smile. 'Chin up chicken, don't you go all hysterical on me.'

Rachel shook her head, 'You know me better than that. But God, Mike, I'm worried. It's so out of character.'

'Yes, it seems like it, but I rather gather Emma has been acting differently lately. I just hope it's not drugs or boys or some combination of the two.'

'So do I! What happens now, Mike? Will you have to go to Brisbane?'

'Not unless it's unavoidable. I can't do much at this stage, and I would rather keep away from Clarrie and Keith if possible. I will go tomorrow if they haven't found her. I keep thinking she's too sensible to have done something silly. The only real danger is if she is in the thrall of some bad person.'

Both sat deep in thought, then Mike got to his feet. 'There is someone else I could try. He'd know what if anything is going on. That is if Emma has got into trouble with drugs or boys.'

'Zak.'

Mike grinned at her. 'Zak. I don't know if I can reach him or what he is doing, but I can try.' with that, Mike disappeared into the office.

Later as they had dinner, they were both quiet, busy with their own thoughts. Then Mike said, 'If we've heard nothing by morning sweetheart, I'll have to go. You understand, don't you?'

'Oh, Mike! Need you ask? Of course, I do. If you want to go now, it's alright with me.'

'Nah. No point tonight. I'll leave first thing.'

Chapter 14

Rachel lay awake. She couldn't sleep but didn't speak to Mike. He needed his sleep, she reasoned, if he was driving to Brisbane early. She turned over cautiously only to find Mike's eyes wide open, glittering in the semidarkness as the full moon lit the room. Without a word, he pulled her to him.

'God, woman, what would I do without you?' They made gentle love. It calmed them both, and they fell into a dreamless sleep.

The phone ringing had them both awake in an instant. With his heart in his mouth, Mike picked up the receiver at the same time, registering the time as 2.30 am.

'Daddy, please, I'm sorry. Please come and get me. I'm scared.' Emma sobbed.

'It's alright, sweetheart, it's alright. Just tell me where you are.'

'Roma, I don't like it here at night. Please come.'

'Emma, listen to me, where exactly are you, sweetheart?'

Emma continued sobbing for a moment, then managed to say, 'I—I'm in the little park outside the Big Rig p—p—p—place.

'Ok, sweetheart, stay right where you are; I'll get a police car to come and pick you up. It will be okay. You're not in any trouble. Just stay there, please, promise?'

'Y—y—yes. Daddy, I'm sorry.'

'It's okay, I'm going to ring them now. I'll use the mobile. Do you want to talk to Rachel while I talk to them?' He passed the phone to Rachel.

'Hello darling, you will be safe and sound soon. We promise. I expect it's not nice there when it's dark everywhere. Are you cold?'

Rachel could hear Emma sniffing loudly, trying to get herself under control. 'A—a bit. I'm a bit hungry too.'

Rachel couldn't help a small smile. Emma loved her food and was going through a growth spurt just now too. She seemed always to be hungry when she had been staying.

'Well, I am sure Dad will tell them to get you nice and warm and maybe a cup of something hot. We'll stay on the line talking to you until the police car picks you up, so don't worry. Ah, Dad's back. Do you want to speak to him again now?'

'I don't mind, just don't be angry with me, please.' Rachel put the phone on speaker so they could both hear and talk with her.

'Of course not, sweetie, we're just relieved you are safe. We'll let your Mum kno—'

'Do you have to?' Emma interrupted.

'Yes, we do. Love, she is beside herself with worry, as we all have been,' said Mike, who was listening in.

There was a moment or two of silence, then Emma said,' I suppose you do, have to. I mean.'

'We do, darling. Your poor mum is at her wit's end.'

'Really? I don't think she cares that much.'

'Of course, she does—'

'Police car's here. I better go.' Emma rang off.

Mike started to get dressed. 'I'd better go and pick her up. I'll bring her back here until we've got to the bottom of all this. It sounds as if she's had a blue with Clarrie, but Clarrie herself didn't think so.' Mike turned troubled eyes to Rachel. 'I don't know what to think.'

'Your parents seem to think she's just being a melodramatic teenager, as some are.'

'But you think there's more to this than meets the eye, don't you?'

Rachel shook her head. 'I'm like you; in the dark, really. It's just… I don't know. It's just so unlike Emma. I think there's something going on we aren't aware of.'

Rachel went into the kitchen and made Mike a coffee to take with him. He protested, but she pressed it on him, reminding him that he had a long drive when he was feeling tired and stressed.

Wrapping a dressing gown around her body, Rachel stood watching his headlights disappear into the predawn darkness. Ruby sat beside her, and Rachel patted the dogs head. 'Well, Rube, I think I'll go back to bed. We'll see what happens later.'

Chapter 15

As it turned out, Rachel couldn't get to sleep again for some time. Then when she did, she was besieged with bad dreams. They weren't dramatic enough to be nightmares, but they were troubling. The kind that are disturbing but unable to be remembered upon waking.

It was late morning before Mike and Emma returned home. Mike had rung her briefly to say they were leaving and to have the coffee on. Rachel went to meet them as the car pulled up. Emma almost fell out of the car in her rush to come to Rachel. She threw her arms around Rachel's neck and, burying her head against Rachel's chest, burst into a fresh round of sobbing. Rachel could see there had been many tears as Emma got out of the car. Her face was blotchy, and her eyes were swollen and red.

Rachel let her cry for a moment, then gently prised her away and looked into her face. 'Come on, Em, that's enough tears. You're safe here, come on, darling, it can't be that bad.'

With Emma still crying, Rachel led her into the house and sat her down at the table in the kitchen. She made her some Milo and gave her some toast as well, then suggested Emma go to bed for a little while. She could see she was exhausted. Emma just nodded, and Rachel went through with her to the bedroom she slept in when staying.

'Do you want to shower or just get into bed?'

'Just get into bed,' Emma whispered, lips trembling. She peeled off her outer clothes, then before Rachel could blink, she climbed into bed in her T-shirt and pants and pulled the covers over her head.

Rachel hesitated, then leaning down, kissed the top of Emma's head and left the room, pulling the door shut quietly behind her.

Returning to the kitchen, Mike looked up at her with a haggard expression on his face.

'What did Clarrie say when you rang her from the police station, Mike?'

'To start with, she was relieved, then angry. She demanded to speak to Emma, but Emma refused to speak to her. It was very fraught. Finally, I managed to calm things down. I told Clarrie to give Emma a couple of days, then we will sort out her returning home, and hopefully, this will all blow over. Clarrie wanted to come straight out here and take Emma back, but I put my foot down. I told her it would make matters worse, and I think in the end she could see that.'

'Hang on a minute, I'll see how Emma is; I'll be back.'

Rachel tiptoed into Emma's room. Emma was in a deep sleep. Exhaustion had claimed her. Feeling relieved, Rachel returned, and sitting down opposite Mike, she reached across the table and took his hand in hers. Mike looked puzzled, but after stroking the back of his hand for a minute, Rachel said. 'Mike, I don't want to alarm you, but there is much more to all this than a row with Clarrie, I'm sure of it. When Emma was here a couple of weeks ago, she made several odd remarks. Then she didn't want to go home. Something is really troubling her.'

'What do you think it is? What did she say?'

I can't remember her exact words, but both times it was something like men being sleazy and liars. It wasn't something I'd expect Emma to say, but we were all here, and it wasn't something I really thought about until this blow-up. Mike, you don't think—you don't think Keith would interfere with her, do you?'

Mike's face darkened. 'Hell woman, I hope not. I'll kill the bastard if he has.'

'Mike. Mike, calm down. I may be completely wrong. Let's not jump to conclusions. Please just keep calm. Like you were telling Clarrie.'

Rachel was still holding Mike's hand, now he gripped her fingers tightly.

'Oh, Jesus Rach. What will we do if he has? Emma can't go back there, that's for certain. What will we do?'

'Let's just hope it isn't that. We'll sort it, my darling man, don't look so worried. We're in this together, ok?'

Mike's eyes filled with sudden tears, 'to think I nearly lost you, Rach, through my own stupidity.'

'You weren't the stupid one. You were doing a difficult job as best you could. I was the stupid one, thank God, we found each other again.'

Four hours later, Rachel heard the shower running, and soon after, Emma appeared in the doorway. Rachel was preparing dinner, 'Hello sweetheart, feeling better? Do you feel like helping, or do you want a cup of tea or just a sit-down?'

'I'll help; chopping veggies is good, helps me think straight.'

As Emma came and stood beside her, Rachel glanced at her. She had washed her hair, and all traces of tears had gone. She was almost like her normal self.

Rachel filled her in on the various happenings around the place, conscious that Emma would talk if she was ready. Mike came in soon afterwards and hugged his daughter when he saw her, lifting his eyebrows over her head at Rachel. Rachel shook her head. Emma had said nothing. Mike opened his mouth, and again Rachel shook her own. Emma may not want to tell them anything, and asking likely wouldn't make her open up sooner. They would have to wait.

They had just sat down to eat when the phone rang. 'Clarrie again', said Rachel. Clarrie had rung several times during the day, and Rachel had heard enough. She had told her she would let her know how Emma was later, and by the way Clarrie was ranting and raving, had decided that the further down the track they spoke, the better.

'I'll go.' Mike got to his feet, closing the door as he went, something nearly unheard of.

Both Emma and Rachel strained their ears trying to hear what he said, but apart from the low rumble of his voice, they couldn't hear the words.

Then they heard, 'GOODNIGHT CLARRIE' and the phone was replaced with force.

Emma smiled at Rachel and at her father when he came back in. It was the first smile she had given. 'Thanks, Dad. I don't want to talk to her. Not now, perhaps not ever.' She fiddled with the food on her plate. 'Well, not yet anyway.'

Mike patted her shoulder. 'It's okay, sweetie, but we will have to talk at some point. You realise that, don't you?'

'I know, Dad. I know, but not tonight, please. I still feel so tired.'

'I think an early bed for you, young lady.' Rachel said.

Emma stifled a yawn. 'Please, could Ruby sleep in my room?' Rachel and Mike exchanged a look. The children had made this request before, but it had not been allowed, 'she really is scared of something,' Rachel thought.

'Just this once.' Mike and Rachel said in unison.

Emma was gone to her room shortly afterwards, with Rachel promising to put Ruby in her room when they went to bed.

'What are you thinking, Mike?' asked Rachel later as she got into bed.

'I'm thinking I am too tired for anything except cuddling up to you and sleeping.' Almost before the words were out of his mouth, Mike was asleep.

Chapter 16

Rachel woke with a start and lay listening, then she heard the kettle give a short, muted whistle. Emma was up. Rachel looked at the clock. 2.25 am. Rachel got carefully out of bed so as to not wake Mike. Pulling on a dressing gown, she padded into the kitchen.

Emma swung 'round looking tense, then relaxed. 'Am I scary, am I?' Rachel smiled gently at Emma.

'Course not Rachel.' Emma took the few steps that divided them and gave Rachel a big hug.

'I love you, Rachel. I wish—I wish— wish you were my real Mum.' The tears were threatening again.

Hugging her back, tears sprang into Rachel's eyes too. 'I love you too, and I may not be your birth mother, but I look on you as my daughter. So long as we love each other, well, that's all that really matters. Don't you think?'

Stepping away from Rachel, Emma nodded, blinking back her tears. 'I feel safe and loved here with you and Dad; Ruby too, but—' Emma stopped speaking and looked lost.

'Do you feel like talking now, or do you want to leave it until the morning, sweetheart?'

'I think now if you don't mind. Dad will get upset. Then perhaps you can tell him for me?'

Rachel pulled a chair out, and Emma did the same, sitting close to Rachel. 'I don't really know when it started, but Keith… ' Emma stopped.

'Take your time.' Rachel said gently, but her heart was racing. What was Emma going to tell her?

'He has made me feel uncomfortable lately and made a few odd remarks about my figure growing and stuff like that. He scares me. He gives me these odd looks, then the other day, he put his hand on my bottom and started to stroke it. I was wearing shorts, and he put his hand inside the leg—' Emma shivered, then tears came again. Rachel went to speak, but Emma gulping continued.' I pulled away and went and found Mum. She had just come home from the supermarket. I told her, and she just laughed and told me not to be silly. She said I was being a drama queen. Keith wouldn't do anything like that. Then a few nights ago, Keith had been to some dinner in the city, I think it was, I was awake. It was late, and I heard him come upstairs. Then my bedroom door opened, and he was standing by my bed. Then Mum called out, 'Is that you, Keith?' and he left in a hurry. I am so scared of him, and Mum thinks I am making it up. I've been avoiding him, and then I decided to come here. I'm safe here. The first time I tried to come, I couldn't work out how to get here. In the end, I got on the bus. I had just enough for the fare to Roma then when I got there I was too scared to think, I wanted to get a lift out here, but I couldn't find one. So I sat in that little park for hours, wondering what to do. I was so afraid Dad would be angry and make me go back.' Now Emma started to cry in earnest.

Rachel held her close, murmuring softly, 'it's alright, we'll take care of you. Don't cry. Dad won't be angry. He knows there is something wrong. You're safe now.

They sat like this for a time, and gradually Emma's tears stopped, 'Were you making yourself a hot drink when I came in? Shall I make you one now?' Rachel asked her as she dried Emma's tears for her gently.

Emma gave a wan smile and took the handkerchief away from Rachel. 'No, I think I can go back to sleep now. Thank you, Rachel.' Standing up, she kissed Rachel then went to her room, leaving Rachel sitting at the table, her head in a whirl. After a bit, she got to her feet and went back to the bedroom. Mike was awake and obviously waiting for her.

'I heard Emma talking to you but thought it better I keep out of it just now. What did she tell you?'

'It's Keith. He's the problem. He has come on to her, and she's afraid of him.'

'The BASTARD.'

'Sssh, don't let Emma hear you. Hopefully, she will go to sleep now. Let me tell you exactly what she told me.'

Mike nodded, so Rachel told him word for word what Emma had told her. Mike listened in grim silence, the emotions flitting across his face. 'The bastard. How dare he. And what's with Clarrie? Is she blind?! I can't believe all this, Rach, this is terrible.'

Rachel shook her head. 'All I can think is she's in denial. She doesn't want to believe Emma. It must be hard for her too in some ways—to admit the man she's married to is after her daughter; some kind of predator, pervert.' Rachel sighed. 'I know when Johnny first became difficult, I was the same. I just couldn't comprehend what was happening. It didn't matter that it was staring me in the face. I just couldn't believe it.'

They sat up in bed talking for a long time till finally they laid back and fell asleep, their arms around each other for comfort. Both feeling horrified and worried, wondering what they should do.

The next morning, they all slept later than normal and may have stayed asleep a little longer, but Clarrie rang, waking them up. Rachel got to the phone before Mike.

'Rachel, I want to speak to my daughter at once.' She said without preamble.

'She's still asleep, Clarrie—here's Mike; he wants a word.'

Mike was looking furious again as he took the phone from Rachel. Just then, Emma appeared, and Rachel gently steered her into the kitchen and closed the door.

Emma looked frightened, 'Did you tell him? Dad won't send me back, will he?'

'Yes, sweetheart. I had to tell him. He is very angry both with your mother and Keith. Not you. I am sure we can sort something out. Don't worry, sit down. I'll make you a drink. What would you like?'

'Could I have a hot chocolate? Is that too much trouble? I know you and Dad have coffee.'

'No trouble, then we had all better get dressed.' As Clarrie had woken them all, Emma was in her pyjamas, and Rachel and Mike had on dressing gowns as they normally slept in the nude.

Rachel had just made Emma's drink when Mike came into the kitchen with a face like thunder. Before he could say anything, there was a tap in the back door, and Sid poked his head around it. 'Oops! Sorry, folks. Bad timing, I'm guessing. I'll go away. It can wait.'

'No, Sid, don't be silly. Come in. Coffee won't be long; what brings you here this morning?' Mike said.

Rachel turned the coffee machine on then fled to get dressed. She wasn't used to floating around in just her dressing gown. Emma, too followed her out and went to get dressed, leaving the men to themselves in the kitchen.

'What's your lass doing here then, Mike, school time, isn't it?'

'Yes. I'll tell you soon, Sid. What's up? You have some news?'

'Yep, Barry thought he could keep watch on the duffers or whatever they are. He got me to park an old ute up near the track, and he's spent the last week or so sleeping in that.'

'That's brave of him.'

'Well, we hid it as best we could. I didn't want him to get into any sort of blue with the buggers. The thing is, I'm not at all sure they are after cattle.'

'How's that then?'

'Well, they appeared again last night. They parked just near the road, there were three of them, and they were in a 4x4 with a horse float. One of them took off with the quad bike while the other two just sat and waited. Barry crept out of the ute and got as close as he dared. He couldn't really hear what they were saying, but he could see quite clearly; the moon was bright enough. I guess that is why they chose last night. After a while, the guy came back empty-handed and just said, 'couldn't get near the bitch' then they talked for a short time, packed up and off they went.'

'Did Barry get the registration on the car?'

'Nah, sorry, mate. The angle was wrong, and I had impressed on him no heroics!'

'Yeah, I wouldn't want him to get hurt. How are you doing?'

'I'm good, no dramas. Anyhow, I reckon they're not after cattle. The only thing I can think is they're after one of your horses.'

'I reckon you're right, Sid, but why?' Mike looked puzzled for a minute, then he said. 'It's got to be Rachel's horse, Smokey.'

'What's got to be Smokey?' Rachel entered the kitchen having got dressed.

'We're talking duffers, Rach.'

'What's Smokey got to do with it, I don't understand.'

Sid explained what Barry had seen. Rachel looked from one to another. 'I think you're right, Mike,' she said quietly, 'it's the only explanation.'

By now, Emma had come back. 'Why would they steal Smokey? Why not one of the others? She is the hardest to catch. All the others come and ask to be haltered. Rachel is the only one she'll go to.'

'Because of her breeding, they think they will succeed where others have failed maybe,' said Mike thoughtfully.

'It still doesn't add up, though, does it, Mike? I don't think anyone that knew we got her would be interested. They'd also know she's barren.'

Mike scratched his head. 'God knows, I'm sure I don't. Surely no-one would be daft enough to think they could race her again.'

They all sat around the table, theories passing from one to another, but they couldn't come up with anything that made sense. Then Sid looked up at the big kitchen clock and, downing the last dregs of his coffee, said he'd better go. Mike walked him to his ute and just told him Emma had a blue at home and was staying with them a few days.

Chapter 17

After Sid had gone and Mike had returned to the kitchen, Rachel could feel the waves of tension coming from Emma. She was waiting for her father to say something. Mike glanced from Emma to Rachel, then back. He strode across the kitchen and put his arms around Emma, hugging her tightly. 'My poor little girl. Don't worry, sweetheart, we will sort something out.'

Emma burst into tears, 'Oh Dad, I was so worried you'd be cross with me.'

'You silly sausage. Why would I be cross with you? I was very worried, we all were, and it wasn't the best plan to end up in Roma in the middle of the night. But you are here now. You're safe. We just have to work out what's best. Okay?'

'Look, the best thing I think is for me to talk to Clarrie and see if we can't sort this out sensibly. I'll go pack an overnight bag and be on my way shortly; is that okay with you girls?'

Rachel was about to say yes when the phone went again. Mike went and answered it, and immediately they heard him explode.

'WHAT SORT OF CREEPY ROTTEN BASTARD ARE YOU? YOU TOUCH MY DAUGHTER AGAIN, AND I'LL MAKE YOU FUCKING PAY. There was silence for a moment then, 'Oh you reckon, do you? Got all the answers, have you? Put Clarrie on. Maybe she'll make more sense than you, you moron.'

Emma and Rachel both stood still listening. Rachel had seldom heard Mike angry and certainly not this angry. His police training meant he kept his anger in check, and he didn't normally swear much.

Silence then it was obvious he was speaking to Clarrie. They seemed to be going around in circles from what the listeners gathered. In the end, Mike said an abrupt goodbye and hung up. Coming back into the kitchen, Rachel could see the strain on his face.

'Now listen to me, Emma, your mother wants you back—' Emma opened her mouth to protest, but Mike cut her off. 'Wait, listen. She has agreed you stay here for a few days, then I will take you back and maybe have a talk to both your mother and Keith. It wouldn't be good to take you out of school on a whim. They do take boarders, so that is something we could find out about when I take you home. Would you be happy with that and you could spend more of the holidays here if you want? If you stay here, you are going to miss out on all the other things you're involved with. The sports group, the swim club, your music, you'd have a long bus journey to go to high school from here too, darling. It would be hard. What do you say?'

Emma stood looking at her father for a long time, her mind in a whirl. She nodded then and, turning, went outside saying she'd let the chooks out.

'Oh Mike, what did they really say?'

'Well, Keith was blustering on about the law and that Emma had just taken against him. He said it was all lies, as she doesn't like him. Clarrie wasn't much better. Until I mentioned the Department of Child Safety, and suddenly she was a lot more conciliatory and then she agreed to Emma staying here a few days.

The trouble is, Keith knows the law inside out and also knows people in high places. He and Clarrie have the legal right for the kids to live with them, and I get the feeling it may be quite a battle to reverse that. Also, Emma has school. She is doing well, despite all that is going on. I really don't know what is best. I don't want to end up in a fight because there is Ben to consider too. He is happy enough, though of course he's fed up Emma is here, and he isn't.'

'Oh Mike, what a muddle. But we'll get through it, and maybe this will be a wake-up call to Keith, and he will behave himself.'

"Only time will tell. Now I'm going outside to do a few jobs.'

'I'll come out too. There is nothing that can't wait in here. I'll see what Emma is up to.'

Emma was sitting on an old garden seat her father had repaired long ago. Rachel sat down beside her. Emma turned towards Rachel with haunted eyes. 'I'm sorry, Rachel. I shouldn't have come.'

Rachel put her arm around her shoulders, 'It's alright darling girl, we're glad you did, that you felt able to.' They sat silently for a few minutes, then Rachel said, 'Do you remember when your Dad and I made you those swings? Then we sat down on this very seat, and it broke, and we both fell on the ground.'

Emma laughed, 'I do. We loved you even then, Rach. Though we hadn't hardly even met you. You were such fun. Still are.' she added hastily.

'The lady in the mobile library thought I was your Granny. I wasn't happy about that.'

'We've never thought of you like that; she was a silly woman.'

Both feeling lighter in their mood now, they went in search of Mike. He was repairing a broken hammer, putting a new handle on it.

'Hello girls, I'm going to fix up the fence where the duffers or whatever they are have been coming in. Left it hoping to catch them, but if they're not after cattle, I think we should put some of the steers down there. Come on, I could do with some help.'

The rest of the day passed happily. They all went in the ute to fix the fence, then came back, saddled up the horses and drove the newly weaned steers down to the creek paddock. When they got back, Mike said he thought they should move the horses into a small paddock that was at the back of the house behind the chook run. The small area was used for any sick cow or calf that needed more attention or medication. However, it wasn't that big, and Rachel worried it wasn't big enough to support them for long.

'We'll just have to hand feed them if they get too short of grass then, won't we? We've got hay left; it's been a good year for fodder. I just think it would be better until these mongrels are caught or give up. I've come to the conclusion that Sid is right. They are after one of the horses rather than any cattle.'

'Ok, go with that. The dogs will make a racket if there are any strangers about too then. Of course, there is Ted, he's getting a little deaf, but he's about if we're not.'

The horses weren't too sure about their new quarters. None of them had ever been put in there before, but they settled down happily enough.

Later, Emma helped Rachel get the dinner, and after the meal, they sat around the table talking. The phone rang, and they looked at each other. *What now?* Mike answered it. 'It's okay, mate. It's okay. Do you want to speak to her' Coming back into the room, he said to Emma, 'It's Ben, he wants to talk to you.'

Emma pulled a face, Ben and herself had always argued, but underneath had been best mates. However, in recent times they had grown apart, partly because of Emma reaching puberty and partly because Ben didn't understand the Keith and Emma situation.

Dragging her heels somewhat, Emma went to speak to her brother. She shut the door behind her, and Mike raised his eyebrows at Rachel. 'She doesn't want us hearing her by the look of it,' he said.

Emma was on the phone a long time, and they could only hear the cadence of her voice, not the words. But there didn't seem to be any argument. Rachel got up to clear the table, and Mike helped her.

They had sat down again by the time Emma came back, and they could see she'd shed a few tears. 'You okay, honey?' Mike asked.

'Yes, Ben says he will look out for me. He just wants me back home, says he misses me but admitted he was jealous I was here and he wasn't.'

'It's good that he will look out for you, Em. How does he get on with Keith? He seemed okay when they were here.' Rachel asked.

Emma shrugged her shoulders in a typical teenage gesture, 'Ok, I think. They don't really take much notice of each other. Keith isn't into any sports; he watches a bit of racing on TV sometimes, but not that much. Ben likes his footy and is always going on about it. Mum says he's a footy bore.'

'Ben didn't upset you then, sweetie?' Rachel was wondering about the tears.

Emma looked almost embarrassed. 'No, he was nice. He isn't always. It took me by surprise. By the way, neither Mum nor Keith knows he rang me. He had his mobile in the bathroom and turned the shower on. '

Rachel and Mike exchanged looks, but neither of them said anything.

Chapter 18

The next day, the three of them went into town for supplies, and Rachel had her hair done. Emma went with Mike to the supermarket for the things they needed and a few other places before they were to meet up with Rachel at the bakery where Jane, Rachels oldest friend worked, in fact, it was her business. It had been owned by a man from Roma with Jane as manager, but he gave up a couple of years ago, and now it was Jane's business. She lived with her family a hundred meters down the road. There was a small seating area outside and just inside the shop, but it was very busy when they got there. Jane saw them and waved them through to the back of the shop.

'You can wait here, and I'll give you the nod when a table becomes empty.' She indicated a small office.

There was only one chair in there, so Mike leant on the doorframe, and Emma sat in the chair. They didn't have long to wait; just as they walked through, Rachel appeared. They were all tucking into freshly baked pies when Jane came across and pulled up a chair. 'Time for a quick break, I think. How come you're here then, Emma?'

Emma looked at her father first, then Rachel. She didn't know what to say. Rachel squeezed her knee under the table gently and said to Jane, 'Emma has had a bit of a blue with her Mum; nothing serious, but we all thought a bit of breathing space might be good. Didn't we, Em?'

Jane laughed. 'Yep, teenage daughters, know what that's like. Sorry Emma, but we all go through it!'

After that, no more was said on the subject. The talk turned to the duffers or rustlers or whatever they were; no one was sure anymore. 'What is it they are after, Mike?' Jane asked.

'We can only assume it's one of the horses, and if it is, it would have to be Smokey. She's the only one that is really valuable. Or rather was. Her breeding is good, but they could never get her in foal, and tests showed they were never going to. She's too old to race now, and in any case, she wouldn't stand it physically.'

They were just leaving the bakery a short time later when a large, powerful motorbike cruised down the street and stopped by the curb about 50 metres in front of them. Rachel gave an involuntary shudder. She hated bikes. Their ute was parked just in front of them, and they started to get in Emma in the middle when the motorcyclist got off his bike and strode towards them. As he approached, he took off his helmet. Mike glanced up then exclaimed, 'Jesus, man, what are you doing here?'

Taller and more unkempt than Rachel remembered, but still with an air of repressed strength and menace, it was Zak. The police officer who had gone undercover in the gang that Rachel's son Johnny had run.

Mike and he were by now clapping each other on the back and shaking hands, obviously pleased to see each other. Zak now turned to Rachel, his face crinkling in a friendly smile.

'Hi Rachel, remember me? This is a much happier meeting than the last time or two.'

'I could hardly forget you, Zak,' Rachel said dryly, though she softened it with a smile. 'You never did tell me your real name.'

Zak laughed, then a deep rumbling sound, 'I reckon Zak, it will stay. I was so pleased when I heard you guys had finally got it together. This bloke here, well, I've never seen him look better. You look pretty good too. Mike, you're a lucky bastard.'

All this time, Emma, who had got into the middle of the ute, had stayed still, watching from within. Now Mike spoke to her. 'Emma, come and meet an old mate of mine, Zak. Zak, my daughter Emma.'

Emma got out and shook hands, then the four of them stood awkwardly for a few moments then Mike said, 'what brings you to these parts then, Zak, or can't you tell us?'

'Nah, nothing to tell, Mate. Was out this way, just thought I'd make a detour and catch up with you two. Heard you were trying to contact me a few days ago about your daughter; it seems it's all sorted. I was coming out to the farm, seems as if I won't need to do that now.'

'Rachel spoke up then. 'If you want to come out, why don't you come to dinner? After all, it would be a different kind of visit than before. How about it?'

Zak hesitated, then smiled warmly through his bushy beard, which seemed larger and wilder than before. 'You're on. I'll catch you guys later.' With a nod, he turned and went back to his bike.

Mike watched him as he put his helmet, on then got in the car. Emma and Rachel already had. He looked thoughtful as they set off home. 'What is it, Mike?' Rachel asked.

'I don't think Zak ever just drops in on people for a catch-up. It just doesn't ring true to me.'

'Who is he anyway, Dad? He doesn't look much like a cop to me. He looks like a swaggie or dropout, scary.'

'He's a cop alright, at least I suppose he's still in the force though he's near retiring age. Maybe it was true, and he has retired and is just drifting. Impossible to tell with Zak. That's why he was so good undercover.'

'Well, since I asked him for dinner, I had better think about what I'm going to cook. Something hearty by the size of him, I'm thinking.

'I don't imagine he gets much home cooking unless his lifestyle has changed a lot, so I'm sure he will enjoy whatever you cook, darlin'.'

'I'll help' Emma seemed to be feeling much brighter today. The truth was she had been intrigued by her father's mate and was hoping he'd have some good stories to tell.

When sometime later Zak arrived, he had brought some beer and wine with him. He almost looked embarrassed when he said, 'I hope it's alright. I've got my swag. I thought we'd make a night of it so I'd sleep here. '

'Cripes Zak. You can have a proper bed. No need to camp out.' Mike looked embarrassed now.

'Nah, Mate, I'm used to sleeping out. I'll be right on the verandah.'

'Might be a bit cold, you sure?'

'Yep. Now, are we going to just look at this beer or drink it?'

Rachel had done roast beef with loads of veggies and an apple crumble to finish. She hadn't had time to do anything out of the ordinary, but judging on how much Zak ate and enjoyed, it seemed as if Mike was right about how much home cooking he usually enjoyed.

Emma had been right; Zak was full of stories of things he'd seen and done. Though he was very careful in what he said, just small incidents of things that had happened in his work. Nothing that gave any secrets away. Emma found her eyes closing, and Rachel told her to go to bed. She looked as if she might argue but finally gave in, and off she went.

'What's going on with your daughter then, Mike?' Zak asked after a bit. Mike told him.

Zak considered what Mike had told him. 'Doesn't surprise me. It happens.' he finally said.

'Not to my daughter, it doesn't.' Mike said angrily.

'Calm down, Mike. Zak didn't mean anything by it. I'm right, aren't I, Zak?' Rachel said, looking from one to another. It wasn't lost on her that the first time she had seen him, Rachel was convinced that Zak was a thug and a bully.

'Sure are Rachel. I've just become too cynical in my old age. It takes something to surprise me these days.'

'Yeah, I know. I am just rather fazed, that's all, and then there is the odd fence breaching thing going on and worrying about Mum.' Mike looked very tired suddenly.

'What's this about your fence then, Mike?' Zak leant forward, looking interested.

Mike repeated all that had gone on. Zak sat thoughtfully after Mike had finished, then said, 'Mind if I have a look round tomorrow? Just out of interest, of course, nothing official.'

'You not retired yet then?' Mike asked.

'Well, yes and no. Don't think I'm cut out to retire, so, though I have retired, I haven't. If you understand me?'

'Not really.' Rachel said with a yawn, 'boys, I'm tired. If you'll excuse me, I'm off to bed,' yawning Rachel got to her feet. 'I know we haven't finished clearing up, but the rest can wait until the morning.'

Both men got to their feet, and Mike gave her a kiss. 'Won't be long, darl.'

Rachel was asleep an hour or so later when Mike slid into bed beside her. She didn't wake.

Chapter 19

Rachel was surprised to find when she entered the kitchen the next morning, having left Mike still sound asleep, the kitchen was spotless. She was just looking round in astonishment when Emma walked blearily into the kitchen.

Looking around, she said, 'that was a good tidy up, Rachel. Did you do it all?'

'I didn't do any after you'd gone to bed. The boys must have done it all. I wonder if Zak's awake.'

Rachel put the coffee on and the kettle for Emma for tea when there was a tap at the back door, and Zak put his head in. 'Off in a minute. Thanks for a great dinner, Rachel, see you young Emma, say G'day to Mike for me.' He withdrew his head, and Rachel raced to the door.

'Zak, wait. Mike was going to take you and show you the fence and things. He'll want to see you. What about breakfast?'

'I've been and had a squiz, and I don't eat breakfast.'

'Coffee?'

Zak hesitated, 'smells good. Ok, thanks. If you're sure?'

'You scared me witless the first time I saw you with Johnny, Zak, but I'm beginning to think you're a pussycat underneath all that.' She gestured to his bushy beard and generally rough appearance as she poured coffee.

Zak gave a snorty sound, a cross between a laugh and a cough, 'I've never been referred to as a pussycat before!'

'What's this about cats?' Mike came into the kitchen, pulling a shirt over his head. Rachel had ensured that this time, knowing they had a guest, she had got dressed before coming into the kitchen. Emma started to giggle away in the corner. 'I didn't know grownups had silly conversations.' she said.

After Zak had gone, they settled down to breakfast. Mike looked at Emma seriously. 'Emma sweetheart, you do realise that I am taking you back to Brisbane tomorrow, don't you?'

Emma nodded and bent her head over her bowl of cereal, but not before Rachel had seen the tears cloud her eyes. She put out her hand and patted Emma's shoulder. 'Dad will make sure it's alright. You know he will.'

Emma nodded again. They could see she was struggling to not cry, so Mike swiftly changed the subject. 'Zak didn't say anything this morning about the duffers or whoever they are, did he? He said he was off to have a look this morning, and I am guessing that he had been when I came in.'

'No. Not a word. You two did a good job clearing up last night, by the way. It must have been late when you came to bed. I didn't hear you; thanks for that.'

'Zak's idea and I must be getting old. Zak drank more than me, but I feel a bit hungover this morning, to be honest.'

Rachel laughed. 'That doesn't happen often. I'll forgive you.' She stood as she said this and moments later found herself sitting on Mike's lap where he had pulled her down. He kissed her and would have made it a long one, but Rachel pulled away with raised eyebrows indicating Emma.

Mike looked rather sheepish and was about to say something when the phone rang. Rachel was nearest and went to answer it. It was Henry, and he was obviously distressed.

'Any chance you could both come up tomorrow or the next day, Rachel? Catherine has taken a sudden turn for the worse, and she's asking after you and Mike.'

'Oh no. Henry, I'm so sorry. Here's Mike. He wants to talk to you.'

Rachel handed the phone to Mike, who explained to his father that he was taking Emma home the next day, but if he left early, he would drive straight from Brisbane to their place. His father wouldn't have a bar of it. 'No, Mike, stay in Brisbane and get everything sorted regarding Emma. Your mother would be horrified if you neglected Emma because of her. Just come when you are able.'

Rachel, who was eavesdropping, said, 'I could come up tomorrow if you like Henry. Ted can look after everything here, for a time anyway.'

The next morning Mike left with a tearful Emma. Rachel, having waved them off and checked everything was as it should be, left with Ruby.

The journey seemed to take longer without Mike, and as she was driving her old ute, it was not so comfortable. She was very pleased when she finally pulled up in front of Mike's parent's house. The first person she saw as she got rather stiffly out of her car was Wendy. She came out of the fly screen door, frowning at Rachel and Ruby.

'Hello, Wendy.' Rachel was determined to be friendly, 'How are you?'

'Hello, Rachel. Thought you'd show your face then, did you?'

'Yes, how is Catherine?'

'You'd better see for yourself, not that—' she broke off as Henry appeared in the doorway and enveloped Rachel in a bear hug.

'Good to see you love. Catherine will be so pleased you're here.'

'So am I,' said a voice behind Henry, and it was Nancy's turn to hug Rachel.

'I'm glad someone is.' Rachel said with feeling. Wendy, who was hovering nearby, scowled then, turning to Henry, said, 'I'll come back tomorrow see what I can do. After all, Nancy obviously needs help.'

It was Nancy's turn to scowl then at Wendy's retreating back. Henry just shook his head.

'What was all that about?' Rachel asked as a few minutes later, having unloaded the car of bags and dog, she followed them both inside.

'Wendy seems to think she is the self-appointed nurse for Catherine and that we can't manage without her.' Nancy sounded rather fed up.

'I think there is more to this than meets the eye,' said Henry, 'but time will tell. To be honest, Catherine has never had much time for her. They are chalk and cheese, and Catherine is getting increasingly cranky every time Wendy comes near.'

'Oh dear, that's the last thing she needs right now.'

By this time, they had walked along the hallway and were hovering outside Catherine's room. 'What don't I need?' Catherine came through the door as they got there. She was dressed in a tracksuit and had obviously just left her bed where she had been lying down. Rachel almost gasped but stifled it in time. Catherine was shrinking away before their eyes. Never a very big woman, she was now tiny. There was no flesh left on her face and hands; even her hair which had always seemed luxurious was getting sparse. Tears gathered in Rachel's eyes as she gently hugged her mother-in-law. Looking at Henry, she could see the strain in his face too.

'Shouldn't you be in bed?' Rachel asked her gently.

Catherine shook her head. 'The time will come, but not today. I'm so looking forward to talking with you and spending time in your company dear. Now tell me about young Emma.'

Rachel sat and talked to Catherine until Nancy called them all to come and eat. It was dinner time.

Before she went to bed, Rachel rang Mike, who filled her in on his day. It had been stressful, but in the end, he managed to talk to Clarrie in what he hoped was a sensible fashion. He also went and spoke at length to the school and had arranged for Emma to board next term at least. There weren't many weeks left until the next holiday. Clarrie had promised to keep an eye on things, but she was in denial that there was a problem with Keith and insisted Emma had overreacted on several occasions. Mike had pointed out it was important for Emma to feel safe above all else, and there should not have been any time or anything happening in which she felt scared or worried. Mike hadn't seen Keith. He was fairly sure he was avoiding him.

Chapter 20

The next day, Rachel spent the morning helping Nancy as much as she could. Although Catherine had got up when Rachel arrived the previous day, she was very weak and agreed to stay in bed. However, Rachel said she would help her shower and wash her hair when she felt up to it, so mid-morning, that is what she did. Catherine was more than happy to let Rachel help her as it took some of the strain off Nancy, who had borne the brunt of the extra work. Wendy appeared just as they had got Catherine dressed and sitting in a chair in her room.

'Oh, I could have done all that. No need for you to Rachel. After all, you have other things to worry you, from what I hear.'

'It's not a problem. Anyway, Mike has got it mostly sorted. He'll be here tomorrow.'

'Really? I would have thought those sorts of things were more difficult than that. I wouldn't expect they could be sorted out in a few minutes.'

Rachel looked at her, speculating how much Wendy had heard and how much she was just stirring. 'As I just said, we are sorting it. We know what we are doing.' Rachel crossed her fingers behind her back as she said this.

'Very clever then, aren't you? You know about Catherine's illness too. Expert in all fields, it seems.' This was all said outside Catherine's room. Rachel edged away, not wanting Catherine to hear the exchange. Now with a toss of her head, Wendy opened the bedroom door and went in. Not wanting to have an exchange with Wendy in front of Catherine, Rachel went into the kitchen where Nancy was busy at the stove. 'Coffee? You look like you may need it. I overheard Wendy just now. She gets bitchier and bitchier. I've never really taken to her, but as the years have gone by, she has got worse and worse. She spoils Craig rotten; the poor kid doesn't stand a chance of being likeable. I rather think she thought she was onto a good thing when she got with David, but life hasn't worked out as she would like. She wanted him to take his share out and set up on his own. Did you know?'

'No, I didn't know. When was this?'

'Before Craig was born, or maybe around that time. Before you and Mike got together, anyway.'

'I expect that is why she's like she is then. I don't suppose she was exactly overjoyed when Mike was left all that money by his Uncle then?'

'No, she ranted and raved. David did stand up to her then, telling her to shut it. We were all in turmoil because of Catherine not being well, and we didn't know where Mike was to tell him he was a rich man.

Then, of course, in a way, you were in the mix!'

'It took me some time to pluck up the courage to ring here. I was so afraid Mike would never speak to me again and that I'd lost him. Thank God I didn't!'

Nancy came across to Rachel and gave her a big hug. 'We're all so glad you're part of the family Rach, we all love you!' The unexpected hug and little speech undid Rachel, and for a few moments, tears spilled down both their cheeks. 'Catherine wouldn't want us to cry, but sometimes it's good, rather than bottling things up.' Nancy sniffed as she returned to making the coffee.

Henry appeared in the kitchen then and, having heard Wendy was with Catherine, sat down to have a coffee. 'I ought to go and relieve Catherine, but a quick drink won't hurt,' he said.

However, moments later, Wendy came out of Catherine's room and, sticking her head in the doorway, said, 'It seems as if I'm not needed here, so I'm off.' She looked furious and flashed Rachel a murderous look, then disappeared. They watched her stomping across the yard with heavy strides.

The three of them exchanged looks, then as one, they all made for

Catherine's room. To their surprise, Catherine was sound asleep in her chair and looked peaceful. They were all perplexed until Henry whispered he thought the dressing table wasn't how it should be. Odds and ends were scattered about on the top, and a few drawers weren't pushed right in.

'Was it like this when you were here before?' Henry whispered.

'I didn't take much notice.' Rachel whispered.

'Nor did I.', Nancy added.

'What are you all whispering for? I'm not asleep' Catherine spoke up behind them, making them all jump.

Henry moved swiftly to her side. 'Sorry, my darling, we thought you were. It's nothing to worry about.'

'You thought Wendy may have taken something. Well, she had a good search but went empty-handed. She thought I was asleep like you did. I'll have to try it more often, see what happens' Catherine gave a wicked little grin.

Henry looked ready to explode, but Catherine calmed him down, 'I don't know what she thought she'd find, but she went off empty-handed. I made sure I'd put my valuables in the safe last time we made a trip to Darwin, and I haven't had them out since.'

'That was a couple of years ago!' Henry looked astonished. 'I never noticed that you weren't wearing those lovely earrings I gave you a while back.'

'Tsk, don't worry about it, dear.'

Later Rachel and Nancy talked about Wendy. They were both sad and angry about her behaviour.

'I don't know how she can be like that. After all the things this family has done for her.' Nancy shook her head in bewilderment.

'It's strange how awful some people can be when all they've had is kindness.' Rachel remembered Johnny and how threatening he was. Nancy shot her a quick look but said nothing, and the rest of the day passed peacefully.

Chapter 21

The next morning, Mike rang to say he'd be another day. He was talking to the Child Protection people. This was against Clarrie and Keith's wishes and in part against Emma's, who, faced with the turmoil her actions had created now, was saying maybe she had overreacted. Henry had answered the telephone and told Mike Catherine seemed to have rallied since Rachel had come and to take his time. Rachel wasn't so sure that Catherine was any better and rather thought it was because she was hanging in, waiting until Mike was there. She was getting weaker almost, it seemed, by the hour and slept most of the time. The only medication she would take was the occasional painkiller. She was adamant she didn't want anything that would 'dull her senses', as she put it.

Although she had spent a little while sitting in a chair in her room yesterday, she didn't feel up to it that day and stayed in bed. Rachel and Nancy took turns to sit with her and do the normal household chores. Trish came over for a time, but there was no sign of Wendy.

Rachel was finding it harder than she expected. It reminded her so much of the time her husband Sam had cancer. It had been so quick, good from his point of view, as it meant he didn't suffer too long. But it also meant that Rachel didn't have the time to come to terms with it, as she may have done if he had lived longer. Now it seemed as if history was repeating itself. Nancy told her that a week ago, Catherine had been out in the garden not doing much physically but certainly pottering about, not much different than when she had visited Rachel and Mike. Now suddenly, she seemed too weak to do more than sit in a chair in her room.

By the time Rachel got into bed that night, she was feeling very emotional. Mike had rung, and she had managed to hide her feelings quite well, though she felt he may have picked up her unhappiness. He said he was coming the next day, and Rachel clung to that knowledge. He said he was happy that Emma was being looked after for now, at any rate. A meeting had taken place with Clarrie and Keith, then Emma had been called in, and the agency seemed happy. Mike had his misgivings, but he didn't tell Rachel that. He also thought he should stay longer but was very worried about his mother, so he made the decision to travel to them. It would be a very long drive, but Mike wasn't deterred.

The next morning, he rang from a service station on the Warrego Highway to say he would be with them late afternoon/early evening. He knew the journey would be getting on for eleven hours and was trying to take it steadily so as to not get too tired. Not having slept well, though he was already struggling. He had, of course, left before dawn and had been fine until after Toowoomba, now sleepiness seemed to be dogging him. He told himself it was because the route was more familiar. Going to Brisbane from where they lived was a long drive, yes, but he'd been there and back in the day on numerous occasions, leaving early and arriving late had never mattered, but now the desire to get there seemed overwhelming.

Lunchtime saw him stopping again and drinking a strong coffee. He had to admit he was tired and worrying thoughts were swirling round and round in his head. Half an hour after his coffee stop, he gave in and pulled over. A quick nap, and he'd be right. Two hours later, he was woken with a sharp rapping on the driver's window. Mike sat up, horrified to realise he'd slept so long and disorientated as to where he was and what was going on. He'd woken from muddled dreams and was now thoroughly confused. The sharp tapping came again, and Mike could see it was a police officer standing outside that car. He let the window down.

'Are you alright, sir?'

'Yes, yes, fine, thank you. I was tired, so I pulled over.'

"Very wise, sir. Can I see your driver's licence, please?'

Mike, still befuddled with sleep, felt for his wallet in his back pocket. It wasn't there! Where the hell was it? He hadn't left it back at the last stop, surely? Panic was setting in when he found it between the seats. It had slipped out of his pocket. As he handed it over, he was aware the policeman was looking very stern. 'Have you had a drink, sir, or have you taken any drugs?'

Mike felt irritated even though he knew the policeman was only doing his job. 'Of course not. I used to be in the force. I know the rules; in any case, I don't use drugs.' He sounded more aggressive than he really was. Having just woken up rather abruptly and feeling stressed as he was with all the things going on in his life, Mike's patience was rather thin. The young officer was keen to show his metal. It was the first time he had been out in the patrol car alone in the country area, which was all new to him in any case.

He couldn't smell any alcohol, but this man might have taken drugs, he'd taken quite a while to wake, and he seemed confused. He held out the swab for Mike to run around his mouth. 'Please run this along your tongue, sir.'

Mike was angry now. He just wanted to get to his parent's place and see Rachel and his Mum. He guessed they'd be expecting him anytime soon. He was going to be late, very late. He snatched the mouth swab away from the officer, who kept telling him what to do, which made Mike even more frustrated.

'I won't be long, sir. Wait here.'

Mike sat fuming but knew it would be counter-productive to argue or make a fuss. The minutes ticked by. What on earth was the young whippersnapper up to?

It seemed an age before he reappeared and handed Mike's licence back to him. 'Thank you, sir. Where are you headed?'

'I have still quite a way to go if you don't mind.' Mike started the engine; he wasn't about to have any more chats with this young copper.

'Wait a minute, sir, I'd like to check around your car if you'd just turn your engine off.'

'What the hell? Just do it then and let me go for Christ's sake.'

Again, the young copper took his time. Mike knew he was doing it deliberately, but with as much willpower as he could muster, he sat still and quiet and finally, he was told he could go. The whole business had taken another half hour. It would be well into the evening before he got there. He had handsfree, but there was no signal, so it was sometime before he could ring and tell them he was going to be late. Very late. As he got nearer, he had to slow down as there seemed to be roos everywhere, and quite a large proportion seemed to have a death wish. That slowed him down even more. The last thing he wanted was his car to get trashed by a kangaroo. Finally, at eight-thirty, he drove up to the house and climbed stiffly out. Ruby came to meet him wagging her tail, but everything else seemed eerily quiet though the house was well lit, no one was about. Then he saw a strange four by four parked a little further on, and his blood ran cold.

He rushed in the front door just as Rachel came out of the kitchen/living room. She went straight into his arms. 'Oh, Mike. Thank god you've come. '

'What's happened? Is it Mum? Is she okay? She's not, she's not…' words failed him.

'No, it's your Dad. He's had a mini heart attack, the doctor thinks. He's in bed now too!'

'Oh God, Rach, what happened?'

'Well. Wendy came this morning and kept throwing her weight around. Just being obnoxious to everyone except Catherine. Henry got wind of it and remonstrated with her, then shortly afterwards, he sat down suddenly in his armchair complaining of chest pain. We called the doctor, who said hospital, but Henry refused to leave your Mum. We were all worried about you too, which hasn't helped. You got held up?'

Mike nodded grimly. If he had been there earlier, maybe it wouldn't have been so bad for everyone. Rach kissed his cheek, 'Come through and see them. Good thing they have a huge bed as they are in together. The doctor wasn't keen on that idea either, but they are both very strong-willed people.'

'They've been together so long it would be criminal to separate them now.' Mike said as he followed Rachel into his parent's room. They were both propped up and looking towards the door as they entered. Nancy was sitting by the bed, and Tommy was hovering by the window.

Mike strode over to the bed. 'I'm sorry I took so long to get here. I had to stop for a sleep and had rather a longer nap than I meant to. Then there were roos, all sorts.' Mike refrained from telling them about the policeman. They didn't need to know that.

Henry looked very pale under his tanned face, and Catherine seemed even smaller than a few weeks ago. Her face had taken on an almost birdlike quality; she looked frail.

'It's alright, son. You couldn't have done anything much had you been here. David needs to take control of his wife and her vicious tongue.' Henry said. 'You're here now; that's all that matters.'

Mike sat himself down beside the bed and took hold of his mother's hand that lay on the cover.

'How're you doing, Mum?'

Catherine mustered a smile. 'Not too good today Mike. I'm getting to the stage where I will be glad when it's all over. Not that I'll know then, really, will I?'

'Oh Mum, ' Mike's eyes filled with tears, 'I hope it won't be for a little while yet. I don't—we don't—' Mike's throat was too closed to say more.

Catherine patted his hand. 'It's alright love, I know what you want to say.'

Rachel left the room and went and cut a plate of sandwiches for Mike, whom she guessed correctly had hardly eaten all day. When she returned to the room though Nancy and Mike were leaving and coming through to the kitchen, only Tommy was staying behind.

During that day, they had all sat down to work out a roster between the family so someone would be with Catherine all the time. It was this that had sparked a row with Wendy. She didn't think it necessary and said she wouldn't be able to help and nor would David. Nancy said that was fine, then Trish spoke up as the whole family had gathered to work the roster out. Trish said words to the effect of, she was sure it didn't matter, Wendy was more hindrance than help anyway.

The row that ensued hadn't been pretty. It was obvious that Trish and Wendy disliked each other intensely, then Jacob and David got into the mix, sticking up for their respective wives. Finally, Henry, who had sat watching the proceedings with something akin to horror, had roared out, 'Enough! Shut up the lot of you. What is the matter with you all? Catherine is *dying,* for God's sake, and you are all squabbling like a lot of school kids.'

Jacob and David looked ashamed, and both started to apologise, but before much more was said, Henry clutched his chest. He looked grey and was visibly sweating. Nancy jumped up and went to his side, Tom without a word, went and rang the doctor. Rachel related all this while Mike ate his sandwiches. Nancy then said, 'it was so awful Mike and Tom is so upset by it all, he doesn't know what to think.'

'Let's just play it as cool as we can, for now, Nancy, we don't want Mum or Dad upset anymore just now, do we? Rachel and I will stay and do whatever we can. By the way, we do have all the necessary first aid equipment, don't we? A defibrillator?'

'Of course, but we thought Henry needed a hospital. He had other ideas.'

'Well, it would take him away from Catherine's side, and they'd both hate that', said Rachel.

Soon after this, they retired to bed. Nancy said she and Tommy would be on hand, and as now Henry was there with Catherine, it wasn't so important for someone to be right in the room so long as they were nearby. He had a bell by his side should he wish to call anyone.

Chapter 22

They fell into a routine of sorts after that, with Nancy and Rachel doing the bulk of any nursing duties. Trish came and cleaned, and Tom and Mike took over Henry's role, which in later years had been to oversee things rather than hands-on. Mike hadn't wanted to do this as his other two brothers were partners in the place, not him, but Tommy was adamant. He wanted Mike to stand in Henry's shoes, and no one else was up for an argument just then. Of Wendy, there was no sign. Jacob was very contrite over his father's illness, but David had gone into a shell, and it was impossible to know what he was thinking. So a kind of odd routine took place.

Catherine was the main concern. One day she would be much better, it seemed, then the next, she slept all the time and seemed almost comatose. The doctor and nurse were on call, of course, but were too far away to pop in at any time. The family knew the basics anyway and had a comprehensive medical cabinet. However, it was putting a strain on them all, worrying about doing the right thing.

Ten days later, Catherine passed away peacefully in her sleep.

Henry was alone with her at the time, and Rachel, who was about to enter the room, heard a low moan. Henry was holding her hand, the tears pouring down his face. It was unexpected. It had seemed just the same as the last few days, with Catherine asleep, only waking from time to time. It was only four months since she had found out she had cancer, but the Doctor told them when he came she must have had symptoms for quite a long time before she went to see him. She had been aware of what it might be but told him at her age she didn't want surgery or a fuss. Henry was, of course, devastated but stoic. Catherine and himself had talked at length about it all, and he knew it was what she wanted.

Later the same day, Ted phoned to say his wife had fallen and hurt herself and he wanted to take her to hospital. He suspected she had broken her leg. He had tried to ring the Newberry's, but Barry had answered and said his parents were away. In view of the cut fencing and that there were some first-time calvers, Ted was worried about leaving the farm even for a few hours, though if it meant Roma, it would be longer. He had rung the local doctor, Merv, but he was over eighty kilometres away, and Ted's wife was in a lot of pain.

Rachel had answered the phone as it happened and said, 'Go, Ted, just go. We'll sort everything, don't worry.' She heard his sigh of relief down the phone.

She returned to the kitchen, where everyone in the family was gathered. It was a very quiet gathering; even Wendy, who had hardly been seen lately, was quiet. Trish and Nancy were both very teary, so had Rachel been until she answered the phone. Mike, she knew, was very upset, maybe because he was the youngest, he was closest to his mother. Everyone knew that and accepted that. It was just how it was,

Now Rachel bent down and spoke into his ear, explaining what had happened. 'Jesus,' he muttered, 'what do we do now? There's Mum's funeral, and Dad's not coping and—'

'Shhh,' Rachel cut him off. 'I'll drive back. It will only be a day, or so then I can come back here. If Allen's around at Sid's, he'll come over, I'm sure, but one of us needs to go and see what's what.'

'You sure, sweetheart? It's a lot of driving for you. I just don't feel I can leave just now.'

'It's okay, Mike, you stay. I understand; of course, I do.' This conversation was held in murmured voices as the rest of the family were trying to each have a say over the funeral proceedings and the arrangements for the wake. Suddenly Wendy said loudly, 'Rachel and Mike seem to have their own agenda. Would you like to share it with the rest of us?'

Putting her hand quickly on Mike's arm before he exploded, Rachel said. 'Actually, Wendy, I have business to attend to away from here, though of course, that's none of your business. Now, if you'll excuse me, folks, I'm going to pack.'

There was a stunned silence as Rachel left the room, closely followed by Mike. He sat on the bed, watching her pack a few things. She wasn't taking much, hoping to be back soon. 'Is it wise to leave this late in the day, darlin'?' Mike asked as by now it was mid-afternoon.

'Well, it's over five hours drive give or take a few minutes. It's 3.30 now. I can be home by nine.'

Mike wasn't convinced but knew once Rachel had decided something, it was nearly impossible to get her to change her mind.

Rachel shook her head, 'the sooner I go, the sooner I'm back, also it means the place won't be left for too long, and it will take the pressure off Ted. He's been such a help to us the last couple of years. The least we can do is help him where we can.'

Mike nodded, but he didn't want her to go. His need for her by his side seemed so important just now. He gave himself a mental shake. He was a grown man, for God's sake. He just worried about Rachel driving; it would be dark soon now in winter.

Not long afterwards, Mike watched Rachel disappear down the drive. She had taken his car as her old ute wasn't really up to much. She had only come over in it as he was in Brisbane. He made a mental note to get her a new car.

The first couple of hours passed quickly, then Rachel was overcome with tiredness as Mike had been and finally pulled over for a few minutes. She had a strong flask of coffee with her, and after getting out and walking around the car, she had a small cup of coffee and drove on. It was overcast, so it seemed even darker than normal, and Rachel drove slowly, having seen kangaroos' hopping alongside the road in several places. The drive home seemed to go on and on. There wasn't that much traffic on the road. Rachel couldn't decide if that was good or bad. Semi's and smaller trucks mostly, but it all kept her awake as tiredness overtook her again. She was still half an hour or so from home when her mobile beeped. Mike had hands-free, so she was able to speak freely. 'Rach, where are you? Why aren't you back yet? I tried the house phone. Are you okay, Rachel?'

'Mike, calm down. It's alright. I didn't want to take a roo out, and I've had to stop for tiredness, but I'm fine. It's just taking longer than I thought, that's all.'

'Thank God, I was worried there for a bit. Where are you? Will you phone me when you get home? You won't forget, promise?'

'I promise Mike. Relax alright? Another half an hour, maybe just twenty minutes. Okay?'

Thirty minutes later, she turned into their drive with a sigh of relief. It was just past ten o'clock. As she drove towards the house, she could see the old homestead now. The holiday let was all lit up. She remembered it was booked. It was one of the things Alma did was to clean and make it ready between lettings. Rachel hoped they hadn't needed anyone to do anything that day.

She was shattered, and grabbing her bag and letting Ruby out of the back, she climbed the verandah steps. In the dark, Ruby, who was ahead of her, stopped and growled. Rachel stopped. The hairs on her arms and neck stood up. It was like… it was like…. the time Johnny sat in the dark on this very verandah. 'Who's there?' Rachel's voice came out squeaky. There was no reply, but a dense shadow moved away to her left. At least she had the impression it did.

Was her imagination playing tricks? No. Ruby was still growling.

Rachel fumbled in her bag and brought out her mobile. It had a torch somewhere on it, she remembered, not that she'd ever used it. There was a light switch just by the door into the house, but Rachel couldn't reach it from where she was, and she wasn't game to take a chance. Suddenly the verandah was bathed in light. Rachel's eyes took a few moments to focus, and when they did, she gasped.

Who should be standing there but the travelling artist Patrick, looking sheepish but also very pleased with himself. Before she had a chance to react,

Pat had swept her into his arms and kissed her full on the lips. Then stepping back, he said, 'Aw, be-Jesus, you are a sight for sore eyes, so you are.'

In spite of her feelings of fear, and she had to admit, annoyance, Rachel found herself grinning at him. With his lovely Irish lilt and cheeky grin, he was irresistible. 'Pat, you scared me! What the hell are you doing here?'

'Waiting for you, of course. Is Mike not with you?' Pat peered over her shoulder into the darkness. 'Hello Ruby, remember me?'

Ruby had continued to growl deep in her throat. Pat had always had this effect on her. The truth was, he was rather scared of dogs, and Ruby knew it.

'Ruby, stop. You'd better come in Pat and explain, and so will I.'

Ruby followed them down the hallway and into the kitchen. 'Sit down, Pat and I'll make tea or coffee. Mike's at his parents' place; his mum has just died. Did you know we're married?'

'Yes, I heard. Lucky bugger that Mike.'

'It seems that when you saw him when he went bush. It was down to you he came back.'

'A long time ago.'

'Yes indeed.' Setting a mug of tea in front of Patrick, Rachel had a good look at him. He'd lost weight, and his hair was thinner, and there was a lot of grey in it. The five or so years since she had last seen him had taken their toll.

'You okay, Pat? Is there a reason for this visit, or are you just passing through? And where's your bike?'

'Bike's round the back. Just called in, really. Well, wondered if I could maybe stay a while. I see you have a cottage down where the men's quarters were. Is it occupied?'

'Yes. I'm afraid it is Pat. We have a retired drover and his wife living there. She had an accident, Ted had to take her to hospital, that's why I've come back. I was with Mike and his family. We didn't want to leave the place unattended—' for a reason she couldn't be sure of, Rachel didn't go into details.

They sat both sipping their tea, busy with their own thoughts. Then Rachel said, 'If you promise to behave, you can stay here in the house for a few days. I'm not sure when Ted's back, but it would help me. I can go back to Mike and family sooner then maybe.'

'Jesus, what a wonderful woman you are, to be sure. I'll tell you something else, you look more beautiful than ever. I didn't think it possible, but by God, it is. Mike shouldn't let you out of his sight.'

'That's enough of your Irish Blarney, Patrick. Else I shall turf you out to sleep outside. You can have this room.' Rachel showed him the room Mike's parents stayed in when they came. It was made up and clean, whereas the other room still had Emma's things she kept at the farm scattered about. 'Are you hungry?'

Rachel hoped he would say no as she was so tired. Maybe he picked up on that because he said he was okay, and Rachel left him to it. Going to the phone, she rang Mike.

'I was about to try you again. Hell, woman, I've been so worried!'

'I'm sorry, Mike, it's all taken longer than I thought, and we have a visitor.' Rachel went on to explain about Pat. As she guessed Mike wasn't exactly overjoyed, in the end, she called Pat to the phone. He stood first on one foot, then the other, listening to Mike giving him instructions. Then, having said, 'Yes Mike' quite a few times, handed the phone back to Rachel with an enormous wink. Rachel thought that was outrageous but took the phone and didn't rise to the bait.

It was a very tired Rachel that finally crawled into bed. She fell into a deep sleep almost before her head hit the pillow. Her unexpected guest, on the other hand, lay wide awake making plans.

Chapter 23

The next morning Ted rang, having guessed that either Rachel or Mike would be there. His wife had to have an operation, and as her leg was very swollen, it wouldn't happen for at least two days. He was torn as he felt he should be home but didn't want to leave his wife.

'It's okay Ted, I have an old friend here. He can hold the fort if I go back before you get home, so don't stress. '

Ted was relieved she could tell by his voice. 'Oh, by the way, Alma said to tell you it was two young couples who have rented the Old Homestead, not one as we thought. She said they seemed nice enough but were out and out city types.'

Rachel smiled to herself... Rachel could imagine that they had probably wrong-footed either themselves or Alma when they arrived.

Ted and Alma had lived in the outback all their lives, and neither of them liked crowds of people. They had been to Brisbane once many years ago and had been like fish out of water. They found it hard to understand why anyone would like to live in a densely populated place. The countryside and a simple way of life is what they understood and were comfortable with.

At breakfast, Pat regaled Rachel with his experiences over the last five or more years since they had last seen each other. He stopped talking and sat looking at Rachel. 'What was that, Pat?' Rachel asked, looking up from spreading jam on her toast.

'You were miles away. I don't believe you heard a word I said.'

'Sorry Pat, I've got a lot on my mind, and there are quite a few things you need to know.' Rachel told him about the fences being breached, though she didn't tell him why they thought someone had done it. She glossed it over as being duffers and not very good ones… She didn't know why she felt like keeping their theories to herself, but Patrick had always been rather a loose cannon. She was just being careful. Then she went on to tell him about cows calving and the holiday let and that Sid wasn't in the best of health, so not to call on him to help with anything unless it was necessary.

'Aw be-Jesus woman, here's me thinking I'll have a little rest and a catch up with you, and you put all these things on me!'

'We'll pay you, of course. I wasn't expecting you to look after the place for nothing. Mind you, we will provide bed and board.'

Rachel decided to spend the day at home, then would set off back the next day. She was hoping Alma would be able to come home then or at least the day after, so Patrick wouldn't be alone for long.

'I don't know how long before we get back, Pat. Henry has taken it badly and is unwell himself, but we will return as soon as we can after the funeral. Can you stay until then? Mike will want to see you for sure.'

Patrick looked a little uncomfortable, 'Sure, me darlin', I'll be doing me best to stay on, so I will.'

Rachel looked at him keenly, he didn't sound that sure, but one never really knew with Patrick, she decided. He always seemed to have surprises up his sleeve.

Rachel was rather shocked when she saw his bike, however. It looked rather the worse for wear, and taking Patrick's appearance in a bit more, she realised he looked very ill-kept. He had always worn his hair long but was clean, neat and tidy. Now his clothes looked as if they all needed repairing, as did his bike and sidecar. He kept his painting kit in there, but even that looked rather bare and uncared for.

'Things a bit tough, are they, Pat?' she asked him later that day.

He shrugged. 'Ah, woman, you know how it is. Sometimes up and sometimes down, haven't sold much lately, that's all. To be sure, it'll get better again one day, so it will.'

'You need to find someone to share your life with and settle down, Pat.' As she said these words, Rachel could have kicked herself. Patrick had told her years before she was his ideal woman. She didn't want to stir that up again.

Pat stared at her for a few minutes, then shrugged again. 'To be sure, the woman of my dreams loves another. But then you know. Remember that.' He added sadly.

Rachel frowned. What did he mean by that? She was about to ask him when Sid drew up in a cloud of dust. He had Norma with him.

''Well, if it isn't Patrick. How're you goin' mate?' said Sid shaking Patrick's hand, then Norma was given a brief hug and Patrick, Sid, and Norma exchanged news, and for a few minutes, they were taken up with small talk. Then Sid turned to Rachel. 'Sorry to put this on you, Rach. Oh, how's Catherine, by the way? 'Rachel swallowed the sudden lump in her throat.

'She passed away yesterday. I came back because of Alma—put what on me?'

'Oh God, I'm sorry. We thought she was a lovely lady the few times we met her, didn't we, Norma?' Norma nodded. 'Oh dear, this really is bad timing.'

'Get to the point, Sid. The suspense is killing me.'

'Well, the two young couples you have staying in the old homestead, they came through the gate onto our side in their big four by four and had a go putting it through its paces. Driving up that steep slope over near the road charging down towards the creek, scattering the cattle down there. Made a real nuisance of themselves. Allen went after them, and they were quite rude though they came back to your side. It was the two guys, not the women. One of them sounded like he had a funny accent, Allen said. Would you mind having a word?'

'Oh God, Sid, I'm so sorry. It never occurred to me anyone would use our private gate.' The gate was a shortcut between the two properties instead of the longer route by road. Neither the Newberry's nor the Grimshaw's used it all the time as the track was very rough in places, and they only managed to grade it intermittently.

'Maybe we should lock it.' Rachel said thoughtfully.

'Nah, that'd be a pain. Just have a word before you go back, Rach, will you? Sorry to dump this on you right now. How is Mike baring up?'

'Not so good, I don't think. He was really close to his Mum; being the youngest made it more likely, I think. They are nearly all pretty distressed; as you say, she was a lovely lady.' They had all migrated to the kitchen, and Rachel set about making drinks for everyone while Sid bombarded Patrick with questions.

Norma came and stood by as she made tea and coffee for them all. 'You okay, Rach? It must be hard for you. Brings back memories, I imagine.'

To her horror, Rachel's eyes flooded with tears. She hadn't really had time to think about herself. Now Norma's words released the emotions she had kept under control. She nodded, 'Pat turning up is a bit of a distraction. He looks rather down on his luck, doesn't he?' she said to turn the conversation away from herself and the Grimshaw family.

Norma looked across at Patrick, who was regaling Sid with some story or another. 'Umm, he does seem to have lost some of his sparkle, maybe.' Sid had just burst into uproarious laughter.

After the Newberry's had gone, Rachel looked at the clock, 'I had better go and see these silly people, Pat, before it gets dark.'

'Do you want me to come with you?'

'No, I'll be fine, but if you could shut the chooks up and feed the dogs and check the horses, I'd be very grateful.'

'Is that all?'

'For now, yes.

'By the way, why are the horses in that small paddock? It wasn't used for much before, as I remember. I see you have to keep giving them hay to supplement their rations.'

'Oh, it's just to make life easier for Ted while we are away.' Rach shocked herself at how easily she had lied. Why *had* she lied? Why not tell the truth? Patrick wouldn't tell anyone, but as only the Newberry's and themselves knew the real reason, Rachel felt it should remain that way.

Jumping in the car, Rachel drove the short distance to the old homestead. The light was going in the sky, but it wasn't dark yet. However, the whole place was lit up like a Christmas tree. Pulling up in front of the house, Rachel got out. A young woman who was sitting on the verandah jumped to her feet and let out a large screech like a cockatoo that they had a visitor. It was the only way Rachel could think of her voice. Another young, very scantily dressed woman and two young men all appeared. To start with, Rachel thought the young men weren't wearing anything at all and didn't know where to look. She focused on their faces. They all introduced themselves and shook hands, soft hands she noticed; the handshakes were very perfunctory. A bit like shaking a damp cloth, Rachel found herself thinking.

'Would you like a beer?' Antony, one of the young men, asked.

'No, thanks, I'm not stopping. I just came to say, please stay this side of the fence lines. The gate you went through yesterday took you onto my neighbour's property, and you scared his cattle. He wasn't best pleased, nor would I be if you do the same here. It does tell you on the information sheet in the house where you can and can't go. '

There was a silence for a minute as the four of them looked at each other. 'We didn't see any info sheet', said the other man, Dan, 'how are we meant to know? One place looks much like another to us.'

'Ya, and it's so dark at night we have to leave lights on. The girls are frightened.' Antony chipped in again.

Now it was Rachel's turn to feel as out of her depth as she could see they were.

'No, there is no light pollution here. You can actually see the stars and constellations. The night sky is quite amazing. Come outside and have a look tonight, but turn your lights off first.'

Amy, the scantily dressed girl who Rachel guessed, was in her late teens, shuddered, 'No way with all the creepy crawlies about and snakes and dingo's and god knows what.'

'Suit yourselves but just remember to keep to areas you are allowed. This is a cattle stud, not an off-road race track.' Rachel had tried to be pleasant, but she was finding it hard. 'Would you like me to show you the little map we left so everyone knows where they can go?'

'Nah, don't bother. We think we will head back tomorrow anyway. This hasn't turned out as we expected.' Antony said.

‘Okay. Fine. Well, a safe trip back‘ Rachel turned to go.

‘Hang on a minute, can we have some of our money back? We’ve booked for another five days. If we leave early, can’t we have a refund?’

Rachel turned back, her patience running out, ‘I am afraid it doesn’t work like that. If you decide to go early, it’s your choice, no refund.’

The four of them stood looking mutinous, but seemingly they had nothing more to say, and Rachel got in her car and drove back to the house. Until she was out of sight, she felt their eyes boring into the back of the car. Silly, she thought, I’m getting paranoid.

Chapter 24

The next morning, Rachel wanted to get away early but thought she should go over to the homestead and make sure everything was okay before she left. Consequently, she pottered about thinking she couldn't go over very early, then Patrick appeared looking very sleepy.

'I thought you said last night you'd be off early. I wasn't expecting to see you this morning.'

Rachel refrained from saying that it would have been very late for letting the chooks out and seeing to the horses. Instead, she said, 'I thought I had better check the old homestead before I go, see if everything is ok.'

Patrick yawned and stretched, 'Do you want me to come with you?'

'Well, I would like to show you. You haven't seen it since we renovated it. I'd like to hear what you think.'

Patrick was flattered, 'Ok me darlin' I'll be with you in a jiffy.'

He went back to his room and reappeared with his camera, 'still got this old girl. Right, I'm ready.'

On the face of it, everything looked normal when they got there. Pat was impressed with the work that had been done with the outside. The front door was open, and looking inside, even before they entered, Rachel could see that they had left as much mess as they could muster. Dirty plates, cushions scattered across the floor, dirty footprints. The kitchen area looked as if a bomb had hit it. Every room was in a mess. They hadn't actually broken anything, but they had left the place filthy. 'Aw, be-Jesus, what a devil of a mess. The rotten buggers.'

Rachel was livid but knew she couldn't do much about it. 'This is going to take a while to sort out. I had better stay and do it; I don't know when Alma will be up to much, and this is booked again in a week or so.'

'Really?' Pat was surprised as he had thought they were too far out for a holiday let.

'Yep, it's surprisingly popular. We've been surprised too. It seems city people like to think they are sampling the outback. Not, of course, that this is outback. But it's far enough in the sticks for most of them.' She sighed and pressed the heels of her hands against her eyes. 'Oh, God. I'll have to ring Mike and tell him I'm not making it back today or tomorrow, by the looks of all this.'

'Don't despair me darlin' I'll help today. Then you head off tomorrow, and I'll finish up here.'

'Oh, Pat, are you sure?'

'Course. Is there anything to eat here? I haven't had any breakfast yet.'

In the end, they went back to the main house as Rachel needed cleaning things, and she also wanted to talk to Mike. He would be expecting her later that day.

Pat had always been rather hit and miss with jobs when he had helped other times, but he put his back into it, and by the late afternoon, they had more or less finished. 'Pat, you've been a star. Thank you so much, I know I asked you to look after the animals, but this was beyond the call of duty.' Rachel said when they finished up the clean and returned to the main house again. 'Coffee?'

"Please me, darlin'. I could sure use a cup. What about supplies?'

Rachel supplied basic things like tea, coffee, sugar, a few tins of staples too and eggs. Though as they came from her chooks, that wasn't a problem. The four that had just left had taken all the supplies with them. A gesture of their discontent. Rachel thought.

'I'll have to go into town and bring stuff back. There isn't enough in my store cupboard either, just now.'

'Give me a list, and I'll do it if you like. I can get most of the stuff in the sidecar if I clean it out. I can store my painting gear on the back verandah for now, can't I?'

'Pat, that would be so good of you. Of course, you can store it and stay as long as you like.' Rachel was feeling very pleased she could get back to Mike the next day. She thought about giving Pat a quick hug then thought better of it. She could tell he still fancied her by the way he looked at her. Pat seemed to read her mind as grinning he leant towards her and gave her a kiss on the cheek and an awkward hug at the same time.

After they had eaten dinner, Rachel sat down and made a list for Pat. 'I haven't any cash to give you, to pay for this stuff, Pat. But if you tell them it's for us, they'll invoice me, so no worries'

Pat looked thoughtful for a moment, then said, 'Would it be okay if I buy a few odds and ends for myself and pay you back when I've sold a picture or something? Or knock it off any wages I might have earned from you?'

'Times are hard then, are they Pat?' Rachel asked gently.

Pat looked down, but not before Rachel had seen the look of distress on his face. 'It's only temporary. I'll be alright soon, to be sure. Ye know what they say about the luck of the Irish.'

Rachel patted his arm, which lay on the table. 'We'll give you a hand to get back on your feet when we get back from the funeral, so don't stress.'

Pat got to his feet abruptly. 'To be sure you're too good, so you are. You deserve better friendship than I can offer; that's a sure thing. Just remember I'm sorry.' With those words, he almost stumbled out of the room. Rachel thought she saw tears on his cheeks. She sat feeling nonplussed, then getting up, went and knocked softly on Pat's bedroom door. He didn't answer.

Rachel thought she wouldn't be able to sleep as she got ready for bed. She had spoken to Mike, and apart from not looking forward to the journey back, she was also now worried about Pat and his strange remarks. However, she was asleep as soon as her head hit the pillow.

She woke refreshed, and as she got dressed, she decided that both herself and Patrick had been very tired the night before, so it was nothing that important. When she got into the kitchen, she discovered Pat had got the coffee going, though there was no sign of him. Sitting down at the table, she found a hastily scribbled note.

It read: *Dear Rach, This morning the light is too good to miss, so with my camera, and painting things I have set off to paint. I have let the chooks out, given the horse's hay. I've had a scratch breakfast. Drive carefully. I'll see you later. Love as always, Patrick.*

Rachel wasn't very surprised, though maybe a little, she told herself, but then they would be back again in a few more days. The funeral Mike had told her was in two days time, and Mike didn't think he wanted to hang around afterwards.

Driving in daylight was much easier. She stopped once to let Ruby out so they could both stretch their legs, but they were soon on their way again and arrived in time for a late lunch. Only Mike was about as she mounted the verandah steps. 'Mike!' He gathered her in his arms as she spoke. Having kissed her, he continued to hold her, burying his face in her hair. 'God, woman, I've missed you so much. Don't go rushing off again, will you? Don't think I could stand it.'

'Not if I can help it, no. I've no plans to go anywhere without you either. Ruby has missed you too. She wasn't very comfortable with Pat.'

They went inside, and soon Henry and Nancy appeared, wanting to hear the news. Rachel was shocked by how much older and greyer Henry was than just a few days ago. However, it distracted him for a short time hearing about the trouble with the guests and Patrick turning up, though, of course, they had never met. Later he excused himself and shuffled off. He really walked like an old man, and again Rachel was shocked. Tom then appeared, and together the three of them told Rachel all that had gone on while she was away. Catherine was to be buried in the family plot, which was just across the other side of the horse and cattle yards. A priest was coming out from Barcauldine to perform the service. The family were all agreed that Henry was looking greyer by the day, and they wanted him to see the doctor again, but he flatly refused. The doctor had come out to see him a couple of days before Catherine died and had given him a spray for angina and told him to take it easy, knowing that hospital would be more stressful for him than staying home.

'How's Wendy?' Rachel asked. This was met with silence for a few moments, then Tom said, 'It's a real pity David ever met that damn woman. She is a troublemaker, no mistake.'

Mike and Nancy both went to speak at once. Mike stopped, and Nancy carried on. 'She came across to the house and more or less demanded to know who Catherine's jewellery was going to and her other personal effects. Tom and I were here having a coffee. Mike was outside with Jacob and David ear tagging some youngsters; she was very nasty. She accused me of sucking up to Catherine, so I got everything. She rubbished Trish said she was a no-good layabout and didn't deserve anything and….'Nancy trailed off.

'Come on, what did she say about me?'

'She said that you only married Mike so you could get your hands on some of the Grimshaw money, you only pretended to know about cattle, it wasn't much wonder your son was a druggie and….' Nancy trailed off again, looking horror-struck. 'God, Rach, I didn't mean to tell you the last bit. Mike didn't know about that, did you?' Nancy turned towards Mike.

Mike sat looking thunderous. 'No, I didn't. I would have been across and given her a piece of my mind if I had, the rotten bitch.'

Rachel shook her head, 'it's not worth worrying about her. As you said, Tom, she's a real trouble maker, and if any of us rise to the bait, we'll be playing into her hands. Whatever game she is playing, that is.'

'You're right Rachel, Henry should be our focus just now. Poor man, he's so lost. I've never seen him like this. When Catherine was so ill before, he was strong and determined that she would get well, and she did. I suppose it's different this time. She's gone, and he doesn't know how to cope.' Nancy, having said this, suddenly burst into tears, 'We all miss her so much.'

Later, as they snuggled up to each other in bed, Rachel and Mike talked it all over again. Mike was still fuming about Wendy and some of the things she had said. He wondered if David knew how Wendy was behaving as he wasn't really around anytime when she was being bitchy to them all.

'I don't know Mike, but he must have some idea of how she behaves. At least you would think so. '

Mike nuzzled his face against Rachel's neck then, drawing back, said,

'Tell me more about Patrick turning up. You say he looks a bit down and out?'

'Yes, he looks as if he has fallen on rather hard times. Maybe we can help him in some way when we get back. Promote his paintings or even buy something? I'd like to help him in some way. After all, it was him that made you come back home, wasn't it?'

Mike was quiet for a few moments then said, 'Yep. I suppose it was, he just told me life was too short, and he reckoned you, and I made a good pair. I can't really remember what he said exactly now, but it worked.'

Mike was about to say more when he realised Rachel had drifted off to sleep. Mike smiled. He was so pleased to have her back in his bed. Then with a jolt, he suddenly realised just how lost his father was now without Catherine. Tears came into his eyes. He never wanted to lose Rachel.

Chapter 25

Afterwards, Rachel struggled to remember details of the funeral. She found herself assailed by memories of her first husband's death and funeral. It had been a very bad time. Compared to Catherine, he had been young at forty-nine, but Rachel had grown close to Catherine. She had seemed so vital and full of life even though she was well into her eighties. Neighbours came from far and wide as both Catherine and Henry were so well known and respected, and Rachel found herself constantly introduced to people she had never met. The day dragged on and on. Wendy was very busy, Rachel noted with a pang. She seemed almost to be revelling in it all.

At last, the day was over, everyone had shed tears, and Henry looked completely exhausted. He announced he was going to bed even though it was only six o'clock and shuffled off to his room. He was bent and bowed and big man though he was he seemed diminished in size so much Rachel felt he was smaller than her.

The family and all the children watched him leave the room. Nancy offered to help him, but he shook his head and patted her arm. 'No, my dear, I'll be alright.'

After he had left, there was a depressing silence. Shawn and Julia, Nancy and Tom's children both got to their feet and said they were going back to the pub in Barcauldine where Shawn was staying because the house was rather full. Julia went with him, as the two didn't see each other that much anymore.

Then the others, Ian and Bob, Jacob's children, and David's children, said they were going back to their own houses. Emma and Ben hadn't come as it was felt it was too far and too difficult to manage in school time. The truth was Mike and Clarrie had rowed about it, but Mike was too emotionally drained to argue for long, and he had given in.

In the end, it was just the four brothers and their wives all sitting looking at each other. Tom cleared his throat, 'Mum made me write this down before she died and told me to wait until she was gone before I read it out. It's not exactly a will as everything except her personal things is left to Dad as you would expect. It's just her jewellery and a few bits and pieces she treasured.' Clearing his throat again, Tom read out what his mother had told him. She hadn't all that much jewellery but what she did have was beautiful and expensive. She had always said she didn't need it out there on the farm, but it was good to have nice things. She had left something for everyone, be it a broach or a bangle or pendant. However, she had left the special earrings Henry had bought her to Rachel. They were eighteen carat rose gold and were quite large, larger than Rachel normally wore. They were hoops with an exquisite horse's head in the middle. Rachel was quite overcome. 'Mum said perhaps you would leave them for Emma one day, Rach?' Tom said.

Rachel nodded, the lump in her throat making speech difficult. Wendy had been left a set of silver bangles. They were very pretty, and when worn together, looked very good, now she spoke with ill-concealed venom.

'I knew it! You gold digger. Why should you get those earrings? I told Catherine I'd like them. How could she!'

Everyone, including David, looked at her with disgust. Then David got to his feet and, taking her arm, pulled her up. 'Time we went. Thanks, Tom.' And he almost frog-marched Wendy from the room. As they exited, the others could hear her raging at him.

For a while, no one said anything. They were all embarrassed and emotional. Nancy and Trish were both sitting with tears running down their cheeks. Rach was leaning with her head on Mike's shoulder, sobbing quietly. Tom, Jacob and Mike all looked like they might cry too, and it was a while before they all pulled themselves together. Wendy's outburst on top of everything else and the way she was ranting at David as they went away was the last straw.

'Thank God Dad had taken himself off,' said Jacob, 'it wouldn't have done him much good if he'd heard all that.'

Mike stirred himself and gently disentangling Rachel, who was still sitting crying quietly. He sat up straight.

'I'm sorry, everyone, but I think Rachel and I will leave first thing tomorrow. There are things to deal with at home, and Wendy seems to have her knife into Rachel. Maybe she will be calmer if we're not around.'

It was decided, and first thing after a scratch breakfast, Rachel left with Mike not far behind her, as, of course, they had both their cars there. Trish came to wave her off, and Nancy was in tears. There was no sign of Wendy, much to Rachel's relief. Tom and Jacob were both talking to Mike across the yard and waved as she set off. It had been hard saying goodbye to Henry, who was like a broken man, *which maybe he is,* Rachel thought, as she got to the end of the drive and turned onto the highway.

She drove slowly, waiting for Mike to catch up with her. It seemed ages before he did, and she was getting worried when at last she saw him in the rear-view mirror. Not long afterwards, they had a comfort stop. Mike gave her a hug as she got out of the car. 'Alone at last,' he said.

'Not really,' Rachel waved her arm round the layby they had stopped in. It had several cars and caravans in it.

'You know what I mean. I love my family, of course, I do, but it's good to have you to myself. I think I understand now how Dad might be feeling. I never really got it before; Mum and he were close, and as a little boy, I remember feeling a bit jealous at their closeness. Mum told me once Dad was her soul mate. Until I met you, I never really understood.'

Rachel nodded, she understood, and she knew exactly how Mike was feeling, and her heart ached for Henry too. He'd been married to Catherine for so long it would feel as if a big part of him was missing. Forever gone.

Rachel heaved a sigh of relief as she turned into their driveway. Maybe they could all settle back into some sort of normality now. Then she reminded herself there was Emma to worry about, the horses, Patrick, Ted and his wife;

the worries seemed to pile up. Mike was ahead of her and was getting their cases out of his car out as she pulled up.

'No sign of Pat,' he said.

'He's probably painting somewhere.'

They unpacked and sorted themselves out. It was quite cold in the house, and Rachel had a grumble that Pat hadn't kept the big kitchen range going. She bustled about while Mike said he was going out to check the cattle. Moments later, he came back in, 'Chooks are still shut-in, Pat hasn't let them out this morning, and there is no sign of him.'

'I'll check his room.'

As soon as she opened the door, Rachel knew he had gone. The bed was made, and everything was neat and tidy, but there was nothing of Patrick's to be seen. As she turned away, Rachel caught a glimpse of a note on the pillow and, picking it up, read it hurriedly then shouted at the top of her voice.

'MIKE OH MIKE, WHAT'S HE DONE!'

Mike came rushing back; he'd been about to go outside. 'What—'Rachel thrust the note at him, and Mike read it.

'*Mike and Rachel,*

I am a rotten bastard, so I am, taking advantage like I have. One day maybe I'll make it right. I've never stolen before, technically not now, but I owe the bastards, so I do, and they had me over a barrel. I am more sorry than you'll ever know. Pat.

Rachel and Mike both looked at each other frozen to the spot, then Rachel said, 'The horses are they okay?'

Mike had the same thought, and together they rushed out to the back paddock. Jock, Dusty and Danny were all grazing peacefully, but Smokey was nowhere to be seen. Hardly believing it, they both searched around with their eyes, but they knew she had gone and that Patrick was responsible. He had managed to get to her and put a halter on her. He could be very quiet and gentle, and when Rachel had been home, he had fed Smokey some apples and generally made a fuss of her. It had been on the pretext that he'd like to paint her one day. 'The rotten, bloody bastard. I could kill him' Rachel almost shouted. *Poor Smokes, I hope she's okay,* was her second thought. Mike was already on the phone with Josh, and then the two of them looked around to see if they could find any clues as to what had gone on.

There wasn't much to see. Smokey's halter was gone, or so they thought, but it was hanging near the gate into the paddock. The rope was still tied to the fence.

It was too dry to see much, but there were scuff marks and faint tracks in the dust. Mike looked further and thought he could see faint tyre tracks too. 'The only conclusion is that Pat was somehow involved with these thieves.'

'How could he? I thought we were friends, the bastard. How could he?' Rachel repeated as the full impact of Pat's betrayal hit home.

'I'll ring Sid. He may have seen or heard something, or Barry might have done' Mike got his mobile out again. 'Sod it. The battery is flat. I'll have to use the landline.' He hurried to the house. Rachel watched him go, then, without warning, she found hot tears running down her cheeks. Tears of anger, sorrow, and an overwhelming feeling of having the rug pulled from under her feet. Everything seemed to be going wrong at once. She angrily wiped the tears away. She wasn't one to wallow, and far worse had happened in the past. *Get a grip, girl,* she told herself. If that was how Pat behaved, well, so be it. He had really burnt his bridges this time.

Mike came out of the house with a grim smile on his face. 'We might be in luck. Barry wasn't well yesterday, and Norma drove him in to see Merv. It was early evening when they returned, and about a kilometre before they got to our turnoff, they met a horse truck. It was going very slowly, and Barry managed to read part of the number plate as he was sure it was like the one he had seen before. However, they kind of put it on the back burner when they got home as Barry was feeling tired, and Norma insisted he stayed at home. He went straight to bed and fell asleep, and they kind of forgot about it. Anyway, since I rang Josh, Barry has spoken to him and told him what he can remember, and it has been put out to everyone, interstate too. I reckon they'll go over the border either to NSW or possibly the Territory.'

'But that was nearly 24 hours ago. They could be anywhere by now.'

'Maybe, but from what Barry said before, it's a pretty old truck. If they are thinking of racing her illegally or breeding from her, they'll want to look after her. My guess is they will put up somewhere and change trucks. They may have to rest up because she may be stressed too. She's a highly-strung horse. She won't take too kindly to all this. It took us a long time to get her settled here, remember? And even now, it's really only you she trusts.'

Rachel shook her head sadly. She felt so helpless. She had grown to love Smokey very much. Granted, she wasn't an easy horse, but she loved and trusted Rachel, and they had a good partnership going.

The day drew to a close with no news. Josh had promised he would let them know as soon as he heard anything, but deep in their hearts, they both felt it was a longshot. With thousands of square miles and no real information in which direction the truck may have gone made it even longer odds than either of them liked to think about. Then, as they were just about to get into bed, the phone rang. They looked at each other. Was it Mike's family, Emma, or Josh about the horse? Mike answered. Rachel watched the expressions flit across his face. Not good news, but not bad either, she guessed.

'Well, was it Josh?' Rachel asked anxiously.

'Yes, they found the truck abandoned not far past St George. The local's think they must have had a different truck waiting, but at least it gives us a direction they were heading.'

Rachel sat on the side of the bed. 'They could be heading further south, or they could be heading to Scone. So many studs around there, horses everywhere easy to put in one more and no one notices.'

'There's this Horse festival thing they have. I think it's on about now, Mid May, but it would be too late for them to put Smokes in anything.'

'Well, maybe that was plan A, but they failed to get her, so maybe it's plan B; whatever that is.'

'That's assuming that is where they are headed, of course.'

They talked round and round in circles and finally fell asleep, still not having decided on anything that made sense.

Chapter 26

Rachel got up with a splitting headache the next morning, and Mike had fallen asleep in a funny position, so he'd got a stiff neck. Breakfast was a rather muted affair. Neither of them was feeling on top of the world.

Then Nancy rang to see how they were and was shocked when she heard the news. Then she told them that Wendy and David were still arguing and Wendy was threatening to leave him but said she'd make sure to get her share out, 'whatever that means,' said Nancy. Also, Henry wasn't at all well, and they were very worried about him. Rachel had answered the phone but had handed the phone to Mike. She could overhear what Nancy was saying, though. She now tugged at Mike's sleeve. 'Why don't you suggest Henry comes and stays here for a bit? The atmosphere must be rather toxic with Wendy throwing her weight around,' she said when she got his attention. Mike asked Nancy what she thought, and she said she'd run it by both Henry and Tom.

Mike had just sat down again to finish his coffee when Sid came barrelling up in a cloud of dust. 'Any news on Smokey?' he asked as he came into the kitchen. After Rachel had poured him a coffee, a debate ensued as to what the thieves intended to do with Smokey. They speculated with Sid as to the final destination the thieves had in mind and what they intended to do. When Mike mentioned Scone, Sid sat straight in his chair. 'I have rellies down there. Not very close, and I haven't seen them in years, but I could put some feelers out. Unofficial ones, of course.'

'Aw mate, could you? That'd be great,' Mike responded.

Sid got to his feet. 'Can't promise anything, but I'll give it a shot. Thanks for the coffee, Rach. Hell, I came to ask after your Dad Mike, sorry about all this. I must be getting old, I forgot. How is he?'

Sid sat down again for another ten minutes, then finally he went. The telephone went again. This time it was Ted. His wife was finally having her op. It had been put off again and again as it was too swollen. All being well, they would be back soon. Though as Rachel pointed out to Mike, Alma wouldn't be able to do much. 'Doesn't matter. It's better if we have to go anywhere for there to be someone around,' Mike said.

They had quite a bit of catching up to do. The jobs seemed endless about the place, but both of them felt restless and unsettled. Rachel took herself off to the old homestead and finished tidying up. They had new people coming in the next day. Rachel was hoping they weren't like the last ones.

By lunchtime, Rachel felt tired, which was unlike her, and when Mike came in shortly afterwards, he said he felt tired too. 'I think it's the reaction of the last few days,' he said.

'Last few weeks more like, 'Rachel responded regretfully.

The telephone rang before Mike had a chance to answer her. It was Josh.

'I don't want you to get our hopes up, but we may have a lead on Smokey', he said. 'As promised, Sid rang his cousin, second cousin or some such. Anyway, he works for one of the big outfits down there; but there have been some new rather brash punters bought the place next door. Sid's cousin Pete, or whatever he is, says his boss had some sort of altercation with these people recently, so he has a bit of an axe to grind. Pete says his boss reckons that they haven't a clue and that there is something very fishy going on. He thinks they hardly know the back to the front of a horse, and maybe it's a front for money laundering. Some horses are worth a lot of money and—

'But what's this got to do with Smoky?' Mike was getting impatient.

'Well, they want horses on the place to look authentic and the better bred, the better for them. Anyway, if they are as green as Pete says, they just might think they can get her in foal where others have failed. I really don't know what to think, Mike, but I am waiting on a call I put through to the local force, and we'll see how we go from there. We might all be barking up the wrong tree, of course, and Smokey is miles away from there.'

They talked some more, then Josh rang off saying he would keep them posted. Mike and Rachel looked at each other, wondering if, indeed, Josh would have anything to tell them.

Later that evening over dinner, Mike, who had been deep in thought, said, 'You know what? I think I will take a little trip to Scone myself and see what I can find out.'

'If you are going to do that, I'm coming with you.'

'I thought you might say that. In which case, we will have to wait until Ted and Alma are back and settled. I don't feel like leaving the place unattended at the moment; too much seems to be working against us just now.'

As if on cue, the telephone went. It was Tom, wanting to speak to Mike. Henry would like to come and stay for a bit, and Tom and Nancy would bring him down and have a few days with Mike and Rachel. 'If that suits you?' said Tom.

'Sure, when are you thinking of coming?

'The end of next week, got several things to sort before we come, is that okay?' Mike said it was, and then they talked about Smokey and Mike's plans to go to Scone and see what they could find out.

'Be careful, Mike. You don't know what you're getting into.' Tom advised.

The next morning Ted rang to say that Alma had been given the all-clear to return home that day, though she would have to return the following week for a progress report. 'We'll set off the next day.' Mike told Rachel.

'I'll have to find out where we can stay, somewhere that can take a dog!' she said, looking at Ruby.

'I don't think we should take Ruby. It will make us stand out for one thing, and I'm not so sure it would be kind to her. She has stayed here with Ted and Alma before. She'll be right.' Rachel knew Mike was right, but she still didn't like it.

Chapter 27

The drive to Scone was a long one, so they took it in turns and ten and a half hours after they left, they finally got there. They had found a very small guesthouse tucked away from the main part of town. It was already dark, so they put their bags in the room and set off to find something to eat. It was Sunday and the last day of the festival. There was a firework display to end proceedings, and lots of places were either crowded or weren't serving dinner, so in the end, they opted for the RSL as they were sure of getting a good feed, and Mike also thought maybe he could put out a few feelers. However, he didn't find out anything useful, and as they were both exhausted, it wasn't long before having eaten they made their way back to their accommodation and bed.

Quite early the next morning, Mike's phone rang. It was Pete, Sid's cousin, as Sid had let him know Mike and Rachel were coming. They arranged to meet later that day. So Rachel and Mike decided to explore the town and maybe visit a few studs on the pretence of being interested in breeding or buying a racehorse. They found the town a delightful place, and the studs, which seemed to stretch forever, all looked extremely well looked after. White railings, archways over the driveways into some places, horses everywhere, it was an extremely beautiful setting. However, they found they would have to make appointments in many cases, so they thought better of it. Then later, when they met Pete, they realised the enormity of the task they had set themselves. It was like looking for a needle in a haystack unless they had something firm to go on.

Pete told them that the people of the stud next door to the one he worked for had put up a lot of money to get themselves into the horse world. But really, it was only the owners that his boss thought weren't quite honest, and it had all stemmed from an argument over the boundary. The new owners had the fencing repaired, and Pete's boss was convinced they had moved the boundary fence onto his land. Only a few metres, but nonetheless, he wasn't best pleased. However, as Mike pointed out, that was a long way from stealing horses. Pete agreed and then said that the staff who worked there were all honest as the day was long and had all been there many years except the stud manager and the head groom. He was backtracking rather, Mike felt and guessed it was more to do with the fact that he and Rachel were actually there rather than several hundred kilometres away.

'Have you met either of them?' Mike asked

'Manager, no. Though I know what he looks like. Head lad or strapper, yes. At the sales the other day. Can't say I liked the bloke. He was full of shit. Ooops, sorry Mrs Grimshaw—but he was.'

'In what way?' Rachel said with a smile at Pete's apology.

Pete looked uncomfortable, then said, 'Well, he was bullshitting about what horses they have and how they've imported some top horses for breeding from Hong Kong and Europe and that they would soon be the top breeders in Australia. Just a lot of bragging, really.'

'You found quite a lot of what he said to be exaggerated or impractical?'

'As I said, it was over the top bragging. He'd had a bit to drink, more than a bit, I'm thinking, so it may have been in his imagination.'

They talked a bit more, but Pete had to get back to work, and they could see he wasn't thrilled to be talking to them, so they let it go. Pete disappeared quickly and sitting back in her chair, Rachel looked at Mike. 'What do you think?'

'I don't know. It seems rather far-fetched for people like this mob to steal Smokes. Why would they, if they have plenty of money to import horses? On the other hand, is it, as Pete said, bullshit, and they are just talking themselves up? Also, we aren't sure Smokey is even in this area. I think we might've run away with ourselves.'

Rachel sighed, 'You're right. Now we're here and realise the huge number of horses in this area, it does seem as if this was a very silly idea. For some reason, I thought we would look around here, and she would just appear somehow. After all, she is an outstanding horse… well to me she is.' Suddenly Rachel felt like crying.

Mike patted her shoulder. 'Buck up, sweetheart. She'll turn up. We'll find her somehow.'

'I'm for going home tomorrow. I think this has been rather a wild goose chase.'

'I think I'm with you there, but I tell you what, let's drive by this place. We haven't been down that side road that takes us by it so let's do that now and see what we can see. We've got my binoculars. Even if we can't get too close, maybe we can see something, then as you say, we'll head home.'

The stud looked brand new from the outside. New driveway and gates, all freshly painted, the fencing looked new too. It was called the Golden Orb Thoroughbred Stud, which was written in bold gold lettering over an archway above the main gate.

'Let's drive in and see what happens', said Mike.

They didn't get very far, about halfway up the driveway, before they were intercepted by an angry-looking man on a golf buggy. He drove up on their right and stopped on the drive in front of them, forcing Mike to pull up quickly. It was a good thing they were going slowly, trying to see as much as they could. All the paddocks seemed quite a distance away, and the main buildings were up ahead. Getting out of the buggy, the man strode up to Mike's window. Mike let the window down, but not all the way.

'This is private property. You have to have an appointment if you have business here.' He almost shouted in spite of the fact he was right by the window.

'We're interested in buying a colt to race and wondered if you had anything that might suit us.' Mike said smoothly.

The man looked a little less belligerent but still angry. 'We haven't any colts for sale just now, and as I just said, you need an appointment.'

Rachel spoke up now, putting on her most charming smile. 'I'm so sorry, Mr?'

'Brown.'

'I'm so sorry, Mr Brown. We didn't realise, and our time in Scone is nearly over; someone told us you have exceptional young stock, so we thought we'd come on the off chance.'

'You'll have to come back some other time. It's not convenient just now.'

'Couldn't we have just a quick look? Then we'll be out of your hair. After all, if we can find the right horse, we are prepared to pay.' Rachel had put on her most pleading voice and smiled as sweetly as she could.

The man melted a bit. 'I'm sorry, ma'am. If you'd like to ring and make an appointment, I'd be happy to help you." He fished in his back pocket and came out with a rather rumpled card, handing it to Mike through the window.

Mike looked at the card before passing it to Rachel. 'Thank you, Mr Brown, we'll be in touch.'

'You can turn round here. It doesn't matter if you drive on the grass.'

'Ok, thanks.' Mike then did a U-turn, driving on the grass as the man who called himself Brown had said. As they drove slowly back down the drive, Mike said, 'Well, that's two things to be suspicious about. One, he didn't want us to go further up the drive to turn round and second, I'm fairly sure he gave us a false name.'

Rachel looked at the card which Mike had passed to her. All it said on it was 'Jethro Brown, Manager. Nothing else at all. 'Mmmm,' said Rachel, 'it doesn't say anything about the stud. It looks more as if it's just a card not related to anything to do with horses. It could be anything.'

'Well, I smell a rat. There's something going on here. Maybe it's nothing to do with Smokey, but they are up to no good, I'm sure. I'm going to drive to the cop shop now and have a chat.'

That was what they did, but they came out feeling it was rather a waste of time. It took some persuading to speak to a senior officer, but finally, Mike managed to see a Detective Sergeant who it turned out had been contacted by Josh. Mike told him what they had seen and heard and also said they were heading home the next day. Rachel got the distinct impression the sergeant was relieved when Mike told him that.

As they drove back to their bed and breakfast place, Rachel pointed out that they still hadn't driven down the small gravel road that ran down one side of the Golden Orb Stud. Mike promised they would do that before they left the next day.

Rachel had brought a takeaway supper which they ate in their room, being careful to clean up after themselves and not spill any of the Chinese food. It turned out to be very tasty, and soon after that, they went to bed. Exhausted and not looking forward to the long drive home the next day. It all felt rather an anticlimax.

Chapter 28

Five-thirty the next morning, they were both woken by Mike's mobile ringing. It took a minute for Mike, befuddled with sleep, to locate it and pick it up, by which time it had stopped. 'Emma' he said and tried to ring back but it went straight to answer phone. Both were feeling alarmed by now, then Rachel's mobile started to ring, she snatched it up. 'Emma!'

'I tried to ring Dad, but he didn't answer. Please come and get me. I don't like it here anymore.'

'Oh, Emma, sweetie, what's happened?' Rachel could tell Emma was on the verge of tears. 'N-N-Nothing really, I just hate it here, please—'

'I'll give the phone to Dad, Em, alright?'

Pulling a face, Mike took the phone from Rachel, who now she was awake needed the toilet, which was where she headed. She couldn't hear much from in there, but Mike seemed quite calm by the time she came out.

'Is she alright? Silly question. She wouldn't ring if she was.'

'She is just finding it hard. I really wish I had managed to get her in for boarding but maybe later. For now, she has to live at home, and she and Clarrie aren't getting on. Keith doesn't say much, but she feels he is watching her all the time. It seems like a pretty toxic atmosphere. Look, do you mind if we go home via Brisbane? I know it means a longer trip, but I just feel I need to see her?'

‘Of course, Mike. I’d have said the same thing if you hadn’t suggested it.’

They showered and got packed up. They had already told the proprietors that they were leaving early and found two breakfast bags full of goodies outside their room as they left.

When they got in the car, Rachel put her hand on Mike’s arm. ‘Don’t worry about driving down that side road. We need to get to Brisbane.’

Mike leaned across and gave her a peck on the cheek. ’Love you.’

Up the New England Highway, they drove. Tamworth came and went. When they got nearly to Glen Innes, they stopped at a pub in Glencoe for lunch. It was very cold, and they were glad of the steaming bowls of soup they ate. Then on to Glenn Innes, Tenterfield, Warwick, the journey seemed endless. ‘If we weren’t on a mission, I would have liked to explore these places.’ Rachel remarked as she navigated her way through the side streets of Warwick.

Mike, who had been dozing, roused himself and said, ‘Don’t worry, I’ve put our names down to be grey nomads in a few years’ time.’

As they drove out of Warwick, they stopped and swapped over the driving again. Mike said they were only an hour and a bit from Brisbane, and he knew the city much better than Rachel. For herself, she was pleased as she felt tired and a bit deflated. She knew it was silly, but her expectations had not been fulfilled, and they were no closer to finding Smokey than before. Even so, she was as worried as Mike about Emma, and she was as anxious to see her as Mike was.

When they got to Brisbane, Mike checked into the same hotel as he did when he periodically came up to Brisbane and where he had stayed recently trying to sort Emma out. From there, it wasn’t far to the suburb where Clarrie, the children and Keith lived. Rachel had never been before and was surprised by the large luxurious houses in the area. Having checked in, they had driven straight to the house as by now it was after three o’clock. Mike figured it wouldn’t be long before the children would be home, but he wanted to speak to Clarrie first. The children made their own way home if they didn’t have any after school activities.

When they got there, it was plain no one was at home. There were no cars, and the place had an empty feel. So they settled down to wait. Mike leant across the middle console and put his arm rather awkwardly across Rachel's shoulders. 'I'm sorry about this. I know you wanted to find Smokes. We'll just have to go back soon.'

Rachel smiled at him. 'Emma is more important, silly man,' she then put her lips to his and kissed him. Their kiss deepened, then they both jumped as there was a loud tap on the window and Ben was standing grinning like a Cheshire cat.

'Hi Dad, Rachel, thought you might drop by. Emma said she rang you, but you were having tea somewhere. Scones and cream, was it?'

Mike and Rachel couldn't help laughing. 'No, son, we were at a place called Scone. It's in NSW.'

'What were you doing there?'

Mike and Rachel told Ben about Smokey, the whole sorry tale, and Ben was rather upset more for Rachel than anything as he knew she loved the horse so much. All this time, they were standing on the driveway, Mike and Rachel having got out of the car when Ben appeared. Suddenly a Porsche swept into the drive, nearly running into them. It pulled up with a screech of tyres on the bitumen drive. Clarrie got out, looking both angry and flustered. 'What the hell do you think you are doing? Why are you here? What a stupid place to stand.'

Mike's turn to look angry, but Rachel stepped in before he had a chance to say anything. 'We're on our way home from down south and just thought we'd break the journey and say hello.'

'Oh. I thought you'd come to check up on us. Emma has been very difficult, and I wouldn't put it past her to run to you, making more wild accusations. Now that you're here, would you like a cup of tea? Or a glass of wine? If you're waiting to see Emma, she shouldn't be long.'

Mike had opened his mouth to protest at the beginning of Clarrie's little speech but decided to let it pass. Rachel looked at him and winked. She knew what he was thinking.

They climbed the few steps up onto the verandah, and Clarrie unlocked the front door, but instead of opening it, she turned to them and, indicating the loungers and armchairs that were there, said, 'Perhaps you'd like to wait here. I'll bring drinks out in a minute.'

Rachel and Mike exchanged looks, then Ben said, 'Can't I show Dad and Rachel my room and the new lego spaceman I just made?'

Clarrie looked embarrassed but held her ground. 'No, Ben. Not now. You can bring your lego thing out here.' With that, she slipped through the door and was gone.

Ben, though, was having none of it. He threw open the door his mother had just shut and stormed after her. 'I want to show them now! And I can't carry the spaceman out. He'll fall to pieces.'

Now Rachel and Mike felt embarrassed, though why should they? Rachel said afterwards; she wasn't sure. 'It's alright, mate. We'll see him another time, and you can show Rachel your room then.' Mike tried to calm Ben down.

'It's not fair, why can't I? You're so mean. I hate you.' Ben shouted out to his mother, who by now was deep inside the house.

Rachel sat on the big cane sofa and patted the seat beside her. 'Come on, Ben, come and tell me about your day.'

But Ben disappeared into the house. Rachel had caught a glimpse of the inside, which was opulent. Money had not been spared, it was obvious. Mike sat beside her. 'Clarrie is always difficult when I've come here. It's almost as if she's ashamed of the place, or maybe she's ashamed of the fact I was once married to her. I don't know.' Mike rubbed his hand over his face.

Rachel snuggled up to him. 'She's an idiot then, but I'm pleased about that because I have you instead.'

Emma came in the drive and, on seeing first their car and then them, gave a squeal of delight and shot up the stairs, almost throwing herself upon her father and Rachel.

'I'm so pleased to see you. Where's Ruby?'

'At home, sweetheart, we've been down south. We're just on our way home.'

'Oh.' Emma looked like she might cry. 'You can't stay then? It's Friday tomorrow. I was hoping you'd be here over the weekend.'

Rachel and Mike once again exchanged looks, 'We just popped in to see you, really. After your phone call, we just thought we'd check in with you.' Mike sounded unsure of himself.

Rachel opened her mouth to speak, but Emma got in first. 'Fine, do as you like. I know I'm not important.'

'That couldn't be further from the truth Emma. We've come out of our way to be here, and Rachel gave up a chance to find Smokey.'

'Why, what's happened?'

'Smokey was stolen four days ago, and we think she is in a place called Scone, which is where they have a horse festival, and there are lots of stud farms. So we went to see if we could find her.'

Emma looked horrified. 'Oh God, Rach, how awful. Did you see her or anything? I know how special she is to you. I'm sorry.'

Emma was sitting between them, and now Rachel hugged her. It's okay, sweetheart, you didn't know about Smokes. And yes, I'm feeling upset. She won't be easy to handle, and she will be cranky and frightened. A bit like you, I'm guessing?'

Emma nodded, tears threatening. Just then, her mother appeared with a tray that had glasses of white wine on it. Ben was behind, carrying another tray with a platter of olives, small crackers, little nibble size pieces of cheese and other delicacies.

'You needn't have gone to all this bother. We only popped in to see Emma and Ben.'

Clarrie settled herself in a cane armchair and, raising her glass, said cheers. Rachel and Mike only mumbled cheers in return. Then Clarrie said, 'Ben tells me one of your horses has been stolen, but you think you know where it is. Bit hard on you just after Catherine's funeral. How did that go? I was sorry to hear about your Mum, Mike. Sorry, I should have said so before.'

Emma spoke up now. 'Ben and I thought we should organise flowers or something, but Keith said no.'

'Your Granny only wanted flowers from Henry. Everybody else donated to cancer research, so it's okay.' Mike didn't sound okay. His throat had closed up, and he felt anger at Keith. However, he took some deep breaths and, turning to Clarrie, said, 'now we're here, we thought we'd take these two out for dinner. '

'Not tonight, there's school tomorrow, and they'll have homework.'

Mike looked ready to burst, so Rachel stepped in quickly. 'We will have an early dinner, and they will have plenty of time for homework. Besides, that means you'll have a nice dinner just you and Keith'

'Keith's got a meeting. Oh well, if you eat early, I suppose it will be alright.'

'Thanks, Mum,' Ben said, then Emma thanked her mother too, though it was muttered, and she didn't look at her mother when she said it.

'We'll go now and change and shower then be back for the two of you in an hour,' Mike said, getting to his feet. He'd hardly touched his wine, nor had

Rachel. She didn't like it, though she noticed the label on the bottle that Clarrie had bought out and realised it was from a very expensive winery that had won many awards.

An hour later, they arrived back to pick up two excited children. 'We don't get to go out like this.' Ben said.

'Don't you? Surely Keith and Clarrie take you out sometimes, don't they?' Rachel asked in surprise. She'd never thought to ask them before. Somehow it had never come up.

'Sometimes Mum will take us to Wet and Wild on the Gold Coast or bowling, but not very often. We haven't been anywhere for ages. We never go out for dinner, and when Mum has taken us out. Keith never comes. Then she is worrying about getting back to him.'

'Oh dear, that's a bit sad. Never mind, we'll have a good time now.'

They did have a good time. Emma and Ben talked and talked; about school, their friends, what they wanted to do when they left school. Ben wanted to join the police force. Emma wanted to be a jillaroo. Rachel stole a glance at Mike when Emma said this, and he winked at her, but they listened and didn't pour cold water on any of their plans. They took the children to an Italian Restaurant nearby, but it was still later than Mike had promised by the time they got them back. Clarrie wasn't pleased but thanked them at the door. She was very business-like but very distant. Mike had promised that they would pick the children up and take them to school in the morning. When he told Clarrie this, she snorted. 'They don't need taking; they walk, or rather Ben does, and Emma catches the school bus.' Mike said it was what he was going to do, and that was that.

Later as they lay in bed, Mike and Rachel reviewed their time with the children. Mike had a talk with Emma during the evening, and it seemed as if nothing was any worse than before. She was resentful of her mother being married to Keith in the first place, and both Rachel and Mike could see that as she grew and her hormones were up and down, she could be difficult. But they were aware that she was genuinely afraid of Keith and Mike resolved to sort it out with her school as soon as he could. They had said she could board next term, but only during the week. Weekends she would have to go home.

Chapter 29

The next morning, they picked Emma and Ben up as promised. Ben seemed happy enough but promised his father he would look out for Emma. Emma, who had been very quiet, suddenly started to cry. 'I hate school, and I hate living in the city. Why can't I come and live with you?'

A moment or two after this, Mike pulled up outside her school, and they all got out.

Rachel hugged Emma. She was struggling not to cry herself. She was as close to Emma as it was possible, even if she was just a stepmother, she told herself. Then Mike was hugging Emma and telling her to hang in there. It would be alright, and he would certainly have another talk with Clarrie. It would be sorted out as soon as they could.

As they drove away, Rachel said gently, 'I don't really know what more you can do, Mike, given how Clarrie is and how Emma is. I don't really see how this can be resolved, not easily anyway.'

'I know, but I have to reassure Emma, and I will speak to Clarrie again too and the school. I may have to come back to Brisbane again soon, sweetheart.' Mike glanced across at Rachel as he said this. He felt bad as he knew she was still worried about Smokey, and of course, Henry was coming soon, and Nancy and Tom would be staying a few days too.

Rachel smiled at him. She guessed what he was thinking. 'It's okay, it will take my mind off Smokes having them come, and who knows, she may not even have been in Scone.'

Their route took them down the Ipswich motorway a short distance, then the Warrego Highway to Toowoomba. Just as they got to the range, they came to a stop; a semi and a car had collided, and it wasn't good. The highway was steep and narrow in that section, and they knew they would be there for some time. Two hours later, they made it into Toowoomba. Having sat still for so long, Mike insisted they have a short break and stretch their legs, toilet too. It had been in their minds not to stop until Oakey, but that wasn't to be. They had planned on getting home mid to late afternoon, but it was actually evening before, tired and hungry; they arrived home to a very excited Ruby.

Mike had phoned ahead and told Ted when they were getting near, he had expected them much earlier, of course. He had been up to the house and put the lights on and had lit the fire, so the kitchen was lovely and warm when they finally got inside.

Rachel bustled about to get something to eat. Mike came up to her and gently pushed her into a chair. 'Sit, woman, will you. Grimshaw's special scrambled eggs coming up in a minute.'

Rachel smiled gratefully. 'You must be tired too. You've done the bulk of the driving today. Do you remember the first time you made me scrambled eggs?'

'I sure do, and you ate them as if you hadn't eaten for a week. I think I fell in love with you then. If you couldn't resist my scrambled eggs, you couldn't resist me. '

Rachel smiled at the memory. She felt warm and loved and—the next thing she knew, Mike was gently shaking her. 'Wake up. Eggs are served.'

The last few weeks had taken their toll, and having both had a quick shower, they tumbled into bed. Three-quarters of an hour later, the phone rang. Mike flew up in bed, his heart racing; looking at the clock, he realised it was still only nine-fifteen.

'Hello?' he croaked.

'Sorry Mike, were you asleep?' Josh apologised.

'Yes. Never mind, what is it, Josh?'

'I've just had a phone call from the police in Scone. There are reports of a grey mare galloping down the main road through the town. She came out of a side road, a team have been dispatched, but so far the news is sketchy.' Mike sat up, wide awake now. 'I just thought you'd want to know. Sorry I know it's a bit late. I just wondered if it was your horse, but I suppose this sort of thing happens down there.' Josh suddenly sounded deflated. He'd been so sure it might be Rachel's horse he didn't stop to think. Then again, he was surprised the police had bothered to ring him. They must have felt it important.

'Thanks for the update, Josh. Let us know if you hear more, but maybe tomorrow.'

'Sure, sorry, 'night', Josh rang off feeling foolish.

Rachel was blinking blearily at Mike when having hung up, he turned towards her. 'Was that about Smokey? Have they found her?'

Mike shook his head. 'No, sweetie. Close your eyes and go back to sleep. You look like I feel; shattered.'

Mike put out his bedside lamp and, lying down again, he felt Rachel snuggle up to him, and moments later, she was breathing deeply. Mike, however, lay for a long time thinking about the strange place down in Scone and wondered what, if anything, was going on there.

Chapter 30

Rachel woke and looked at the time. 6.15 am. Being the start of winter, the mornings were dark, but she was usually awake before now, and so was Mike. He was still asleep, so she crept out of bed carefully. She didn't want to wake him. For herself, she felt more refreshed from a good sleep than she had for several weeks. She dressed as quietly as she could then, going through, let Ruby out. During the summer months, Ruby slept on the verandah, but she was allowed to sleep in the warmth of the kitchen during winter. It was a clear frosty morning. Everything was covered in a thin film of white. In places where the sun reached its early morning rays, the white had a pink tinge to it. It looked like a giant hand had gently outlined the chooks pen and house, the yards and buildings with a pink paintbrush. The sky was clear, almost translucent, the palest of pale blue. Rachel stood looking and enjoying the beauty while Ruby snuffled about, seeking out smells, then rolling on the frosty grass for good measure. Rachel, her contemplative mood over, went and let the chooks out then fed the other dogs who were looking for their breakfast.

By the time she got back inside, she felt cold as she hadn't stopped to put a coat on. Mike was sitting yawning at the table. She hadn't expected him to be awake yet, and he made her jump.

'Oh Mike, there you are!'

'Where else would I be?'

'I left you asleep. I'm guessing you haven't slept as well as me?' Rachel poured them both a coffee, but as she put Mike's down beside him, he pulled her onto his lap. 'God, woman, you're cold.'

'There's quite a frost, but come on, I want to hear about the phone call last night.'

'It was Josh; something about a loose horse careering about Scone's main street after dark, I think. Josh said it was a grey horse. He wondered if it was Smokey,' Mike didn't want to get Rachel's hopes up; he thought it was unlikely to have been her. After all, they wouldn't have let anything like that happen, especially if she had been stolen. Rachel nodded, looking sad. She thought Mike was right, she made to get up, but Mike held her fast, working his hand under her shirt. 'You're so cold. I think I may have to warm you up.'

'Sounds interesting, but we have loads to do— Mike stopped her objections by kissing her.

It was an hour later when the phone rang. They were both getting dressed for the second time that morning. Mike answered, and Rachel watched his face as he, first of all, looked surprised, then pleased, then incredulous. 'Well, that is amazing. Yes, we will make arrangements. Thank you, my wife will be thrilled.'

Turning to Rachel with a broad grin on his face, he said, 'That was the local police down in Scone. The loose horse was Smokey. It took quite a time to corner her. She was pretty wild, scared, I expect, but finally, they captured her, and sure enough, it was her. She is being looked after at the veterinary facility down there. She has a few cuts and minor scrapes, but nothing serious. They'll keep her for a few days and let her recover., she's pretty wound up and cranky. We'll have to organise transport home.'

'Oh, Mike!' Rachel threw her arms around his neck and kissed him. 'Steady girl, I think I might need a little rest first!'

'Mike!' They were both still laughing when Ted tapped on the door. Rachel almost felt like kissing him too, she was so pleased, but she knew he would be highly embarrassed. 'Come in, Ted. We're a bit behind this morning. We haven't eaten breakfast yet. Would you like a coffee?

The day passed in rather a blur for Rachel. She was so busy thinking about Smokey, where had she been and how come she was loose. She wasn't an easy horse to handle; she either liked you or she didn't, and that resulted in her being temperamental. She tolerated Mike, but it was Rachel she loved. Ted was treated with disdain by the horse. She had only taken the titbits from Patrick because Rachel had been with her. But Patrick had been droving in the past. In fact, he'd had many jobs, so Rachel hadn't been that surprised he had managed to capture her. But why had she been loose? If they had gone to the bother of stealing her, why let her go? It just didn't make sense. Mike had talked to the vets who were looking after her, and they said they would keep her for the best part of a week, at least until her swollen foreleg recovered a bit. They said it wasn't serious. She had just knocked it badly somewhere. It seemed to them that maybe she was being loaded onto a float, and she managed to break free and then somehow got clean away. She had a halter on, and the remains of a rope was attached to it.

Early evening Tom rang to say to expect them the next day if it was still alright to come, which, of course, it was. Then Mike rang Emma, and they both had a talk to her. She was very tearful, but when they spoke to Ben, he said nothing bad had happened, really. They were both pleased to hear Smokey had been found. Emma even said she would tell her mum and, as she hardly seemed to have a normal conversation with Clarrie, they hoped it was a good omen. Mike remarked to Rachel that it had made Emma think about something outside her own problems.

'Perhaps things will get better from now on,' Mike said as he came out of the shower later that evening.

'Hopefully, coming here will be good for Dad, and if I can get Emma into boarding during the week, that will be good too. We'll get Smokes home too, and I don't think they will try that again. Stupid bastards, what in the world did they think they were doing and why let her go?'

'Beats me, I can't understand it either. Maybe we'll never know.'

Chapter 31

It was mid-afternoon the next day when Henry, Nancy and Tom arrived. Both Rachel and Mike were quite shocked by how tired they all looked. 'Bad journey?' Rachel asked as she and Nancy hugged.

'No, not really. We were later leaving than we intended, weren't we, Tom?'

Tom looked grim, then said, 'You can say that again, but at least we are here now, and I, for one, could do with a beer.' He looked at his brother as he said this with a gleam in his eye.

'Coming up and for you too, Dad?' Mike replied.

Soon the men were sitting out on the verandah, catching the last of the sun's warmth before sunset. Cattle, horses, the land would all be mulled over now. Nancy and Rachel had refrained from joining them. Nancy said she wanted to unpack, though, in truth, there wasn't that much to do. Rachel picked up Nancy wanted to talk to her alone, so she waited, pottering about in the kitchen. A few moments later, Nancy joined her.

'How are things really, Nancy?'

Nancy sat down at the table. She looked close to tears.

'Tea? Or something stronger?' Rachel asked.

'I think I could do with a glass of wine or beer, whatever you are having, please, Rach.'

Rachel got out a good bottle of wine and poured Nancy a generous glass. 'It's early to be drinking, but who cares. This is only the second time you and Tom have made it out here, isn't it? Cheers, lovely to see you.'

Nancy's eyes brimmed with unshed tears at Rachel's little speech. She nodded, too emotional to speak for a little. Rachel sat quietly, knowing she had something to get off her chest, and she'd speak when she was ready.

'It's just been so horrible since Catherine died. I know it's only a short time, but it feels like a lifetime. Henry and Catherine were such a strong team. Now Henry just sits and seems so uninterested in everything. He's out there with the boys now, but I'd be surprised if he says a word. Anyway, he's like a zombie. And Wendy, well, what can I say? She keeps coming up to ours and bitching about everything. She had a go at Henry about Catherine's jewellery, saying it wasn't fair. She says that as they have three kids who are younger, they should swap houses with us; she just goes on and on. Henry sits and ignores her though I think it gets to him. He was crying the other day after she left. Just sitting with tears running down his face. It was awful. If we did swap with her, then poor Henry, what would he do? Live with us? It's primarily his house, but we've lived there ever since we were married. I got on so well with Catherine, it was never an issue, and it's a big house after all.' Nancy stopped suddenly, looking stricken. 'I'm sorry, Rachel. I'm not making a lot of sense, and I know you have troubles too.'

Rachel reached across the table and took Nancy's hand in hers, and gave it a squeeze. 'It's alright. It's good to let it out. Bottling things up is never good. I've been guilty of that in the past. Wendy is a bitch by the sound of it. Poor Henry, and you as well, it's the last thing any of you want right now when you are grieving. We are too, but being away helps. Mike was very close to his Mum, and I see the sadness in his eyes, but time does help. A cliché, I know, but true. You are welcome to stay as long as you want. Though I suspect Tom won't be comfortable being away too long.'

'Thanks, Rachel. I am so pleased you and Mike found each other. You have been so good for him, and you're right, the Grimshaw men are all very focused on their work, whatever it may be.'

Having talked to Rachel about Wendy and how things were, Nancy seemed a lot happier, and soon after this, the two of them started to get dinner ready. Henry came in from outside. 'Getting too cold out there for my old bones,' he said. He put his arm across Rachel's shoulders as she stood preparing vegetables, 'I hear Smokey has been found. Good news, my dear, good news. Now I'm off the have a shower before dinner.'

Nancy watched him go with her eyes like saucers. 'That's the most I've heard him say since the funeral. Coming here was a good move; that's plain. What's this about Smokey? We knew she was stolen, but where was she found? Have you got her back?'

Rachel filled her in, and moments later, Mike and Tom appeared. 'Henry looks and seems better already, Tom,' Nancy said.

Tom nodded, 'You look brighter than when we arrived too.'

The evening was convivial as they were all making an effort not to be weighed down with any problems or sadness, and when they retired for the night, they all slept soundly. Even Henry, for whom sleep had eluded lately.

Tom and Nancy ended up staying for nearly a week and looked like different people when they finally left for home. In the meantime, it was arranged for a horse transporter to collect Smokey and bring her home.

When she arrived back, it was obvious that she was pleased to be home. She had lost weight and still had a few places of bare skin where she had been injured, though they had all been superficial. The main concern had been her knee, which had been knocked badly, it was thought, but there was no permanent damage, and though still slightly puffy, it was much better.

When she came down the transporters ramp, she gave a loud whinny, and Jock whinnied back. Rachel took her from the transporter driver and led her out to the paddock. All the other horses were pleased to see her back, and they all galloped off in high glee.

Mike was just fixing the invoice up with the driver when Rachel returned to hand him the halter Smokey had on, so she asked him if he wanted a drink or anything to eat before he started back.

'I wouldn't mind, missus, if that's on offer, thanks. Name's Abe, by the way.' He held out his hand.

He was a real chatterbox, and once he'd had a feed, he sat back in his chair with a cup of tea and looked as if he'd stay until dark, if not all night. Henry was the one he was mainly talking to, and Mike and Rachel were happy to sit back and listen to his stories. They both felt it was doing Henry good.

Henry seemed more like his old self. He had times when he was sad, they all did, but they also knew that Catherine wouldn't want them to be moping about. She had been a strong person and, like Rachel, and hadn't believed in dwelling on the past or on anything which she could do nothing about.

Time passed, Mike enjoyed having his father there, and they spent many an evening reminiscing about things that had happened to Mike as a little boy. He had been something of a scallywag, it seemed, and Rachel listened in, finding out all sorts of things about him she hadn't known.

They woke up one morning and were surprised to realise Henry had been with them for over a month. It had been a good suggestion, Rachel reflected. Henry looked much better. Mike had stopped stressing about Emma so much; things seemed to be on a more even keel with the children. They didn't expect anyone would try to steal Smokey again, and next door, Sid seemed to be getting back to his old self. Also, as far as they knew, Wendy had behaved herself, keeping her distance from Nancy and Trish. 'I hope this isn't too good to last', Rachel thought that morning as she let the chooks out.

Chapter 32

Two weeks later, Rachel would recall her thoughts as everything happened at once. First of all, Henry suddenly announced he thought he had better go home. It was lunchtime, and Tom had rung and asked to speak to his father when Rachel answered the phone. Henry looked angry as he came back into the room.

'I'll have to go back. Tom and David have had a big blue. Jacob has tried to mediate, but David is being driven by Wendy, and all hell is breaking loose as far as I can see. Besides, I've been away long enough. You've been so good putting up with me, my dear Rachel, thank you.'

It was arranged that the next morning, Mike would drive Henry home. Rachel said she would stay at home. She had no wish to inflame matters. Wendy didn't like her, and though she would be happy to spend some time with Nancy and Trish, she felt it wasn't worth the hassle. Mike promised he would come straight back as they had quite a few animals calving just now, and there was a lot to be done. Another few weeks and it would be spring, and though they had quite a few visitors in the old homestead through the winter, it was booked up nearly nonstop until the summer. Rachel had been doing all the cleaning over there since Alma had her accident, but Alma was gradually getting back into the swing of things. Rachel didn't want her to overdo it, though.

Mike had only been gone two hours when Emma called. She was crying, and to begin with, Rachel had trouble understanding her problem as she was hiccuping and generally not making sense. They hadn't seen the children since they had visited them in Brisbane, as Clarrie had taken them with her to see her parents during the school holidays. Keith hadn't gone as he was too busy, and it meant a trip to W.A. as Clarrie's parents had moved to Perth some years before. Her father had a job there; consequently, they seldom saw the two children or their daughter.

'Emma, sweetheart, take a deep breath and speak so I can understand you.'

'I know Dad did his best getting me into boarding, but I don't like it, and this weekend when I went home, Ben was so horrible to me he says I can't come home and throw my weight around. Keith and Mum have taken him out to dinner and shopping and all sorts of things, and I feel left out. It's not fair. So I said all this to Mum, and she was so cross with me. So cross! She said I was an ungrateful little brat. Keith was having to stump up the money for me to board, and it was my own fault I was boarding and Keith was so fed up seeing my miserable face around the place anyway, and if I didn't look out, they would throw me out and send me to live with you or better still my grandparents in Perth.' Emma stopped at this point and burst into more uncontrollable tears.

'But Emma, when did this happen at the weekend?' Rachel was puzzled, as today was a Tuesday.

'It was yesterday. I had a row with Mum as I wasn't well, so I didn't come back to school until this morning. I still don't feel well either. I have bad stomach cramps.'

'I see,' Rachel said slowly. 'Well, supposing you go to the sick bay and get something for your tummy, Dad isn't here right now. He's taken Grandpa Grimshaw home and will be on the road just now. I'll get him to call you later. Alright? Come on, chin up. When you don't feel well, things always seem worse than they really are. Mum loves you. We all say things we don't mean when we are cross or tired. I love you too, and so do Ben and Dad.'

Rachel could hear Emma blowing her nose vigorously, then she said,' Thanks, Rach, I love you too. I'll go to the sick bay now. You will get Dad to ring me, won't you?'

'Course I will, sweetie.'

'Bye.' Emma rang off. Rachel sat down. She felt almost exhausted after that exchange. Moments later, the phone went again. Thinking it was Emma, Rachel merely said. 'What is it now, sweetie? Go to—'

'Mrs Conway?' A female voice asked.

'Yes. No. I was Mrs Conway. I'm not now. Who is this, please?'

'Ah yes, sorry,' said the woman the other end. 'My name is Olive, and I am ringing as I work for the Child Safety Agency. Can you clarify you were Mrs Conway? What is your surname now? If you don't mind my asking.'

Not happy with the way this conversation was going, especially after the conversation with Emma a few minutes before. 'As it happens, I'm Mrs Grimshaw now. What is this about?'

'Look, I'm sorry, we seem to have got off on the wrong foot. Just tell me did you have a son called John or Johnny?'

Rachel's heart seemed to stop. 'Yes, I—yes,' she whispered.

'I think I need to meet with you, Mrs Con—sorry, Mrs Grimshaw. Can you come into Roma in the next day or so?'

'Please give me an idea what this is about, or I'm not wasting my time driving to Roma.' Rachel said firmly.

She heard the other woman sigh at the other end of the line. 'I really do need to talk to you, Mrs Grimshaw, face to face. Can you make it on Thursday?'

Rachel wasn't prepared to go to Roma without Mike by her side, so she said. 'No. I can come Friday but not Thursday.'

It was plain it didn't suit Olive, but in the end, she agreed, and they arranged to meet Friday late morning at Olive's office. In spite of asking again what it was about, Olive stood firm and said she would tell Rachel when she saw her, but it was nothing to worry about.

Her mind in turmoil, Rachel found it hard to do any of her usual jobs that morning. Memories of Johnny kept intruding on her thoughts. From the little blond boy who loved to ride his pony, help his father, play hide and seek, run around with the dogs; to the monster who made her life a misery and of whom she was terrified. It had ended with his death, not hers, but it had been a close thing.

When at last Mike phoned to say that Henry and himself were back safe and sound, Rachel couldn't wait to tell him about the odd phone call, leaving Emma's call until she had told him about the Child Protection phone call. Then she said she was worried, but it was mostly about Emma.

'But surely they would have called me or used your married name, not Conway. They wouldn't have asked about Johnny either, would they darling? Look, I'll get home as soon as I can, I was going to leave the day after tomorrow, but I'll come straight back. Hang in there. I'll be home soon.'

'Thanks, Mike, please drive carefully. Now tell me about things that end.'

Mike groaned. 'Not so hot, I'm afraid. Wendy seems to have David running around in circles and pressing for them to swap houses with Tom and Nancy. They say Dad can stay but that they have younger children and need the space.'

'That's not true though, is it, Mike? Their house is big enough, and Nancy and Tom have lived there ever since they were married. Henry wouldn't survive under Wendy's house rules anyway.'

Mike snorted a short laugh, 'I like that expression, 'Wendy's house rules, and no, you're right. The shit would hit the fan, as they say. Big time. Tom and Jacob will have to rein David in, I'm thinking, as the atmosphere here is rather toxic. Seeing as it doesn't involve me, I'll be pleased to come home earlier anyway.'

They talked for another few minutes, then Mike rang off. Rachel put the phone down with a sigh, this year hadn't been much fun so far, and it didn't look like getting any better.

She didn't understand what Wendy thought she would achieve in alienating David's brothers and his father; it didn't make sense. She liked David, what she had seen of him, but thought he was probably a little weak. He seemed the least business-like one of the brothers and was maybe lacking in drive and energy.

Rachel sighed. She would be pleased when Mike was back by her side. Those lonely times between husbands was something she couldn't contemplate. Looking back, she was surprised at what she had managed on her own. *I was younger then,* a little voice reminded her.

Chapter 33

Mike rang her briefly the next morning to tell her he was just about to leave. 'Drive carefully, Mike. I'll see you in a while.'

Rachel then settled down. He was on his way, and five and a half hours later, he'd be back, *well, around about that time,* she told herself. She went down to the cottage to have a word with Ted about a few odd jobs that needed doing and ended up having a cup of tea and a chat with Alma. Looking at her watch on the way back to the main house, Rachel was surprised where the time had gone. She wanted to ride the back boundary fence as they were going to put young heifers in there next week, and they needed to check that the fence was still good. She considered going in the ute, but she had hardly been on Smokey since her return, so thought she would enjoy riding her instead. Shortly afterwards, she was enjoying a canter across the paddocks, Ruby running alongside. It was a coolish day with a slight breeze, and the three of them enjoyed the wind and the freedom as they bowled along. There were several places where the wire wanted tightening. Rachel had her tools in her saddlebag; when she reached a spot where there was a heap of rocks near the fence, she was a bit more cautious as once before a snake had made her trip up and falling backwards, she had broken her arm. However, the fence was fine just there. She gave a little chuckle to herself as she rode on, Mike had picked her up from the hospital, and she had been very embarrassed. She hardly knew him then and was acutely aware of the fact she wasn't properly dressed due to having her arm in a sling.

Looking again at her watch, she decided to go into the paddock where the creek ran through. She had time, and she wanted to make sure the fence line was secure where the horse thieves had opened it. She was sure it was but somehow wanted to be doubly certain.

She never felt that relaxed there after finding a dead man once half in, half out of the creek. However, everything was looking good, and finally, she turned for home. 'We should get there the same time as Mike, Smokes,' she said, patting Smokey's neck. 'Come on, Ruby, you'll get left behind,' she said, having got through the gate. They set off at a steady canter. Smokey was pleased to be home; Rachel could feel her happiness with her pricked ears and long swinging stride. She seemed to glide effortlessly over the ground. Ruby was running flat out and was hardly keeping up. By the time they arrived back home, Rachel was feeling very exhilarated; Smokey was hardly blowing, and Ruby jumped straight into the big water trough to cool off and drink at the same time. When she got out, she shook herself all over Rachel, who couldn't help laughing. Having sorted her horse out and put her into the paddock with the others, Rachel looked at her watch, then frowned. It was later than she thought. Where was Mike? He should have been home a little time ago by her reckoning.

Feeling uneasy, she went straight into the house, hardly stopping to discard her boots. There was no message on the answering machine, so no news being good news, she tried to settle down and quell the little worm of worry at the back of her mind. She decided to get dinner prepared as much as she could without actually cooking it. Preparing vegetables and marinating meat would take her mind off watching the clock.

It didn't. The time seemed to go faster somehow, and now Mike was two hours overdue. She gave in to her worry. What could have happened.? He was always good at letting her know if he was going to be late for anything. That fact alone made her worry more. Reluctantly, she tried his mobile, but it seemed as if it was switched off. There was no response at all. She felt hot and sticky with worry. Should she have a shower? But then if he rang, she wouldn't hear the phone, and she could hardly take it into the shower with her. She made herself a cup of tea, then Ted tapped on the door, saying he had shut the chooks up. They were all in, and though it was early, he'd made the best of it.

'Boss Mike not home yet then?' he looked keenly at her.

'No, not yet,' Rachel tried to keep her voice light.

'He'll be right, don't worry.'

'Thanks, Ted, I hope so.'

Ted tapped the side of his nose and repeated. 'He'll be right.'

Suddenly needing company, Rachel asked Ted if he'd like a cup of tea or even a beer, but he shook his head.

'Reckon Alma will have tea ready soon. Best get back. If youse need us, youse know where we are.' With that, Ted was gone. Rachel sat at the table in the gathering gloom of late afternoon.

'Oh, Mike, where are you? Please be safe,' she whispered to herself. Ruby sat as close as she could get to Rachel and nudged her hand. She was trying to comfort her mistress. Rachel put her hand down and stroked the silky head. 'What could have happened, Rubes? Please let him be safe.'

The phone ringing in the quiet was almost frightening. Rachel snatched it up. 'Mike?!'

'Hell, no. Rachel, it's Josh here.'

'What's happened? Mike is hurt, isn't he? What's happened?'

'Rachel, it's okay, Mike's okay. Well, he's had a bump on the head, but he's okay. Just an accident.'

'Oh God, where is he? What's happened? Are you sure he's okay?'

Rachel could hear voices in the background, then Mike spoke. 'Rachel, I'm alright. It's just these paramedic people won't let me come home, they want to take me to hospital, but I'm fine.'

He certainly sounded his usual self, and Rachel found herself suppressing a grin. She could imagine what a difficult patient he was being.

Putting on her sternest voice, she said. 'Now listen to me, Michael Grimshaw. If the paramedics want you to go and be checked over, you go. You, of all people, know how bad a seemingly innocent bump on the head can be. Where are you anyway?'

'On the Warrego, not far from our turn off, had a bit of a prang. They want me to go to Roma hospital.'

'You go with the paramedics, and I will meet you there soon.'

There was a silence for a moment or two, then Mike said. 'God, woman, you can be bossy sometimes. Alright, I'll see you there—and Rach? I love you.'

Unexpected tears sprang into Rachel's eyes. 'Love you too. Lots.'

Minutes later, Rachel was on her way to Roma. She had been down and told Alma and Ted what was happening. Then, calling Ruby to stay with Ted, she got into her old ute and started the journey to Roma. It seemed to take ages. While she drove, different scenarios played out in her head. She realised she had been in such a hurry for Mike to have medical attention she hadn't asked a single question. Johnny's problems had started with a blow to the head. It had changed his personality; she didn't want history to repeat itself.

When finally she got to his bedside in the A&E department, she found Mike sitting up on a bed with a bandage around his head, a bruised face and one arm in a sling. There was a nurse taking his blood pressure, and she turned around as Rachel came into the cubical. 'Here's my wife now. She'll know I don't need to stay.'

'Mike, what in the world happened? Bit more than a bump on the head. What else have you done?' Rachel bent and gave him a swift kiss on his better cheek.

Mike looked serious suddenly and gave an involuntary shiver.' A cattle truck lost control and crossed the road right in front of me. I couldn't do anything about it, it was just there! I don't remember much else for a while, then when I came to, I was trapped. There were cattle blaring and steam rising, and all hell seemed to have broken loose. I couldn't get out. The car was half underneath the side of the truck. It was all jammed up. After a bit, the firemen managed to get me out. I couldn't let you know, don't even know where the phone is. They would have let you know earlier, but I told them Josh would ring you, so they got onto him. But I wouldn't let them contact you until I was out, and it took a while. Sorry, but I didn't want you coming when I was still stuck. I know what you are like.'

'What about the truck driver?'

Mike shook his head, and his eyes welled with tears, 'Poor bugger didn't make it. Though I think he may have been in some sort of trouble when he lost control. It's a straight section of the road. '

Rachel bent and kissed him again. He was suffering from shock, she could see, and was deathly pale.

'Well, here you are and lucky by the sounds of it, what happens now?'

'I was hoping they'd let me come home with you, but they are talking about CT scans and things. '

A few moments later, a young doctor appeared and behind him was a nurse, and shortly after that, Mike was whisked away for a scan. He would be staying overnight, that was plain, and later, in spite of his protests, that was exactly what was arranged. Rachel told him to stop being silly; she wanted him to be fit and well. He was not to not come home without first making sure everything was okay. 'I know how important it is to be one hundred percent sure your head is alright, darling. I don't want history to repeat itself. I've been worrying about that ever since I heard about this accident,' she said anxiously.

Rachel and Mike were very relieved the next morning when Mike was given the all-clear to leave. They had to wait until eight o'clock when the doctor came, and it seemed ages. The hospital coffee wasn't to their liking, so they decided to wait before they had anything to eat or drink. Mike's arm wasn't broken, but all the ligaments were badly torn. He was black and blue all over. Though it was fairly superficial, it was very painful.

They were just getting in the car to leave when Rachel banged her hand on the steering wheel. 'Hell, we are supposed to come back here tomorrow to see that Child Safety woman. I don't think that is on now. I'll ring her now before we leave.'

Olive wasn't answering her phone, then Rachel realised it was still early, and she wouldn't be in her office yet.

'Look, sweetheart, let's drive into the town centre and have that coffee and breakfast we were planning, then try her again. I don't feel that hot, but I'd rather we do that than go home and have to come back. After all, they said Merv and the nurse at home could see to my arm if necessary.'

Rachel looked at him with concern. He looked pale and drawn. He was in pain, she knew, but what he'd suggested made sense, so that is what they did. Rachel tried Olive's number again as they sat down, and this time she answered, breathless. Rachel explained what had happened.

'Oh, dear. Well, if you can come right now, I can see you, but only for a short time, as I have a busy schedule. Can you do that?'

They cancelled their coffee and breakfast, which they had ordered, and went to the office. Olive turned out to be a large lady with a strange taste in clothing, but she greeted them kindly and sat them down. She kept looking at Mike, worried, as she talked.

'I am sure you are wondering what this is all about. I will try to be brief as I can see you need to get home, Mr Grimshaw. Your son, Johnny, Mrs Grimshaw, I have been digging and know quite a lot of his past and how he terrorised you. He did, however, have a relationship with another bikie. A young woman called Eve, and she was in the early stage of pregnancy when he was killed.'

At this point, Rachel gasped. 'Oh, God. I met her at Johnny's cremation. She was very hostile. Are you saying there is a baby somewhere?'

'Not a baby, no, that was five years ago at least. The baby is five years old now, a little boy.'

Rachel's throat tightened, and she felt faint. Olive continued. 'We have only now found out about this child. He was found sitting beside his dead mother in a squat in a tenement building that was about to be demolished. She hadn't been dead that long thankfully, but he is traumatised enough as it is. There were papers in an old bag referring to his father, whom it seems may have been your son. Somehow, she has flown beneath the radar. There was no birth certificate, or at least we couldn't find one. She died of a heroin overdose. The child is currently in foster care, and well looked after. He is small for his age and, at the moment, has no speech. We're not sure if this is because of his mother's death or other circumstances. We've been trying to trace any relatives he may have. DNA will help us with that. What I am asking for at the moment is would you be willing to give us a mouth swab for a test?'

Rachel felt sick and faint, but she nodded, and Olive set about organising that. She was asked when she had last eaten, and as it was the night before, that was fine. Then she had to rinse out her mouth and wait ten minutes before spitting into a plastic container. 'The more, the merrier', Olive said cheerily. Rachel felt far from cheery, and when finally they left Olive's office, Rachel was feeling light-headed and weak. Mike, of course, wasn't much better, and they both staggered into the café they had been in before; the staff gave them very odd looks.

Chapter 34

Several cups of coffee and breakfast later, they both felt much improved. Rachel had only picked at her food, but Mike had eaten a hearty breakfast. They had both been fairly silent, each busy with their own thoughts and didn't really talk until later when Rachel drove them home.

'We'll have to see about replacing my car, and it's time this old jalopy was replaced too, I'm thinking.' Mike said. He was watching Rachel keenly, not sure how she was feeling after the shocks she had dealt with in the last twenty-four hours. He knew she was a strong woman, but it seemed to be one thing after another these last few months. Then he remembered how strong she had been through Johnny's reign of terror, but this was different.

Rachel didn't reply immediately, but then she nodded. 'That'd be good. This old car will die on me one day.'

'Well, we didn't really bargain on it being driven around the countryside like this, did we?'

Rachel shook her head. 'No…' she said vaguely. 'Mike, what do you think about this little boy. Do you think he's Johnny's son?'

'I don't know what to think. I never saw this girl, did I? It's possible, I suppose. But then again, we don't know exactly what her relationship was with Johnny; or if there was anyone else in her life.'

'Mmmm', Rachel was thoughtful. 'All I know is she was very upset and very hostile at Johnny's cremation. We were the only mourners. I offered her a coffee and a chat, but she refused. I stopped for fuel, and she must have followed me as she appeared and asked for Johnny's possessions that he had on him when he was shot. I just handed them over. I didn't want them. It's sad, isn't it? If she was having Johnny's child, she didn't tell me then.'

'Maybe she didn't know or wasn't sure who the father was. Who knows?'

They drove on in silence for a bit. Neither of them knowing what to think. Rachel was surprised at herself, as the thought of a grandchild didn't excite her as she had always thought it would. She realised she had changed a lot over the last five years. *Maybe even before that*, she thought to herself.

'Rach?'

'Sorry Mike, I was miles away. What did you say?'

'If this girl was taking drugs while pregnant, there is a good chance the baby would be damaged anyway, and Olive said he has no speech. It might be he never had.'

'I know. Do you think if he is my grandson, they will expect me to take him on?'

'I don't know, darlin'. Do you think you could take him on if they do?'

Rachel was quiet for a couple of kilometres. Mike waited. At last, she said, 'No. I don't think so. In fact, no, not at all. All the trouble I had with Johnny, I couldn't go through all that sort of trouble again. I feel as if Emma and Ben are almost my kids. I don't want this child; it would make our lives even more complicated. Does that make me a bad person?'

Mike put his hand on her thigh and gave it a little rub. 'Whatever you decide, Rach, it will be fine with me. I love you, and nothing will change that. If you do decide to take him on, then I will support you as much as I possibly can. If not, then that is okay too. We are partners and soulmates, right?'

Tears threatened, but Rachel swallowed them down. It didn't do to drive when crying. The rest of the journey home, they talked about Emma and her problems and put Johnny's son on the back burner for now. It would be some time before the results of the DNA came through anyway, and they had more immediate problems to deal with.

Mike looked done in by the time they got home, and Rachel insisted he went to bed. 'Your body took a huge thump, yesterday sweetheart. Please go to bed and rest. You look like you'll fall down soon.' Mike gave in; he wasn't feeling that great. Ten minutes later, Rachel, who had expected to hear the shower running found Mike half undressed, asleep on the bed. She covered him and crept out of the room. She went down and gave Ted a rundown of events, then phoned the Grimshaw's to tell them. She didn't want them to hear by some other means. Then she set about making some soup for a light lunch. Mike was still asleep when she popped her head in, so she went and laid beside him for a moment; she had been so afraid he wouldn't be here beside her like this, and now he was. Thank goodness, she thought.

They both woke up startled. Ruby was scratching at the door that led onto the verandah. Daylight was fading fast. 'Oh dear, I fell asleep too. Are you alright?'

Mike smiled at her, 'I'll live, but I'm hungry now. What's the time?'

Rachel squinted at the bedside clock then gasped, 'goodness, it will be dark soon. We've slept nearly the whole afternoon away.'

'That is a waste. We could have been doing something else—ouch.' Mike had gone to put his arm around her, and the bruising on his ribs and arm protested.

'Come on, lover boy, let's go eat, I feel hungry too, and Ruby is saying it will soon be her suppertime.'

In the end, they weren't really sure if it was a very early dinner or a very late lunch, but they both felt better and rejuvenated by it.

Rachel was just clearing up when Ted stuck his head in. 'All the jobs are done outside, Missus,' he looked at Mike, who was still sitting at the table. 'They showed your accident on the news earlier this arvo. I reckon you are one lucky guy.'

'I think so too, Ted. Thanks, hopefully, I will be out and about tomorrow. See you then.'

Ted wasn't so sure by the look of Mike and by what he'd seen of the crash site. It seemed inconceivable that anyone had survived. Then the phone rang, and Emma was sobbing when Rachel picked it up. 'Dad. Is dad hurt? What's happened? why didn't you tell me?'

'It's alright Emma, Dad is here with me, battered and bruised, but that's all. Sorry not to let you know sooner. We wanted to wait until we were sure he was coming home, and events overtook us rather. We didn't expect them to put it on TV. We were going to ring you in a minute anyway. Dad had better ring your Mum too, but he'll speak to you first.' Rachel handed the phone over.

Mike talked soothingly to Emma for a few minutes, then told her he would ring Clarrie and disconnected the call. As soon as he had done so, the telephone rang; it was Clarrie, and he then had a huge ear-bashing as he told Rachel afterwards.

When he finally put the phone down, he looked exhausted. 'Bloody television. They might have warned us my name would be mentioned,' he growled.

No sooner had he said this, but Sid and Norma turned up. Of course, they knew all about it as the bush telegraph had been working overtime. However, they wanted to check that Mike was indeed alright for themselves.

It was well into the evening before Norma and Sid left. Norma had brought a casserole 'just in case', she said. Rachel asked if they would like to stay and help eat it. 'No, my dear, it's for the two of you. Mike won't be doing much for a week or so. You'll be too busy to cook, I think.'

Knowing Norma as she did, Rachel accepted it with thanks and put it aside. Not long afterwards, both she and Mike were in bed sound asleep again.

Chapter 35

Mike soon found out that though he had always thought himself very fit and able, his body had taken a huge knock, and it was ten days before he started to feel something even approaching his normal self.

It was a busy time with the cattle, and as they were nearing the end of winter, they moved most of them to the further paddocks where there was more shelter from the hot drying winds and more grazing as those paddocks had been rested during winter.

Coming into the house after a long and busy day out in the paddocks, Rachel saw the answering machine was flashing with a message. 'Play the message, will you, Mike? I'm getting straight into the shower before I start on dinner.'

'Hmm, I thought I was going to shower too. I could soap your back for you?' Mike paused and played the message and then went to tell Rachel what it said. He had a strange expression on his face as he joined her under the hot water.

'Who was it, Mike?'

'The Child Safety woman, Olive. It seems you are that kid's Grandmother.'

'Oh, hell. I was so hoping I wasn't. I had almost forgotten all about it too. We've been so busy.'

Rachel gently soaped Mike's back and massaged his shoulders. He was still tender in places. Having done that, she got out and started to dry herself. Mike joined her. 'I was hoping that would last a bit longer!' he said, wrapping a towel around himself.

'It was meant to. I was distracted thinking about this child. What else did she say?'

'Only would you ring her at your earliest convenience.'

'Oh dear, I suppose I must, but I am so afraid of opening Pandora's Box. I have almost forgotten about Johnny, and the terrible time he gave us all. You have been so brilliant in helping me with all that, and we have a good life, a happy life. We have ups and downs; who doesn't, but what we share is so, so wonderful. I don't want anything to spoil it. I'm scared of that happening, I guess.'

Mike drew Rachel into his arms. 'Rach, you are one of the bravest, strongest, kindest people I know. We have a strong marriage, don't we?' Rachel nodded. 'Whatever happens, with this child or anything else come to that, we will face it together. I am not at all sure they are expecting you to take this boy on anyway. They will just want to keep you in the loop. Now, how about massaging my sore places a bit more or any other place that needs attention, maybe?'

Rachel smiled at him, 'Mike Grimshaw! You are incorrigible. I have a meal to get, remember?'

'I'll help with that, but a little cuddle first?' with that, Mike picked Rachel up then almost dropped her as all his sore places protested. This set Rachel off into gales of laughter, and grabbing her singlet and shorts, she ran into the kitchen before Mike had fully recovered.

Mike followed her with a rueful look on his face. 'You win. Now, what do you want me to do?'

Later as Mike slept beside her, Rachel thought back over their conversation. Mike was right, their marriage was solid, and in the past, they had been through so much nothing would rock their world now. There was nothing to say that they expected Mike and Rachel to take this child on anyway. She would ring Olive tomorrow and have a chat, simple, really, she thought.

The next morning, Rachel waited impatiently for the time to ring Olive. She knew she wouldn't be in her office that early, and time dragged when she wanted to get on. Mike had asked her if she wanted him to stay and be there for the phone call, but Rachel knew he was champing at the bit to get some jobs done and sent him packing. He set off in the ute to check out one of the windmills, which didn't seem to be working properly. Ted was going with him.

Rachel busied herself cleaning, always good to do when stressed, but today it didn't soothe her enough, and she went to her desk in the office and sat down. She sat staring at the blank computer screen for a minute, then opened a bottom drawer and pulled out an old photo album. The photos were mostly black and white to start with, then went to colour. There she was, a young bride smiling up at Sam, Johnny's father. In some ways, Sam had been better looking than Mike and, when they were first married, had been fun-loving and full of life. But when the problems with Johnny started, he became withdrawn and quiet, as Johnny became a stranger and so, in a way, had his father. Rachel sat staring at the photo of the man she had married, so long ago now it seemed, she hadn't really taken on board how much Johnny had changed Sam and herself, too. Deep in thought, she jumped when the phone rang. It was Norma wanting to have a chat and catch up. Although she had resolved to say nothing, Rachel found herself telling Norma all about this little boy whom it seemed was her grandson.

Norma was quiet for a few moments, and Rachel thought she had somehow gone, but then she said,' Oh my word Rachel, what a shock, what happens now?'

'I don't know. I don't know if they expect me to take him in or anything. I don't even know how I feel about it. I ended up being so scared of Johnny, he would have killed me, I don't doubt it, if—Well, you know. I just know there was no love left, and I don't want a reminder of him here, or anywhere, come to that. Oh, Norma, am I being selfish? This poor child must have been to hell and back as it is.'

'Rachel, you are one of the kindest, most loving and giving people I know and never selfish. I fully understand what you are saying. Do you think they expect you to take this child on then?'

'I don't know what they want me to do. It's new ground, but that's the crux of it, really. I'd rather not even see him but feel I must.'

'Poor you, you know where I am should you need to talk, have a woman's perspective and all that.'

'Thanks, Norma. I may take you up on that more than you think. Mike is wonderful, but men do tend to look at things differently.'

They chatted for a few more minutes, then rang off. No sooner had Rachel replaced the receiver than it rang again. It was Olive.

'Good Morning Mrs Grimshaw.'

'Rachel.'

'Rachel, yes, no doubt your husband told you the news? '

'Yes, I understand you have a match. This child is related to me, my, my grandson.'

'Yes, how do you feel about it, Rachel?'

This threw Rachel completely. She hadn't expected to be asked this question. She took time answering.

'To be perfectly honest, I don't know how I feel. Johnny, well, he was a monster at the end. I have tried not to think about it for these last few years, and now it seems I must. What happens now?'

'The first thing will be for you to come into my office again, and I will arrange for you to meet the foster parents that are looking after Caleb.'

Rachel sucked in a breath. She felt Olive was railroading her. 'I am sorry, Olive, I need a bit more time to think about all this. I will ring you in a few days.'

'Oh.' There was a pause, then Olive said. 'I see. I do understand you are reluctant to see your grandson after all that has happened, but I have to admit to being disappointed, Will you ring me in a few days and let me know how you are feeling then? It's important.'

'Of course, I know it's important.' Rachel snapped, 'I just feel you are pushing me. I'll be in touch soon.' Rachel replaced the receiver gently, though she was tempted to slam it down. She felt angry. How dare this woman railroad her like this? She wasn't prepared to make any decisions until she was ready.

Later, when Mike came in, he found her scrubbing away at the kitchen sink and everything gleaming. The curtains from their bedroom were spinning around in the washing machine, and there was a strong smell of polish everywhere.

'I gather you are upset, darlin'. You're cleaning as if your life depended on it.'

Rachel chucked the cloth in her hand down and turned into Mike, who wrapped her in his arms. 'This is awful Mike, I got cross with this Olive woman. I felt she was pushing me too hard. I don't want to see this child. I don't want any reminders of Johnny. He would have killed me, for god's sake. His mother too, Eve or whatever her name was, was so nasty. Why would I want to see their offspring or have anything to do with him? But then I think, poor little boy, all alone in the world, in foster care when he has a grandmother and step-grandfather here who could provide for him and give him a home. I just keep going round and round in circles, Mike. What should I do?'

'I suggest we sit down and have some lunch, then we will write a pros and cons list. Perhaps that will help. You are right about one thing though, Olive is wrong to push you. Especially you, you are more likely to do the opposite when pushed.'

Rachel gave a little rueful laugh and pushed him gently. 'I know I can be a bit stubborn sometimes.'

'Sometimes?! You are the most stubborn person I know, but also the loveliest, most beautiful and desirable grandmother in Queensland, maybe even Australia.'

Rachel stuck her tongue out at him and started to get the lunch organised. Mike, as always, had made her feel better.

Two days later, Rachel rang Olive and told her she would meet the foster parents and talk to them. Maybe they could tell her more about her grandson than Olive because, as it transpired, Olive hadn't actually met the foster parents or the little boy as they were all in Brisbane.

Olive would be there, too, and because of this, it wouldn't happen for a couple more weeks as Olive had a large caseload. She suggested someone else go instead of her, but Rachel said no, she wanted Olive to be there. If not, she wouldn't meet them. 'She started all this, Mike, so I think she should be there.' Rachel explained to Mike.

School holidays were starting, and Mike and Rachel had invited the children to stay. Clarrie said no, they were a short two weeks, and the kids had several sporting things to go to and friends to see. She wanted them at home in Brisbane. Also, Kevin had promised to take them away for a few days. 'He wants to bond with them more.' Clarrie told Mike.

'Not sure I like that expression coming from him,' Mike said to Rachel as they were eating dinner that night.

Chapter 36

As it happened, they would be in Brisbane two days of the last week of the children's holiday, so Mike managed to persuade Clarrie that they would spend what time they could with Emma and Ben. They would travel up on the Friday and spend some time on the Saturday and Sunday before meeting with Olive and Caleb' foster parents on the Monday.

So Saturday midmorning, they met Clarrie, who had picked the children up from their different sports to take them to lunch. Ben seemed the same as ever, but Emma was sullen. She turned away when Rachel and her father went to hug her and when Rachel asked if she was okay, she just shrugged and said, why wouldn't she be. Rachel and Mike exchanged looks, but Clarrie, who was still there, didn't seem to notice. They took the children to a restaurant on the south bank but being a Saturday, it was very busy, and they wouldn't have got in had they not booked.

Once they had ordered and got their drinks, Mike sat back and started to ask them about their trip to Rainbow Beach, where they had gone with Keith and Clarrie.

'It was great, lots of fun,' enthused Ben. Emma sat quietly and didn't speak 'we had surf lessons, and I did really well, better than Em. Keith bought us our own boards each too, except Emma forgot hers one morning, and Keith had to take her back, so I got an extra half hour that morning.'

‘I didn’t forget it, Ben. I had put it in the car the day before, and I hadn’t taken it out. Why would I?’

‘Well, it wasn’t in there, was it? Mum said you must have moved it, else why wasn’t it there. No one else would want to move it.’

Emma shook her head, tears pooling in her eyes. This argument had raged before Rachel realised. She also realised Emma would have been alone with Keith, something they had hoped wouldn’t happen.

Mike opened his mouth to speak to Emma, but Rachel, who was sitting next to him, squeezed his thigh under the table. Mike looked at her, and she shook her head slightly.

Mike quickly changed the subject and told them all about Ruby and the horses. He told them Dusty, and Danny were both getting fat. It seemed a long time since the children had been out to the farm to ride. Then their food came, and the conversation died a little as they ate. Emma, though, only picked at her food and Rachel watching her, felt that something was very amiss.

Later, when the meal was over, Emma got up to go to the toilet, and Rachel got up and went with her. Once alone in the Ladies, Rachel asked Emma what was troubling her.

‘Nothing, Rachel, I’m good.’ Emma shot into the nearest cubicle. Rachel sighed, it wasn’t going to be easy to get Emma to open up, but something was very wrong.

‘Emma,’ Rachel tried again when Emma came out, ‘sweetheart, what is—’ she said no more, as a couple of girls came in chattering away about their boyfriends.

Emma hurriedly washed her hands and seemed about to take flight, but Rachel stopped her. ‘Emma darling, we need to talk. YOU need to talk.’

‘I can’t, Rachel, can’t you see? I can’t.’

Leading her out of the ladies, Rachel steered Emma to a couch in the passageway that led back to the restaurant area. ‘Why can’t you, Emma?’

‘Because. Because I’m too scared.’ Emma started to cry.

‘What are you scared of, darling? Please tell me.’ But Emma just shook her head then, with a big effort, gulped her tears back and said, ‘Nothing, I am being silly. Mum’s always telling me I’m silly and imagine things. I expect she’s right. It’s nothing really.’

Rachel sat looking at Emma searchingly for a few moments but knew she would get nothing more from her, so reluctantly got to her feet. As she got up, Emma grasped Rachel's arm. 'Please don't say anything to Dad, will you?'

It was exactly what Rachel intended to do, but she managed to sidestep the question neatly as the two girls came back out of the ladies, and one of them collided with Rachel. It was deliberate on Rachels part as she was afraid Emma was about to get her to promise to keep quiet.

Then they all went to the Art gallery. Rachel managed to speak quietly to Mike and say she would tell him later, so he didn't ask any questions. Rachel felt she was walking on eggshells all afternoon, as she didn't want any confrontations between Emma and Mike. She knew he was frustrated at not knowing what was going on but wanted to talk to him first. She was relieved when finally the afternoon was over.

No sooner were they alone when Mike said, 'Come on, Rach, tell me all. What's up with Emma?'

Rachel repeated the whole conversation she had with Emma, thinking as she spoke it didn't amount to much. As she had known he would be, Mike was angry, very angry. 'What do you think is going on, Rach? It's that creep Clarrie was daft enough to marry, isn't it? I'll wring the bastard's neck!'

'Mike, calm down. We don't know what is going on, do we? We can't just swan in there and make accusations; you as a policeman should know that.'

'Ex-policeman.' Mike corrected her automatically.

'I think we need to be very careful what we do. We don't want to make things difficult for Ben either. Keith is a nasty piece of work, but I, for one, don't imagine he is violent. I think we need to find out what is going on and play it softly, softly from there.'

Mike sat thinking, then said. 'I married a wise woman, it seems. It makes sense what you say. No good asking Clarrie, is it? She will just say Emma is silly.'

'Well, I'm probably putting my head in a noose here, but shall I try to have a word with her tomorrow. If I can make her think about Emma instead of herself, maybe she can get to the bottom of what's happening. After all, she is responsible for the children.'

Mike was thoughtful again, then he said. 'God, I'm a lucky bugger to be married to you. I think it might just work. It's a great idea, Rach. If anyone can get through to Clarrie and Emma, it's you.' He leant forward and kissed her. 'Thank you, sweetheart.'

'Don't thank me yet, Mike. I may get nowhere at all, but it's worth a try.'

Chapter 37

The next morning when they met Clarrie to spend time with the children, Rachel asked her if she could have a coffee with her away from the others. They had decided to do it this way as Clarrie wouldn't be forewarned, and they hoped easier to get on side.

'Oh, I haven't long. Keith is expecting me home again shortly. He wanted to go to Redcliff for lunch to try out a new restaurant there.'

'Please, Clarrie. I, um, need your advice.' Rachel had her fingers crossed as she said this.

Clarrie visibly perked up. She was glamorously dressed, as usual, and it crossed her mind that Rach, who though neat and tidy wasn't very fashionable, needed advice about her appearance. She would help her to dress less of the country girl and more of the city girl.

Leaving Mike to take the children into a small shopping area, the two women settled themselves in a nearby coffee shop.

'Now, what can I do for you, Rachel?' Clarrie asked importantly.

'I'm not asking for me, Clarrie; I'm asking advice about Emma. After all, she's your daughter, but my stepdaughter and I want her to feel she can confide in me as I am sure she does you, confide in you, that is.'

Clarrie sat looking completely non-plussed. 'What do you mean, confide in me?'

'Well, it's plain something is very wrong, have you not noticed?'

'Of course! Well, actually, not really' Clarrie slumped In her seat. 'I don't think it's anything serious. She's just being a teenager. Boy trouble maybe.'

'Has she a boyfriend then? I didn't know.'

Clarrie looked very uncomfortable now. 'Well, not that I know of, as I said, just teenage angst, I expect.'

'Clarrie, there is much more to it than that, believe me, and it doesn't do to bury your head in the sand and pretend nothing is happening.'

Clarrie bristled, 'I'm not. Are you suddenly an expert on teenagers then?'

Rachel sighed; this wasn't going well. 'No, but I don't want things to go wrong, and that is where they are heading.'

Clarrie was getting angry now. 'I seem to remember your son was a thug, so who are you to tell me how to deal with my own daughter?'

'I care about Emma, and I care about you too. You don't want to lose her, do you? I know what it's like when that happens. Different circumstances but my heart still aches for the dear little boy I lost.'

Clarrie was intrigued now. She didn't really know what had happened, only bits she had read in the paper and the small things the children and Mike had told her.

'How come? What did happen? Was he alright as a small child then?'

Rachel told her the whole sorry story. How she and Sam had longed for children, and after several miscarriages and misery, Johnny was born. He was all they wanted until he fell from his pony and hit his head. It had changed his personality, and he had turned into an impossible child and ultimately the drug-ridden bikie who had terrorized her.

'Look, Clarrie, what I have told you is completely different from your situation, but the bottom line is this. Emma is very unhappy and stressed about something. You need to talk to her and find out what it is. You're her Mum, her best friend, who else should she turn to? No one can ever take your place, and if you don't care for her now, you could end up losing her and believe me, a child is so precious you don't ever want that.' Rachel stopped, then said. 'I haven't put this very well at all, have I? I just want you to talk to Emma. There is something wrong, and I feel it has something to do with Keith. I may be wrong, but please try to find out what it is. You may only have one chance.'

Clarrie had sat with her head down, looking at her hands which were resting on the table. Now she raised her head and looked at Rachel. Tears were glistening in her eyes. 'Thank you, Rachel, for telling me your story. I had no idea. You are right; the children should come first. I'll try to get to the bottom of it all.'

'Good. Now I had better catch up with them. I expect they will have persuaded Mike to buy them morning tea by now. We never did order that coffee, did we? I'll see if they have time for me to have one with them.'

As they stood, Clarrie unexpectedly hugged Rachel, 'I'm glad Emma and Ben have you as their stepmum', and with that, Clarrie rushed away, not wanting to get more emotional.

They took the children to Cleveland for the day, or what was left of it. There wasn't time for much, but they had fish and chips for lunch, and the children paddled a bit, then they played French cricket and fell about laughing at Rachel, who was hopeless at hitting the ball, and when she did hit, it went off in odd directions. Emma relaxed more than she had the day before, and they all felt sad as they made their way back into Brisbane. Emma was tearful when she said goodbye, but Rachel and Mike told her that they may be back in Brisbane again soon, so she cheered a little. Ben was quieter than usual too, but not tearful.

'I had almost forgotten about meeting those people tomorrow; what with one thing and another, Mike, I'm dreading it.'

'It will be fine, Rach, don't worry, we're in this together, remember. Now tell me again what Clarrie said. It was a job to talk before.' Rachel had rather garbled her meeting with Clarrie to Mike, not wanting the children to hear.

Rachel recalled the conversation as best she could. She played down what she had told Clarrie about Johnny but emphasized that she had told her to think of her daughter and to make sure she was alright and not under any bad influences.' I tried to make her see that if she didn't do the right thing by Emma, she would always have regrets. We only have one shot at being mothers.'

Mike was driving and glanced across at her.. 'Do you have regrets regarding Johnny, then?'

'I know there was nothing more we could have done. We tried everything, but yes, of course, I regret the fact I lost my little boy; that he fell off his pony that day. I asked myself lots of times if we could have somehow prevented that from happening. But they are futile questions; what is done is done. I just tried to make Clarrie see she has to support Emma more and not dismiss her as a silly teenager.'

Mike patted her knee as they pulled into the car park of the apartment building where they were staying. 'If anyone can make Clarrie see she needs to do something, it has to be you. She'd have gone off at me like a rocket.'

Chapter 38

The next morning Rachel felt nervous. *No, not nervous,* she told herself, *apprehensive.* She really didn't know what to expect or where this was leading. She was very glad Mike was with her.

They were asked to wait in the reception area, and no sooner had they sat down than Olive came bustling in. Rachel looked at her and smiled. Her clothes were mismatched and too small, and she had a little beret perched on her head that looked a little like a bird's nest. It had the effect of making Rachel feel less stressed. *Maybe she does it on purpose,* Rachel thought to herself. She dared not look at Mike; else, she would have laughed.

Another woman appeared and, after speaking to Olive, came towards them with her hand out to shake theirs. 'Hello, good morning. I'm Amanda Freeman, and I am overseeing your grandson's case. This way, please.' She indicated she wanted them to follow her through the swing doors she had just entered by.

She led them into an office that was large and had a sofa and chairs set up in a corner. A young couple was already sitting there; they got to their feet when they all entered the room. Olive was bringing up the rear.

They were all introduced to each other. The young couple were Sandra and Alec Jones, and they were looking after Caleb for the time being. Rachel had expected a much older couple and was thrown by the fact that they looked so young.

To start with, both she and Mike were a bit tongue-tied. However, Sandra and Alec had no such qualms and were soon telling Mike and Rachel about their little charge.

'He's very sweet to look at, blonde hair, blue eyes, like his Granny, 'said Sandra. This shocked Rachel. She hadn't expected this. Sandra continued, 'It's sad he seems to have no speech. The doctors think it's the trauma of losing his mother in such a way, but he is very good and lets you know what he wants by signing. Well, not normal signing, but his idea of it. He gets scared of things, though. The neighbour's dog frightens him, for example, though we have managed to get him to stay outside now if the dog is in the garden next door. Before, he would run inside and hide under the bed. He is only the size of a three or four-year-old child. The doctors think his mother was on drugs, and that is why he is so small. He is clean, though. They did all sorts of examinations at the hospital before he came to us.'

At this point, the Jones's seem to have run out of steam, and the four of them sat looking at each other. Then Mike asked them if Caleb looked at books or could draw or anything like that. Was he going to school?

Amanda spoke up then. 'At present, no, he is only just getting used to living normally in a house with a family, and as he seems unable or unwilling to speak, we are taking it very, very slowly. Would you like to meet him, Rachel, Mike?'

Mike and Rachel looked at each other. Rachel felt her heart hammering in her chest. 'I—I—I'm not sure. Well yes, maybe.'

'Well, how about you just look in? He is next door playing with some toys. He has one of our staff with him. You needn't fully enter the room if you don't want to or speak; just have a little look. Alright?'

Mike and Rachel got to their feet, and to their surprise, Amanda opened a door on the other side of the room they were in. The room was brightly painted and seemed to be so full of toys it took them a moment to spot a small boy sitting in the middle of them all. He was holding a toy car in one hand and running it backwards and forwards on the floor in front of him. In the other hand, he clutched what remained of a soft toy of indeterminate origin. It was obvious he treasured it.

'Caleb.' Amanda spoke gently. The little boys head jerked up, and Rachel saw fear in his eyes though he sat frozen. Then he looked at her, and her heart melted. Without thinking, she took the few steps into the room and sat down beside him. He was so like the little boy her Johnny had been to look at, but the fear and uncertainty in his eyes was something Johnny had never shown. That wasn't who he was. This little scrap may look like him, but Rachel felt instinctively he wasn't feral like his father had become and never would be if she had anything to do with it. This was like a second chance, and she would take it. Tears brimming in her eyes, she looked up at Mike, who had followed her into the room; he nodded.

'Hello Caleb,' she said softly, 'I'm your Granny. I am so pleased to meet you.'

The big blue eyes regarded her solemnly for a heartbeat, then he smiled a big, big smile. Behind her back, Rachel heard Amanda give a small gasp. Amanda told her afterwards it was the first time any of them had seen him smile. 'Is this little animal your favourite companion?' Rachel asked him. He nodded gravely. 'Has he a name?' Caleb shook his head, all the time looking at Rachel. Then Mike knelt down beside Rachel. Caleb regarded him with a frown, then decided Mike was okay, and though he didn't smile, he looked happy enough. 'Caleb, this is Mike. Your Grandpa.' Caleb frowned again, then nodded vigorously and, to everyone's surprise, put his hand out and touched Mikes arm lightly before withdrawing it quickly. He looked scared then. Mike ruffled his hair, 'Good one, mate,' he said thickly, and Rachel realised Mike was feeling emotional too.

They stayed for a little longer talking to him, and Mike got another toy car and made engines noises. Caleb looked startled for a moment, then joined in making engine noises too. Again, everybody was completely surprised and pleased. A little later, Amanda indicated that the meeting must end. Caleb looked at Rachel with sad eyes, but Rachel hugged him and assured him they would see him again soon, then Mike hugged him too, and they retired to the other room.

The Jones who had remained behind were very surprised but pleased when told about the meeting. They were leaving now and taking Caleb back to their home.

'It sounds as if he will be coming to live with you soon.' Sandra remarked as they said their goodbyes.

'I think so, yes.' Rachel replied.

They then found themselves immersed in mountains of paperwork and questions, Where exactly they lived, how far was the school, was it safe out on the farm? At this point, both Rachel and Mike got a bit defensive. 'It's a farm, for God's sake. We will look after him and make sure he doesn't come to harm, but cotton wool is something we're short of.' Rachel's patience was wearing thin.

'I'm sorry, Rachel, we are only doing our job. We have to make sure we get it right. We have a massive amount of guidelines we have to follow.'

'We would like you to come and visit Caleb a few times too before he comes out to your place. I know distances make it hard, but we don't want to frighten him or upset him, do we?'

'We will do our best to come as often as we can, we have business commitments, but I don't see any reason why we can't come when you'd like us to.' Mike said, looking at Rachel. He could see she was rather edgy and emotional, not surprising after the last few days.

Chapter 39

Later driving home, their thoughts turned from Caleb to Emma. 'I wonder if Clarrie has spoken to her. She's back at school today, so she won't really get the opportunity until the weekend.' Mike mused Rachel, who was still thinking of Caleb and planning his bedroom, only mumbled a reply. 'Rach?'

'Sorry Mike, I was miles away. Yes, I do hope Clarrie spoke to her either last night or this morning. Keith went away to something or another that was going on in Sydney last night, so she should have been able to talk to Emma freely.'

'We seem overwhelmed with children's problems, don't we?'

'Yep, but neither of us would want it any different, would we?'

Mike, who was driving, patted Rachel's leg. 'Good thing we ordered a big new car while we were in Brisbane. There will be five of us when Em and Ben come to stay.'

They had replaced Rachel's old ute with a newer one, but as it was mostly for farm work except for occasions like now, they had decided to spend the money on a brand new four by four which is what Mike's car had been five years before. They had debated whether they needed to do this but were now pleased they had.

It was late evening by the time they got home. They had stopped at the pub in town for a bite to eat, and of course, it was full of locals who all wanted to know about Mike's accident and anything else that may be happening. They had decided to say nothing about Caleb for the time being. Tongues would wag soon enough.

Ruby, who had stayed behind with Ted, was waiting for them and no sooner was Rachel making a fuss of her than the phone rang. They looked at each other with alarm; it was late for a phone call unless something was wrong, very wrong.

Mike answered it. Rachel watched his face. She had picked up from his greeting. It was Clarrie. The emotions flitted across his face. Anger, sorrow, anger again, then he looked incredulous. Finally, he said. 'My God, Clarrie, are you alright? Where are you?'

When he finally put the phone down, he walked straight to the cupboard in the kitchen and poured himself a scotch, which in itself was completely out of character, then he poured another and sat down, putting the second drink on the table too. 'Come and sit down, Rachel and listen to this.'

'Whatever is it, Mike? Are you alright?'

'I will be in a minute. I can't quite believe it, that's all.'

Rachel sat down beside him and picked up her drink. She wasn't a fan of whisky, but then neither was Mike really; he must be very spooked. 'What's happened?' she repeated.

Mike took a deep breath. 'Clarrie couldn't get anything out of Emma except she said that Keith had told her it was their secret and she mustn't tell her mother. She got so upset that Clarrie let it go, but of course, she was really worried then. However, she didn't want Em to be even more upset going to school. Ben didn't know anything, it seemed. So after the kids had both gone to school this morning, Clarrie went into Keith's study. He doesn't like that, and she has always respected it, so because I suppose he trusts her, the door is never locked. She just vacuums in there sometimes and flicks the duster, she said. First, she turned on his computer but didn't know the password. Then looked through his desk, but one large drawer was locked. However, this only fired Clarrie up. She always was inquisitive. So she got a screwdriver out of the garage and forced the drawer open.' Mike shook his head. 'I am really surprised she did that, but I'm guessing she doesn't really trust Keith. Anyway, she found photos, pornographic photos then— 'Mike shook his head and, to Rachel's horror, choked back tears. 'There were some shots of Emma. You couldn't see her face, but Clarrie said she just knew it was her. He must have forced her to pose when he took her back to their apartment when they were away.' Mike put his head in his hands, 'Why didn't I make a big thing of it when she told us about him before?'

Rachel put her arms around him. 'Hindsight is an amazing thing, darling. What else? Has he molested her?'

'Clarrie doesn't think so, but that's not all. There were photos of children being abused, even raped! Oh God, Rachel, this is awful.'

Rachel was at a loss to know what to say. So they sat quietly for a time, Mike, who was very upset, finally said. 'Clarrie has packed a bag and is staying with her best friend, Beth. Ben is with her. Clarrie rang me to tell me and let me know she had phoned the police. They will be waiting for Keith when he gets back.'

Rachel held his glass to his lips. Her hands trembled on the glass.

'Why did she let him do it, Rach? Why did she?'

'I expect he used some sort of blackmail and coercion. She must have been terrified, poor little girl. I suppose he thought she was frightened enough not to tell her mum.'

'Well, that worked too, didn't it?'

They sat up for some time, going over and over everything. They were both more shocked and horrified than they liked to admit. They drank their tots of whisky, then Rachel made tea though it grew cold as they talked round and round in circles. Clarrie had said nothing to Emma yet nor to the school. Mike said he would ring her in the morning and see if he should go and be some sort of support. Rachel, deep down, wasn't sure she wanted him to do that but said nothing. Eventually, they crept into bed.

Chapter 40

After a very restless night, they both looked terrible the next morning when Ted popped his head in.

'That big young bull you purchased a time back is lame, Boss. I think we need to get him into the crush and take a look, see what he's done.'

'Cup of coffee, Ted?' asked Rachel.

'Well,' Ted scratched his chin, he didn't normally stop for coffee, but maybe he would. 'Sit down, Ted, I'll be a little while, then I'll come and take a look' Mike sounded as harassed as he felt.

'I'll go with Ted if you are too long on the phone, Mike.' Rachel had been worrying all night that Mike would take off for Brisbane at first light.

Ted sat down, and Mike went off to phone Clarrie. He was gone for quite a time. Ted grew restless, so Rachel pulled on her boots and said she'd go with him. Just then, Mike appeared but went straight into the office. He looked grim, so Rachel and Ted went out to see to the bull. Rachel let the other dogs off, and with Ruby, it didn't take too long to get the bull into the crush. Being quite lame also meant he didn't take too much persuading. It didn't take long for them to see he had an infection in his hoof, and Rachel went and got the antibiotics they kept handy and gave him an injection. 'We may have to get the vet out if it doesn't look any better tomorrow, though, Ted. We'll put him in the small yard now so we can watch him better.'

Ted was a man of few words, but when Rachel asked him how Alma was because she hadn't seen her for a few days, Ted got talking, and it was hard to get away from him. Rachel only half-listened as she was antsy to get back to the house to see how things were in Brisbane and had only asked partly out of politeness.

When she got back, Mike was sitting at the table in the kitchen staring into space. Rachel sat down beside him and touched his arm.

'Well, how is everything? Pretty bad by the look of you.'

'Worse for Clarrie, she is devastated by what is happening. Seems Keith was part of a paedophile ring from what I can make out. Clarrie isn't that coherent, to be honest. Her parents are coming to look after her and the kids. I said we'd go, but it seems as if it's all covered for now. I said we'd be going back soon anyway because of Caleb, though I didn't actually mention why to them. Keith has been arrested, and they are tracking down others. Some are even abroad. What a mess. Clarrie can't believe she has been so blind, and she feels so bad she ignored Em to start with.'

'I don't think she should be too hard on herself. She was too close to the whole thing, and it's easy to be wise afterwards. So you haven't got to rush up there just now?'

Mike shook his head. 'No, thank goodness, next week when we go back to see your grandson will be soon enough. The police will want to speak to us then.'

'Mike, *our* grandson. He may not be your flesh and blood, but I want you to think of him as yours too. It's the only way I will take him on if we share this equally.'

Mike looked at her searchingly, then smiled. 'I think deep down I wanted to hear you say that, Rach, thanks.'

'You may not thank me down the track, Mike; it won't be easy.'

'I know that, sweetheart, but he will be as important to me as my kids are. Right? You look on them as yours, don't you? Even though they have a mum. Caleb will be the same to me.'

'You know what, Mike Grimshaw?' Rachel's eyes were brimming, 'I love you to bits.'

'Now tell me about this bull; in fact, show me.' Mike said after kissing her.

The next week passed quietly for Mike and Rachel. They just got on with their normal lives. Things were bad in Brisbane, but neither of them felt they could do anything unless they were called to. Also, Mike was in constant touch with his father and brothers. David and the other two did nothing but argue. David was being driven by Wendy, they all guessed but refused to talk sensibly, and Tom and Jacob were almost tearing their hair out.

'When we next get back from Brissie, I think I had better go up and see my folks, don't think Dad is coping that well.' Mike said a few days later.

'If Ted can cope for a few days, I'll come with you.'

'I was hoping you'd say that thanks, darlin'.' Mike looked relieved.

The horses were still up near the homestead and yards, but now Mike and Rachel decided they could go in one of the further paddocks as they should be safe now.

'I'll ride Smokes down; the others will follow. Then you come and pick me up in the ute Mike, how does that sound?'

'Good. See you there in half an hour.'

Ten minutes later, Rachel set off on Smokey, who hadn't been ridden lately, so was feeling skittish. Rachel had ridden all her life and was a good rider, but her mind wandered, and Smokey knew it, so thought she'd try her mistress out and gave an enormous buck, taking Rachel completely unawares and partly unseating her. A second buck had Rachel hanging half off; the third had her rolling in the dust. Smokey stopped then and looked around, reins trailing. Rachel was badly winded and took a few minutes to gather herself together and get to her feet.

Getting hold of the reins as Smokey had only gone a short distance, the others were nearby too; Rachel told Smokey off then looked around for a rock or something to clamber back onto her horse. She was feeling very sore already. *I guess I don't bounce the same anymore*, she thought ruefully.

When a little later Mike rolled up in the ute, the first thing he said was, 'You look like you kissed the ground somewhere along the way.'

'Yeah, I was daydreaming, and Smokes took advantage. Good thing she and the others didn't go far. I don't think I bounce as I used to either.'

'Have you hurt yourself much, sweetheart?' from grinning broadly, Mike now looked concerned.

'I'm going to have some massive bruises, I think. My bum hurts, my arm is sore, and so is my face.'

Mike looked at her cheek, which was already blooming a red gravel rash. 'I think you will be a sight tomorrow, that's for sure. Come on, old lady, I'll help you with the saddle.'

'Don't you dare patronise me. I can manage. Whoops!' Rachel's arm was worse than she realised, and she nearly dropped the saddle instead of loading it in the ute tray neatly. 'Not so much of the old either,' she remarked as they drove slowly back. 'I don't need you to tell me I'm older than you.' It had been a sensitive subject as Rachel was conscious of it when they first got together, but Mike had never worried about it. Rachel was five years older.

Mike patted her leg in response, 'Naah woman, I reckon you can run rings round me any day!'

When they got into the house later, Mike disappeared for a moment, then came back and, taking Rachel's hand, steered her into the bathroom. He had set the bath running for her. It was hardly ever used but was ideal for soothing aching muscles. "Come on, my lovely, get undressed and into the hot water. It will help.'

'Aw Mike, I have dinner to get and—'

Mike set about undressing her and sweeping her up, lowered her into the fragrant bath, all the time telling her to stop fussing about dinner or anything else. The warm water relaxed her sore muscles, and Rachel started to feel better. She hurt more than she had first thought. Mike suddenly said, 'I had better go and start on dinner because you are so tempting lying there I might feel compelled to join you.' With that, he disappeared.

The bath did restore Rachel, but her face looked a lot worse. Her cheek was badly bruised, and she also had gravel rash along her forehead. She was still very sore in a few places as well, though they didn't show so much. A few days later, they were off back to Brisbane, and Rachel worried what anyone might think. Mike laughed it off.

Chapter 41

They arrived late afternoon and were staying two nights. That allowed them time to see Caleb and also meet Clarrie, who had now moved back into the house she shared with Keith. Emma was back at school after having a few days off. Both children were now seeing a psychologist, and outwardly Emma seemed quite calm, almost unaffected. After settling in, Mike phoned and spoke to all three of them. They arranged to meet Clarrie after lunch, then they would pick the children up from their schools and go back to the house for an early dinner.

'It's silly, I know, but I feel even more nervous seeing Caleb today than before. I'm scared his good reaction may not surface this time' Rachel worried as she climbed into bed that night.

Mike pulled her into his arms. 'Silly sausage, he will be one pleased little boy. The only thing I worry about is your face. I hope they won't think I beat you up!'

'Oh God, you don't think they will do you? And supposing it frightens Caleb? What shall we do?'

Mike wished he hadn't said anything, 'I was teasing, sweetheart. Of course, they won't, and I'm sure Caleb will be fine with it, don't worry.' Mike then made love to her and, for a while, took her mind off her face and everything else. However, it took Rachel a while to get to sleep with lots of thoughts swirling around her head.

Consequently, they were up later than they would have liked to be. Mike woke the usual time, but Rachel was in a deep sleep, and he resisted waking her. He lay watching her for a bit, then drifted off again himself.

They started off feeling rushed, though Mike privately thought it was good Rachel didn't have so long to try to hide her bruises. They still showed whatever she did. One or two patches on her face were a deep purple, and others were green and yellow. It was too lurid for any makeup to cover up.

It was Amanda who was waiting to greet them, and this time there was no sign of the Jones. 'What happened to you?' Amanda stared at Rachel, 'an accident or what?'

'My horse, I'm ashamed to say, bucked me off. My own fault, really.'

'Oh. I don't know anything much about horses; they always sound dangerous to me. I don't know what Caleb's reaction will be, but we'll find out in a minute.'

Caleb was again sitting on the floor surrounded by Lego and other toys, but he wasn't playing. He was just sitting and looked up as soon as they opened the door. 'Hello Caleb, remember me, your Granny and your Grandpa?' As she spoke, Rachel went and sat down near him. The little boy didn't smile this time but sat looking at her with enormous eyes. Then he reached out and very gently touched her bruised face, tears gathering in his eyes. 'It's alright, sweetheart, it doesn't hurt. I fell off my horse, and Grandpa has been looking after me.' Caleb looked solemnly at Mike, then gave a big smile and, getting to his feet, hugged Mike and then hugged Rachel. He then sat down again and played with the toys but made it obvious he wanted them to join in, handing them things and indicating what he wanted.

Amanda said, 'you can ask Caleb about coming out to your place if you want to.'

Caleb immediately stopped playing and looked from one to another. 'Caleb, how about you come out to the farm and see if you like it there?'

Again, they were rewarded with a huge smile, and he nodded vigorously. Before coming in to see him, Rachel and Mike had spent some time with Amanda, going over the bones of the plan for Caleb to come and live with them, and this was the first hurdle.

'How do you feel about that Caleb, would you like to come to our house? It's a long way, would that be alright, do you think?'

The big blue eyes regarded them for a few moments, then he nodded and nodded. Rachel was afraid he'd hurt his neck or his head; he was so enthusiastic. Then another huge grin and a hug each. 'Is that a yes then?' Rachel asked. Caleb got up and did a little jig.

They stayed as long as they could, playing with him, and he looked tearful when they had to go, but they explained to him that they would be back in a couple of weeks to take him home. Rachel could see he was disappointed but also that he understood what she was saying.

They were late leaving and consequently were nearly late picking up Ben, who came out of school earlier than Emma. Emma looked anxious until she saw them and speaking to her friends slipped across the school driveway and flung herself into her father's arms and burst into tears, then held her arm out sideways for Rachel to hug her too. It seemed as if she had been holding it together until she saw them, and now the floodgates opened. When eventually they got to the car, Rachel told Ben to get into the front, and she sat in the back with Emma, who was still crying quietly.

She quietened down on the journey to their house, and it took longer because there had been an accident that had slowed the traffic up. 'Feel better now, Em?' Rachel asked her gently.

'It's so good to see you and Dad. You believed in me right from the start, Mum didn't, and because of that, Keith… She trailed off, and the tears started again.

'I know darling, I know. Sometimes even adults make very bad mistakes, and it's really hard to admit to them. I expect that is how your Mum is feeling, and I suspect she will never really forgive herself. She played ostrich and buried her head, but she will regret it always. You and her will have to help each other now. Don't forget she loved Keith and trusted him. This must be very hard for her too. She will feel very betrayed and let down by him. It will have been a huge shock, and we don't always like to admit someone we love is capable of dreadful things.'

Emma looked at Rachel for a long moment, then said. 'I know a little of what happened with your son. So in some ways, you have been through something like this yourself, haven't you?'

Rachel nodded. 'It will get better, sweetheart, I promise. Letting what has happened to you make your life a misery is like letting Keith win, and we can't have that, can we?'

Emma was thoughtful for a time, then they reached the house and pulled up in the driveway. Rachel made to get out, but Emma put her hand on her arm. 'Thank you, Rachel. You've made me feel better.' She kissed Rachel softly on the cheek. Rachel swallowed the lump in her throat.

It was a difficult evening. Clarrie was tearful one minute and angry the next. Not with anyone in particular, just angry with the world at large, but most of all with herself. Ben was quiet, and so, on the whole, was Emma; they had been through their mother's anguish a few times already. The Child Safety people had interviewed Clarrie several times, but she was now completely in the clear. Keith had been very careful, and his obsession with pornography and child abuse was so well hidden that if it hadn't been for Clarrie's determination, he wouldn't have been found out as soon as he was. It was becoming clear he hadn't indulged in these activities for that long, but long enough to be part of a group that was operating in all parts of Australia at least. The police were still building the case against him and had told Clarrie there was still a long way to go. He had been refused bail, much to everyone's relief. Once the school holidays were there, Clarrie was planning on taking the children to see her parents then asked if they could all come out to the farm.

Rachel and Mike looked at each other. Now was the time to tell them all about Caleb and all that it implied.

All three of them were immediately interested and asked lots of questions.

'You say he's dumb, can't speak?' Clarrie said.

"The phycologist thinks it's just he has chosen not to, that he can, but he has been so traumatised he doesn't want to. They think he will in time. Of course, it's difficult to know what he actually thinks when he won't speak, but you can tell if he is happy or sad.'

Clarrie looked from Rachel to Mike, 'well, I reckon you deserve a medal for saying you'll have him.'

'He's my grandson Clarrie' Rachel said quietly.

'Our grandson', added Mike.

Clarrie felt a stab of jealousy. Why had she let this man go? But she knew in her heart that in many ways, they were poles apart, and Rachel and Mike were true soul mates.

Later, as they were leaving, Clarrie suddenly said, 'I'm sorry. You could have stayed here now. There's no Keith. I didn't think of it before.'

'It's alright, Clarrie. Best not, I think, we'll stay better friends that way.' Mike replied.

Clarrie watched them go. Yes, Mike was right. Rachel inadvertently made her feel inadequate. She was such a strong woman, and she and Mike were so close. It wouldn't do to see too much of the two of them.

Chapter 42

The next morning, they drove to the garage to pick up the new car. Rachel told Mike he could drive it back, so she merely dropped him off and started for home. Mike would follow on a bit later once he had gone through all the formalities with the car. When she got back, Ruby was beside herself with joy. Rachel noticed that there were two strange cars at Ted and Alma's and hoped everything was alright.

She busied herself unpacking and sorting washing as, if they were to go to see Mike's folks tomorrow or the next day, they needed to be organised. It didn't seem that long before Mike arrived full of delight over the new vehicle. Rachel listened patiently for a bit, then commented about the visitors that Ted and Alma had got. Mike frowned. 'Yes, I was hoping to leave Ted in charge when we go to see Dad. If he's got company, he may not be too happy, and we have been away a lot lately.'

'He is officially retired, Mike.'

'Yeah, I know, I wanted you to come too.'

'I want to as well. Let's wait and see what Ted says. I'll go down and see him and Alma shortly.'

This proved unnecessary, though as five minutes later Ted banged on the door. Alma was with him, and so was a tall, lean young man, a young woman and two small children.

'Our son Jack and grandkids,' Ted said proudly. 'Tilly too, Jack's missus.'

It wasn't long before Rachel had the two little children sat at the table eating muffins and drinking orange juice. Mike was busy talking to the grownups. 'What are your names, and how old are you both?' she asked her young guests.

'I'm Lenny, and she's Lena. We're twins', said the little boy.

'Gosh, are you?' Rachel pretended to be surprised, but she had thought that was the case. 'So how old are you then?'

'Three and a quarter, and I'm oldest by five minutes.' Lenny sounded very important.

'Five minutes! So does he boss you around, Lena?' Lena looked at Rachel with her huge dark eyes.

'Yeth', she said. As it turned out, Lenny was a chatterbox, and Lena was the quiet one, though Rachel suspected some of that was because she could hardly get a word in edgeways.

Mike and Rachel knew about Jack, of course. Ted and Alma were very proud of him, but he'd never been to visit; they had always gone to see him. He was an only child. 'Whose is the other car, Ted? Have you other visitors that you are hiding away?' Mike asked.

Jack answered first, 'No, I thought Mum and Dad's car had seen better days, so the other car is for them. Tilly drove ours, and I drove the fresh one. Don't quite know what to do with the old one now, though.'

'Might be useful around the place sometimes. Leave it there for now. It's not going to be in the way', Mike said easily.

Jack worked at the mines and was earning good money. Rachel and Mike were impressed by the way he looked to his parent's needs. They talked on some more, then Mike asked how long they were staying. 'A couple of days at least, if that's okay,' Tilly spoke up shyly.

'Couse it is but won't you all be rather cramped? There are only two bedrooms down there', said Rachel. 'Hey, I've just had an idea the holiday let is empty just now you can use that if you want, after all, it is Alma who cleans it!'

They all laughed at that. 'We'll be fine, Missus, thanks', said Jack.

'Rachel', she smiled at him. She had always told Ted and Alma to use their names, but they never had. They weren't comfortable with it.

Later that night, Mike asked about the twins, what they had said to

Rachel and how old were they and so on, 'They are about the same size as Caleb, ' he remarked.

'They are three. Yes, it made me realises just how small for his age Caleb is. Apparently, it's something that happens when the mother is still doing drugs when pregnant. Amanda said she would send a report through, telling us all they know about Caleb's history. She was emailing it, so hopefully, it will be here tomorrow.'

'We will leave for Dad's the day after tomorrow. That will give you a chance to digest what Amanda says, and anyway, I feel we need at least one day at home. I can go round with Ted in the morning and make sure everything's good. We seem to spend more time on the road and away than we do at home lately. While I have been thinking we should do a bit of travelling, all this wasn't what I had in mind. You've never been to W.A., have you?'

Rachel shook her head, 'to be honest, I've hardly been out of Queensland.'

'My God, woman, your education is sadly lacking. I didn't realise we've never really talked about it, have we? Well, that settles it; once we get everything sorted, we'll go.'

Rachel's eyes clouded over, 'We won't be able to Mike if Caleb comes to live here.'

Mike smiled, 'I'm aware of all that, sweetheart. We'll cross the bridges as we come to them. There's this place to consider too. We'll work it out one day soon.'

An hour or so later, Rachel, lying beside Mike, who was fast asleep, thought about his travelling idea and thought about how much she'd like to do it. But Caleb and Mike's children came first and their cattle, the dogs and horses, so how could they? She drifted off to sleep, still thinking how impossible it was but how good it would be.

Chapter 43.

It was lunchtime the next day before Rachel managed to get time to sit at the computer and see if Amanda had sent in any information on Caleb's past. Some, Rachel already knew, but some she didn't, and it made her feel so sad when she read it all through. Caleb was born in Melbourne. It seemed as if Eve suddenly appeared in the A&E department of a big hospital in labour. He was full term but tiny with breathing difficulties and was put in an incubator. Eve stayed in the hospital to be near him but was hostile with everyone. She was prescribed methadone to help her with her addiction. The staff tried to help her, but she refused all offers. The only thing she did allow was that when Caleb's birth was registered, she named the father. Caleb did better than they expected. He was a little fighter, and everybody was pleased when he was allowed out of the incubator into a proper cot though he was still being monitored. Then one night, he was gone, so was his mother, and he didn't reappear until he was found sitting beside her in the squat. Where they'd been in the intervening years and how well he had developed was unknown. A search had been launched, of course, but there had been no trace. He'd had quite a lot of examinations since he was found and though timid, he seemed quite well adjusted except, of course, for his speech. The psychologist was quite certain he could speak, just that for now, he didn't want to.

Mike came in to find Rachel tearful. 'What's up, darlin'? This isn't like you.'

Rachel showed him the email, and his jaw clenched as he read it. 'Poor little sod, he hasn't had an easy time, that's for sure. Well, life will be better for him if we have anything to do with it, don't you reckon, hun?'

'Yes, I thought I would make a start on getting his room ready now, so there isn't so much to do when we get back.'

'Oh.'

Rachel looked at Mike, 'Yes, I know we have to ear tag those calves this arvo, don't we?'

'Sorry, but they need doing.'

'Yeah, I know. This just got me going a little, that's all, there's enough time really for getting everything ready.'

Ted, of course, came out to help, and so did Jack, Ted's son, to Mike and Rachel's surprise. They were even more surprised when he proved to be a great help and knew what was needed and what to do. Separating the calves from their mothers was never easy, but Jack seemed to be one of these people that animals respected and obeyed.

'You wouldn't like a job, would you?' Mike said at the end of the afternoon when cows and calves were reunited, and everything was peaceful again.

'I would love to work out here, but the mines pay silly wages, and I have my family to think of, but thanks for asking.'

Mike grinned. 'I knew you'd say that, mate, but if ever you should decide to do something else, remember us.'

Jack touched his hat and walked away. Ted, who had been listening, said, 'Thanks for saying that Boss, Jack earns good money, but he doesn't enjoy his job. This has been good for him.' He swept his arm around, indicating the paddocks and the distant hills that looked deep purple as the sun set behind them. 'Back on the land, it's in our bones, always will be.'

'I know, mate, I know. Ted, I feel we have taken advantage of you and Alma lately, always rushing off. After all, you are supposed to be semi-retired. Hopefully, we will be home more soon.'

'Nah, don't worry. Alma and I love it here, and you and the missus are very good to us. I like getting out in the paddocks, and Alma likes to help. We know we are very lucky to live here, so no worries.'

Rachel, who had been listening to this exchange, now said, 'We have some news actually, Ted. It seems we will be having my grandson come to live here soon.'

Ted, who was mostly unperturbed and hard to read, positively gaped at Rachel. She went on to explain, Ted, of course, knew a little about Johnny, but this was all news to him.

'Look forward to seeing the little fella', was all he said when Rachel had finished speaking.

As it happened, they got through the task so quickly as Jack had been a great help; Rachel had time to make a start on preparing a bedroom for Caleb. The house had originally had four bedrooms, and the smallest had been Johnny's. It was next door to the room Rachel and Johnny's father Sam had used, but early on, Rachel had turned it into her office as the previous office hadn't been much bigger than a cupboard. Now they would have to make one of the main guest bedrooms into Caleb's room. Mike said they would work something out should they have more guests than rooms, and in summer, no one minded sleeping on the verandah on a trundle, anyway.

Rachel was tired when they set off the next morning, as she had spent a long evening sorting the bedroom out for Caleb. She got Mike to remove some rather dark and sombre prints from the walls. She took down the curtains to wash. She found a bright rug that was folded up and put away and thought it would do, but when she unravelled it, she found wildlife of the insect variety had damaged it too much. In the end, Mike dragged her off to bed, saying they would go shopping maybe in Barcauldine and she needed to sleep. Ruby, who was going with them, picked up on the excitement and barked furiously when she saw them loading the car. She was afraid she would miss out.

Chapter 44

Nothing looked any different when they drove up to Mike's parent's house except driving by the house David and Wendy lived in; Rachel remarked it looked rather deserted.

They soon found out that was the case. Two days before, the three brothers had the most terrible row, and David and Wendy had packed their bags and taken off, children as well, and no one knew where.

Henry was extremely upset, as was Jacob, though Tommy and Nancy seemed relieved if anything. 'I'm sick to death of all the rowing and Wendy telling us to move out and let them live here. We've lived here all our married lives. It's our home and Henry's too', Nancy said to Rachel. 'We knew you were coming, so we thought we'd tell you face to face.'

Mike had gone in search of his father as soon as he heard what had happened, and Tommy had gone with him, so the two women were alone.

'What about Trish?' Rachel asked.

'To an extent, she is fence-sitting. I think she is pleased to see the back of Wendy as they live close to each other, and I know she is fed up with Wendy's vitriol, but she is worried that Jacob has taken David's leaving so hard. I think they were fairly close, and Jacob seems to feel he has let David down in some way. Though how goodness knows.'

'What exactly is Wendy's gripe anyway, and why now?'

'Things have been bubbling under the surface for a long time, but while Catherine was alive, even though he was supposed to be retired, Henry was still boss, really. With Catherine gone and Henry not only mourning her but not so well either, I just think Wendy saw her chance. She has said for a long time it wasn't fair for us to live here, but Catherine would never have had a bar of Wendy. She never said or did anything unkind, but she didn't like her and Wendy knew it. She could have made more effort to fit in, but she never did. We always felt she thought David was some sort of meal ticket for her, and I, for one, am not surprised it's worked out as it has. The trouble is, too, that David has never stood up to her. She has always ridden rough-shod over him.'

'What will happen now?'

Nancy shook her head. 'To be honest, I don't know. If David wants his share of this place out, I don't think we as a family can afford it. We are asset rich but cash poor, like all farmers. We are waiting to see what happens next when the shit hits the fan, as they say.' Nancy was so meek and mild it wasn't the sort of thing Rachel expected her to say. She gave Nancy a big hug. 'Hang in there, I'm sure it will work out' Though as she said it, she couldn't really see how.

Both Rachel and Mike were shocked when they saw Henry. He looked tired when he had been to stay with them, now he looked completely worn out. The constant rowing and nastiness had got to him. He looked grey and not at all well. A short time later, Trish and Jacob came in, and an impromptu family gathering and conference took place. Rachel was ready to excuse herself as she felt it wasn't anything to do with her, but the others all wanted her to stay. By coincidence, no sooner had they sat down than the phone rang. It was David, wanting to speak to Jacob. Nancy had answered the phone, and now she held it out to Jacob, who to start with shook his head. Then David must have said something about speaking to Henry because Nancy said. 'You are in luck David, Jacob has just walked in', she once more held the phone out. Reluctantly Jacob took it.

To start with, Jacob just stood listening, occasionally shaking his head as if in disagreement. Then he looked upset, then angry. Finally, he said, 'It won't happen, David, it can't. You must know that. You are being very unreasonable. It's bad enough you have taken off like a spoilt child when you haven't got your own way. Or rather, Wendy hasn't. For goodness sake, come home and start being reasonable. We can sort something out. If you think your house isn't big enough, we'll build a bit on.'

Everyone sitting waiting for the conversation to finish could hear David's angry voice on the other end of the phone, but not what he was saying. It seemed to go on and on, then finally Jacob said loudly. 'Bloody hell Dave! I've had enough of your bullshit, just get a life, will you!' and he slammed the phone down, sunk into a nearby chair and put his head in his hands. For a time, everyone sat quietly waiting for Jacob to get control of himself, then Trish got up and went and squatted down beside his chair, putting her hand on his arm and stroking it. 'Come on, love. Don't let him get to you so, you've gone out on a limb for him so many times. It's time he stood on his own feet and time he stood up to that witch he's married to.'

Jacob lifted his head and nodded, pulling himself together with a big effort.

'You're right, Trish, stupid bugger. He doesn't know how well off he is here or has been.'

'What did he say, Jacob?' Henry asked.

'More of the same really to start with, then he said he would take us to court if we didn't pay him out his share of the business.'

Mike looked appalled, 'He wants paying out!?'

'Yep, that's the latest; that's the last thing we rowed about.' Tom sounded more sad than angry.

Everyone spoke at once until Henry suddenly banged loudly on the table. He was ashen, but there was a spark in his eyes that spoke of authority and determination.

'Listen to me, all of you. There is no way I will let this happen. Catherine and I built this property up and started this cattle stud with our hard work, and I dare say blood and tears. I am not, AM NOT, going to let this woman take away the legacy that the rest of you should inherit. She can go to hell. Anyway, I very much doubt that the courts would come down in her favour. She's been a parasite ever since she arrived, bloody woman.'

'Dad,' Nancy said gently, 'She did help a lot when she first came.'

'Maybe, but she was always difficult and sometimes rude to Catherine.

We put up with it partly for David's sake and partly because she was helpful in the beginning.

Mike spoke up then. 'The last thing we need right now is for David to go to court and try to take money out of the business. I know I don't have any stake in it, but I would hate to see it all lost. Maybe I can reason with him. I can at least try.'

'David was angry that Uncle Saul left you his entire estate, so he has an extra axe to grind with you, Mike', Jacob said.

Mike now looked bewildered. 'I didn't know that. Is that why Wendy is so down on Rachel, not just that she has joined the family lately, but because of the money?'

'We never thought it was important enough to worry you about it, Mike. We never expected all this to happen. Sure, things have been simmering under the surface for years, but none of us thought anything like this would happen.' Henry looked sad but resigned.

They talked round and round in circles for some time, not knowing what to think or do either. Finally, Jacob and Tom both got to their feet, saying they had work to do. Mike stayed on for a time, then he too went to find his brothers. He looked very thoughtful and bent to kiss Rachel's cheek as he left. 'I need to talk to you later, sweetie', he said in a low voice.

Rachel watched him leave the room with a frown on her face. *What did Mike have up his sleeve*? she wondered.

Trish was the most upset because of Jacob. She didn't like the way David had spoken to him, having felt that Jacob had tried so hard to be fair. Henry announced he was tired and shuffled off to have a rest before lunch. 'Have lunch here, Trish, you look tired', Nancy said.

'Thanks, yes, it would be good. Jacob is in such a bad place just now. I don't know how to cope with him.' The three women got to their feet and started to prepare a cold lunch, setting the table and making a salad. Nancy got a big joint of roast beef out and carved generous slices onto a platter for everyone to help themselves. With three of them busy, it didn't take long. 'I expect the men will be late now', Nancy observed.

When Mike came in twenty minutes later, Nancy asked where the others were. 'They'll be here in a minute. I just want a word with Rachel. Do you mind Rach, come through here?' Mike indicated their room.

Mystified, Rachel followed him. 'What's up, Mike?' she said as soon as the door was closed.

'Now, before you say anything, please hear me out. I don't like what is happening to this family and the way things are going. I can see the farm being diminished or, worse, sold off altogether if David has his way. If he takes it to court, there won't be any winners, and I dread to think what effect it would have on Dad. It's so silly the whole thing has got blown up out of all proportion. So I have been thinking about the legacy Uncle Saul left me. You remember after we had done all the things that wanted doing, there was still quite a considerable amount of money left over?' Rachel nodded by now, guessing where this was going. 'I invested it in shares, and they have done well. How about I reinvest it in this place. What do you think?'

'First of all, Mike, I guessed where you were headed with this little speech and secondly, it's your money to use as you see fit.'

'No, Rachel, it may have been left to me, but it's yours as much as mine, so what do you think?'

'I think you are very kind, warm and generous, and if you can do it and make this place Wendy and David proof, then go for it.'

'Thanks, darlin'.' Mike gave her a quick hug, then, opening the door, strode through to where the others were gathered to eat. Minutes later, he was laying his plans before them all. It was greeted at first with stunned silence, then everybody spoke at once.

Once again, after a few minutes of the hubbub, Henry banged on the table.

'This will take some serious planning if we go ahead. We have to make it watertight. If that wife of his, Wendy, has her way, we will all be poor as church mice. Whatever the outcome Mike, thank you. I feel quite overwhelmed by your generous offer, and you too, Rachel. Right once we have finished lunch, we start organising this deal. I don't want to be caught out by Wendy or David.'

There was heartfelt agreement around the table, and lunch was over very quickly after that.

Chapter 45

A few days later, Mike and Rachel found themselves driving home. It had been a very hectic few days, and quite a lot of time had been spent with the family lawyer who had come out to the farm three days in a row sorting out the financial and legal implications of the whole thing. They had contacted David and made him an offer, which amounted to one-quarter of the property's worth. Only a short time before they had a valuation done, partly because of Catherine's death. Much to everybody's surprise, he had acquiesced without any argument. In some ways, that worried them all more as they had expected a fight, but he sounded quite calm and ready to take the money. He told his father he wouldn't make any further claims, and they all hoped that would be the case.

'Well, honey, I wonder what lies ahead now. We seem to sort out one thing when another pops its head up.' Mike remarked as they neared home.

"Yes, there's Caleb and Emma and, of course, Ben to worry about now. These last few days has made me put all those worries at the back of my mind.'

'Me too. And we haven't heard from Clarrie or anyone that there is anything going on we didn't know about, so fingers crossed nothing terrible has happened while we were away, and they haven't told us.'

However, all was quiet when they drove up to the house. Ruby couldn't wait to get out and explore her territory and make sure she was happy with it all. Ted's shiny new car was outside his cottage, and everything was very peaceful. Now that spring had arrived, it was getting warmer. The cows were under the gum trees across the home paddock dozing, the calves nearby. It looked so idyllic. Rachel had a sudden surge of contentment and happiness. She put her arms around Mike's neck and said, 'I love you, and I love this place. I feel so blessed to be here beside you, Mike and have all this.' She swept her arm at the scene and accidentally whacked Mike's nose.

'Ouch! Woman that hurt, I'll have to get my own back.' Mike picked Rachel up before she knew what he was going to do and started to carry her into the house but was brought up short by a voice saying, 'Well, well. I see you're back then.'

Mike swung around and almost dropped Rachel, who slipped out of his arms, and they both stared. 'Wendy, David, what the hell?'

'That's not a nice way to greet your brother and me.' Wendy said, giving them her sour smile, 'We thought we'd pop by and see you only to find you weren't here, so your man let us in, and we've made ourselves at home.'

'Mike was clenching his jaw, and Rachel felt her anger rising rapidly. 'How long have you been here?'

'Oh, just a couple of days, I have to say, Rachel, your main spare room was a bit chaotic. But it's better now I sorted it. Also, provisions are getting low, you'll need to go to town and stock up, I'm thinking.'

Just then, Rachel saw some of the chooks scratching under the rose bushes at the side of the house, which was where Wendy and David had come from. 'Who let the chooks out of their run?' she said over her shoulder, and she went to drive them back towards their quarters.

'Poor things, I thought they need to expand their area and anyway, the kids like playing with them.'

Rachel was seething twenty minutes later when she finally got the chooks all back in their run. She had planted seeds and seedlings in the veggie patch before they went to see Mike's family, now the chooks had scrapped most of the seedlings up, and where the seeds were planted, it was a mess. David and Wendy's vehicle was behind the chooks' run, facing into the shed where the farm ute was parked. It had a large trailer on the back. There was no sign of the children and Rachel returning to the front of the house where Mike, David and Wendy were still standing demanded to know where they were. David, she noted, was looking very uncomfortable, but Wendy just looked belligerent. Mike was angry but keeping a lid on it so far. 'Across the paddocks somewhere, I think they were talking about having a ride.'

'Well, I hope for their sakes they don't try to get near Smokey. Also, I have to say that letting the chickens out to completely trash my vegetable garden was not the way to make me feel like welcoming you into our home.' Rachel said all this very slowly, enunciating each word carefully as if talking to someone who was either stupid or hard of hearing.

Wendy opened her mouth, but David got in first. 'I'm sorry, Rachel. I'll help you sort it out, and I'm sorry, Mike, if we could just stay for a night or two? Maybe we'd be more comfortable in the other house.'

'We have guests arriving from Brisbane tomorrow, sorry.'

Rachel brushed by the others and went into the house. Everything seemed much the same except for the main guest bedroom, which was where they seemed to be sleeping. The smaller room was where the boys slept, but she had no idea about Christine. Their room seemed untouched, and then she found a sleeping bag in the office. *Thank goodness all private papers were locked away,* Rachel thought to herself. She busied herself getting coffee on the go, her mind in overdrive. A few minutes later, Mike came in having got their bags out of the car. There was no sign of Wendy or David. 'Where are the others?' Rachel asked in a stage whisper.

'I told them to go down to the horse paddock and make sure the kids were okay. Wendy objected, but David put his foot down, and she went.'

'What was said when I was getting the chooks in?'

'David was on about the family paying him out. I don't think he's thought the money came from us, and I'd rather it stayed that way. He said that he was sad it had to happen, but he had to make a go of things on his own for Wendy and the kids. Sick of living in the shadow of Tom and Jacob, he wanted a decent house and to be his own boss etc. etc. Wendy just stood there nodding and smiling and saying yes every few minutes. It was sickening. If I really believed any of that, I'd be happy for him, but it's all Wendy. Their house was bigger than Jacobs and a good house. David was equal with the others…' he trailed off as they heard the family coming back inside.

Christine and John were nice kids, Rachel decided even though she didn't know them well, but Craig was spoilt and whined and complained all that evening. Rachel got two of Norma's famous casseroles out of the freezer. Norma had given them to Rachel when Mike had his accident, saying they would come in handy, and sure enough, they had now. Adding a few veggies to the meal was all Rachel had to do. It was a tense evening, and Mike and Rachel were pleased when David and Wendy retired for the night. They sat at the kitchen table for a while, talking things over. Mike had gone down to see Ted earlier and told Rachel the poor man was rather upset as he wasn't sure he had done the right thing giving the key over to Wendy, who it turned out from Ted and Alma had been quite rude. Wendy had impressed upon him not to get in touch with them as it would be a nice surprise. He hadn't known what to do.

'They will have to move on tomorrow. I can't stand it otherwise, and David and I will end up really rowing, which I don't want to do. I just wish he had more backbone', Mike said despairingly.

'I thought I noticed he was getting very impatient a few times. Maybe he will see the light.'

'Well, if he does, it won't be soon enough; so much damage has already been done. Come on bedtime, I'm shattered', Mike yawned loudly.

Chapter 45

The next morning Rachel was first up. She had been aware of Mike tossing and turning during the night and guessed he'd slept badly, as he now seemed in a deep sleep. She left him and, pulling on some clothes, went into the kitchen to put the coffee machine on and lay the table for breakfast. As she approached the door, which to her surprise was shut, she could hear a voice; a child's voice. She pulled up short in the doorway. Craig was in the kitchen, and so was Ruby. Ruby was tied to the kitchen table leg with a piece of string around her neck. Craig was sitting on top of the table and hitting at her with a stick, saying, 'go, dog, go.' He was saying it quietly, though, so Rachel hadn't heard anything until she nearly got there.

Rachel's blood boiled over. 'WHAT THE HELL DO YOU THINK YOU ARE DOING, YOU LITTLE MONSTER!' With that, she yanked the stick out of Craig's hand and had a job to restrain herself from hitting him with it.

'I am an arctic explorer, and Ruby is a husky,' Craig said, 'but she lazy she wouldn't move.'

At that moment, Wendy, David, Mike and the other two kids appeared looking bleary-eyed and worried.

'What's up? There, there, Craig, don't get upset. I'm sure Rachel didn't mean to upset you.' Wendy put her arms around Craig, and half lifted him off the table. He started to cry loudly.

Rachel, who was busy untying Ruby, looked up from her mission and said. 'Upset him?! Upset him?! What about my poor dog? It's a disgusting way to treat an animal, and I won't have it in my house. The sooner you and this sniffling brat are gone, the better!'

'Who do you think you are, miss high and mighty? You with your jumped-up ideas. You couldn't even raise one child properly. He was a no-good druggie from all I hear. So don't you dare tell me how to raise my kids. We'll be pleased to leave and after I tidied up for you as well; the room we're in was a tip, a complete mess, can't even run a house well, you can't; let alone a family.'

'ENOUGH! DAVID REMOVE YOUR WIFE ELSE, I WON'T BE RESPONSIBLE FOR MY ACTIONS' Mike roared. Rachel thought afterwards that for an instant, Mike was going to strike Wendy. She had pushed him to the limit.

David took hold of Wendy's arm. 'Come on, Wendy. That's enough, go and pack.'

Wendy allowed David to lead her away, though as she went, she was name-calling all the way. Craig had followed his parents, leaving Mike, Rachel and Ruby, who was shivering alone in the kitchen. Rachel crouched down beside her and put her arms around the distressed dog. 'It's alright, Rubes. It's alright. You haven't done anything wrong.'

'What a good dog. Quite a few others would have given young Craig a nip at the least', Mike said. 'Though I suppose she couldn't have reached him anyway.'

'More's the pity' Rachel got up and filled the coffee machine with water.

Rachel and Mike stayed in the kitchen. They could hear angry voices and Wendy shouting at the other two children, Christine was answering her back, but they closed their ears to it all as best they could, not wanting to be involved. Then Christine and John both appeared looking upset. 'We've come to say goodbye, and thank you for having us', they chorused together. Before Mike or Rachel had a chance to respond, David came in behind them. He looked near tears. 'I'm sorry, Bro, it was never meant to be like this. Sorry Rachel,' Mike got to his feet and hugged his brother. He was near tears too. 'Ok mate, you know where we are should you want us.'

Rachel made noises of agreement, but Wendy walked by the door saying loudly, 'Are you coming or not, David?' As he left, Rachel saw the tears glistening on his cheeks; shortly after, the car started, and they were gone.

Rachel and Mike found it hard to concentrate the rest of the day, as they were both feeling out of sorts after such a bad start. 'All before breakfast', Rachel said.

They soon found Wendy had left everything as untidy as she could, though Rachel wasn't put out by that as she got stuck into sorting the room out for Caleb as she had started before. Needless to say, she had to start again, but she didn't mind. It was soothing to be doing that after the twenty-four hours of Wendy and her family.

Originally they had thought they would be picking Caleb up, but Amanda said no, she would bring him as part of her job was to check out the environment a child like Caleb was going to. Amanda said she would stay the night at the pub in town after she had dropped Caleb off and looked around.

A few days later, Mike and Rachel waited nervously for Caleb to arrive with Amanda. 'I feel as if I'm on some sort of trial', Rachel remarked, 'but I suppose it is necessary.'

They knew it would be late in the day before they arrived, but hopefully, there would be enough daylight left to show Caleb the chooks and for Amanda to have a good look too. In the end, they were quite early, much to Rachel's relief. She had been listening for the car and was out on the verandah before it pulled up. Caleb was strapped in the back. He looked smaller than ever and very tense. However, as soon as she got to the car, Rachel opened the door, and the little boy's face lit up. He held his arms out to her. Rachel had a lump in her throat then; as she helped him out of the car, Mike hovered behind. Amanda had been talking nonstop, but neither Rachel nor Mike had taken in what she was saying. They were so focused on Caleb. Ruby had been sitting at the top of the verandah steps, now wagging her tail; she came down the steps to greet the visitors. Caleb's eyes grow enormous, and turning, he clung to Rachel's legs burrowing his head. He was shaking. Rachel remembered the Jones saying he was afraid of dogs. She had forgotten.

Mike gently prised him away and picked him up. 'It's okay, mate, this is Ruby, and she loves you already. She just wants to say 'g'day.'

Ruby had sensed there was a problem and had sat down with her head on one side, and she had a doggy smile on her face. 'See, she just wants to say hello' Caleb, who had buried his head again, peeked at Ruby fearfully, then nodded his head as if to say it was alright, but he still held on tight to Mike. Amanda had taken all this in, and for the next hour, they were taken up showing Amanda and Caleb round. Amanda asked so many questions Rachel felt worn out by them all, but eventually, they made it back into the kitchen. Rachel made Amanda a cup of tea, then she took her leave, saying she would be back in the morning.

Caleb, of course, had said nothing, but he seemed rather taken by the chooks, but at other times he had wanted Mike to pick him up. They hadn't got as far as the horses or the cattle, but there would be enough time for that. Caleb seemed delighted with his room, and Rachel and Mike had bought him some toys and Lego. He watched Amanda go but didn't seem stressed in any way when she disappeared.

Rachel and Mike chatted to him as if he was part of their lives and family and also as if they weren't expecting him to talk back. They had read up about Caleb's lack of speech and felt reasonably confident that they could deal with it and that maybe he would start to speak when he felt able.

They were both surprised how big an appetite he had when it came to supper time. Rachel did spaghetti bolognese, and Caleb devoured a vast amount for a child of his size, or so they both thought. A shower and bed all went without a hitch. Rachel asked if he would like her to read a story, but Caleb shook his head and pointed to Mike, then picked up a book Rachel had found, which had been Johnny's. It was about farm animals. Mike read it to him, then as he was reading, Caleb's eyes dropped shut, and he was asleep.

As they were going to bed a bit later, Mike remarked to Rachel it all seemed almost too good to be true.

Chapter 46

The next morning, Mike woke to a funny sound outside their room on the verandah, which is where Ruby slept now the weather had warmed. After lying and listening for a moment, he nudged Rachel whispering 'shh' as he did so. For a moment, Rachel looked startled, then her eyes grew round as she and Mike listened in disbelief. Caleb was crooning to Ruby very quietly and peeping out; they could see Ruby had her head on Caleb's lap as he sat on the floor and he was gently stroking her head and humming quietly to her. Mike and Rachel both had tears in their eyes and, by common consent, left the boy and dog alone.

Later, when Amanda came, and they told her, she was surprised yet thrilled. She left soon afterwards feeling satisfied all was going well. It had been decided as Caleb seemed so settled already he could stay for the time being. Amanda would assess the situation in a few day's time. There were, of course, some issues; for example, Caleb wet the bed nearly every night, but Rachel was confident it would gradually get better. From that morning onward, Ruby and Caleb became almost inseparable. Rachel missed having Ruby at her heels for much of the time, but she was overjoyed that boy and dog had formed such a bond. Still, though Caleb didn't speak, even to Ruby, he sang to her in his strange crooning way.

In the meantime, Rachel and Mike slowly introduced Caleb to the horses and cattle, and he soon made it plain he would like to try and ride, holding his arms up and pointing. Mike saddled up Jock and had Caleb sitting up in front of him, as he was too small for any of the animals they had. It was evident that Caleb was in heaven, he smiled and clapped his hands, and when Mike brought him back to Rachel, and he slithered down into her waiting arms, he hugged her tight with tears of joy in his eyes.

'We'll have to get him a pony, no mistake,' said Mike, and almost at once, they started to search for one. Rachel worried about it after what had happened to Johnny but then reminded herself that she should move on. History didn't repeat itself that frequently and she would insist that Caleb wore a helmet, she thought.

Luck seemed to be on their side as a few days later, having put the word out, Sid rang to say a friend of a friend had a pony for sale not too far from Chinchilla and gave Mike the telephone number. The next day they set off, hopefully towing the float. The pony was a pretty little skewbald and was laid back and gentle. The man who was selling it had bought it for his grandchildren, but they had outgrown it some time ago. 'Lucky for us', Mike commented, driving home as not only had they bought the pony, but the man had put in the saddle and bridle and other odds and ends. Caleb was very shy when they had been there and had hidden behind Rachel, but once away from the place, he was sitting up excited. Ruby, who had come for the ride, seemed overjoyed too. The pony was called Puzzle, and it seemed to suit him. Caleb proved to be a natural rider and was soon scooting around on Puzzle in the round yard as if he had ridden all his life. In the meantime, Amanda had said they were all very happy the way things were and would leave them to it, though, of course, stay in touch.

A short time after all this, Josh and Jem Jones turned up. Pleased as they were to see Josh, Jem was another matter. Rachel decided when she saw him get out of the police vehicle that she wouldn't stand for his rudeness again.

Caleb saw them get out of the police 4x4 and ran to his bedroom, and when Rachel went to see if he was alright, he was hiding under his bed. She guessed it reminded him of his past and goodness knows what he had gone through, little though he was. She had left Mike to deal with whatever the problem was. She was more concerned with Caleb's reaction. However, after a few minutes, Mike called her to come and listen to what they had told him. By this time, she had persuaded Caleb to come out, and she picked him up and carried him through to the kitchen with her.

Both Josh and Jem got to their feet as she entered the room, Josh greeting her normally and Jem Jones she decided was much politer than he had ever been. Maybe he had been told to behave!

Mike was busy making coffee for everyone, and Rachel sat down with Caleb still clinging to her, his face hidden against her neck.

'Rach, you'll never guess what's happened', Mike said.

Josh then spoke up, 'We've discovered, well not us, but the force, that Smokey was stolen by a racing syndicate that was in danger of destroying the racing industry long term by breeding through artificial insemination, gambling, fixing races, all sorts of things. A really big organisation financed from Asia. Anyway, this gang has been broken up by our boys, and we now know that Keith, your ex's husband Mike, was being blackmailed, so it was him that let slip about the well-bred horse you had here. Someone found out about his liking for children and all that rotten stuff, and Keith was over a barrel. He didn't mind a big bet or two as well, so he was really in the soup. They think that Smokey got a bit hot to handle after you went down there. It was a close call for them, so they decided to move her, and that is how she broke away.

As he was speaking, Caleb lifted his head and was watching Josh with big round eyes, though still clinging to Rachel. 'Hi Mate,' said Josh, who had kids of his own. 'How do you like living here with Granny and Pops?'

Being a small community, everyone knew everything about Caleb by this time. Caleb continued to look at Josh, then finally nodded. 'Tell you what, kid, you can have a little ride in the police car with the siren going before we leave if you'd like to?'

Caleb's eyes grew even rounder, then he smiled at Josh.

Jem cleared his throat. 'I don't think that is allowed, sergeant.'

Josh turned back to stare at Jem, and his patience finally snapped. He'd had a long time of putting up with Jem Jones. 'Now listen here, constable, these people are good people, and this little boy has had a raw deal. If I say he can ride in the patrol car, he can. DO I MAKE MYSELF CLEAR? What's more, I am sick of your 'holier than thou', attitude so just shut it, else my report back won't be good.'

Caleb had hidden his face again during this exchange, and Rachel could feel him shaking. She shook her head at Josh, who shut his mouth, looking unhappy. He realised he had upset the little boy.

'It's okay, Josh, and thanks for bringing this news; Keith has a lot to answer for.'

'Indeed. Hey, Caleb, what do you think of this?' Josh picked up his policeman's cap from the table and gently popped it on Caleb's head. For a few moments, Caleb sat still, his head hidden, then he slowly sat up and felt his head, Josh's cap slipped over, and Caleb's face disappeared. 'Do you know where Caleb is, Granny?' Josh said to Rachel.

Caleb pulled the cap back and gave Josh a tiny smile. A few minutes later, having finished their official business, Josh got to his feet. 'Do you want that ride then, little mate?' Josh bent towards Caleb. Caleb looked first at Rachel, then Mike. They both nodded and smiled, and moments later, Caleb was sitting beside Josh, who, having turned the car around, drove out towards the entrance with the lights flashing and siren going. Of course, it wasn't far, and they were soon back. Caleb's blue eyes were so big he looked all eyes, and he smiled and clapped his hands when he saw Rachel and Mike waiting for him. Even Jem looked impressed by the wee boy's reaction.

Later, when they were getting ready for bed, Rachel remarked to Mike that Caleb seemed to be getting better with strangers, but she wished he would speak.

'They told us it is a deep psychological problem and he will speak when he feels able to, sweetheart, but yes, I agree he hums and kind of sings to Ruby but not us. I wish he would too.

Chapter 47

The weeks slipped by. Rachel was giving Caleb a few basic writing lessons now, but as he refused or couldn't bring himself to speak, anything else was difficult. The psychologist came into their small town once every three weeks to see Caleb, and Rachel sensed even she was slightly frustrated with Caleb's silence, especially as he seemed to be getting on so well in every other aspect. He had grown too, they found, and Rachel had to restock his clothes. She managed to find an Akubra, much to his joy, and he refused to take it off except when in the shower.

Christmas was looming, the holiday let business seemed flat out, and Rachel wondered how she would ever manage without Alma. She was also worried about Mike's children coming. She wasn't sure what the reaction was going to be from any of them. Clarrie wasn't coming for Christmas; the children were, though. Clarrie had been invited. She had opted to spend Christmas with her sister. She was meeting Mike to swap over at Roma. Ben was going to share Caleb's room, and Emma would have her own room. Ben and Emma hadn't met Caleb, and both Mike and Rachel were a bit worried about the reaction of all of them.

It was all good to start with or seemed so; Caleb hid behind Rachel when they arrived but was soon showing by pointing where Ben could put his things. Ben seemed happy enough, but Emma looked unhappy.

At dinner time, Emma was in full flow, telling them all about school and her friends; no one could get a word in edgeways. Caleb sat watching her with huge round eyes, mesmerised by her. Emma largely had ignored him so far, but Mike could see the way Caleb was staring at her was making her uncomfortable. Rachel, too, had picked up on Caleb's fascination and tried to distract him, knowing Emma may not like it.

'Caleb dear, I don't think Emma likes you looking at her quite so much. Now, eat up it will soon be bedtime.'

Emma opened her mouth as if to say something, then changed her mind. Herself and Ben had been given the lowdown on Caleb and a little of what he had been through, though, of course, no one knew the whole story and maybe never would.

Caleb looked at Rachel questioningly, then resumed eating his dinner.

Ben said he was quite happy to go to bed at the same time as Caleb. He would play on his iPad for a while. Emma wasn't ready for bed yet, and neither Mike nor Rachel wanted to force it. It was early anyway.

'I don't understand. Why doesn't he speak? He has a voice box because he was humming to Ruby, and why is Ruby allowed to sleep in his room? She slept in mine when I came before.'

Mike and Rachel exchanged looks. 'Are you jealous, Em?' her Dad said gently.

Sudden tears appeared in Emma's eyes, and she shook her head, then nodded it instead. 'It's not fair he is living here, he's nothing to do with you, Dad, and you didn't even know about him until a short time ago Rachel, and he's taken over Ruby, and you bought him a pony and—and—'

This had all come out in a rush, and Emma was openly crying now.

Rachel sat down beside Emma and put her arm around her. Mike did the same on the other side.

'You silly sausage Em, you've nothing to be jealous of. You're my girl, nothing and nobody can change that.' As he said, this Mike looked pleadingly at Rachel to say something.

'Emma, how would you feel if you woke up cold and hungry beside your mum in a filthy room and she was dead, stone-cold dead. You are small and don't know what to do. There is no phone you can use, even if you wanted to. So you sit for hours, days, not knowing what to do. Then there are some terrible noises. You don't know that the building is being demolished, but the noises come closer and closer, huge noises that you don't understand. Then a figure comes in through the door, dressed in yellow with a mask and a helmet. He looks terrifying. He shouts, then others appear and you are picked up and carried away, and you are so scared, so scared. You were scared of Keith, but maybe not so frightened of him as Caleb would have been. They think his mother had been dead for about two days, maybe three, and it's a wonder he survived at all. He was very dehydrated and weak when they found him. I am sure Ruby understands that and wants to help him recover, which is what we are trying to do. Perhaps he thinks you look pretty and kind, and that is why he stares at you, but he means no harm. Come on, Em, you can help this poor little chap too. Maybe he will start talking to you if you are kind. The psychologist thinks it's just a matter of time before he speaks. We know he can; he's just been too traumatised by all these awful things that have happened to him.' While Rachel was saying all this, Emma stopped crying, and by the end of it, she was looking at Rachel with something akin to horror.

'Oh God, that is so awful. I'm sorry I was being horrible. I didn't understand. Of course, we'll help, Ben and I.'

Later, when Emma had gone to bed, Rachel said as she snuggled up to Mike on the old sofa that ran along one wall of the kitchen, 'I think we should have told your kids more about Caleb to start with, but hopefully, it will be okay now.'

Chapter 48

It was more than okay. Ben and Emma went out of their way to play with and look after Caleb. Mike talked to them both on their own the next morning and told them they weren't to try to force Caleb to speak. It would come when he was ready. In the meantime, they got ready for Christmas. Emma helped Rachel in the kitchen, preparing what food they could in advance. Mike took the boys off to find a suitable tree or big branch they could use as a Christmas tree and also hang fairy lights all around the place. Caleb was full of wonderment they could all see, and several times he actually said 'ooooh', but no other words.

Emma and Ben had long since given up believing in Father Christmas, but with Caleb's arrival, they pretended to believe in him again. Emma whispered to Rachel she was secretly pleased with the idea of stockings at the foot of the bed again, anyway.

Christmas Eve, and they were all invited over to Sid and Norma's as they always had carol singing around their tree. Mike and Rachel hadn't gone the previous year, as they had spent Christmas with Mike's family. Caleb was shy when they got there and clung to Rachel, hiding his face, but when the music started up, he soon lifted his head and stared in amazement. Norma's brother had several children, and the boys in the family had started their own band up some years before and were all semi-professional. They played a mixture of country and western, carols and folk songs. Caleb soon forgot his shyness and sat clapping his hands to the beat and beaming all over his face.

Rachel and Mike sat watching him and wondering if he would speak, but he didn't, though at the end of the evening, when Sid appeared dressed as Santa, he did say, once again, 'ooooh'.

Everybody had a small present, and for Caleb, it was a small mouth organ. Once they had shown him what to do, he wouldn't stop, and Rachel told Norma their friendship was in jeopardy, though she said it with a smile. Josh was there too as he was related by marriage to the Newberry's, and Caleb smiled when he saw him, then he patted his own head, remembering wearing Josh's cap.

They were all tired when they got back, and it didn't take the children long to fall asleep. Looking out down to the cottage, Mike told Rachel it looked as if Ted and Alma had visitors. 'That's why they didn't come tonight, I guess', said Rachel. Can you see if it's Jack's car?'

'Too dark. We'll find out in the morning. You invited Ted and Alma to join us for Christmas dinner, didn't you?'

'Yes, that was the other day. They said they would come. We've got plenty of food, and not eating until late means they and us have all day to get organised.'

Very early the next morning, Rachel and Mike were woken by squeals of joy coming from the boy's room. Caleb had found his stocking. His delight in everything was infectious. Ben and Emma joined in with him playing games and riding the go-carts that had been hidden away from all of them. Rachel had worried Emma would turn her nose up and say she was too old, but that certainly wasn't the case.

During the morning, Rachel went down to the cottage and was rather surprised to find Tilly alone in the kitchen. It was very quiet.

'Happy Christmas Tilly, where is everyone?'

'The kids have both gone down with a horrid tummy bug, and we were up half the night. They are sleeping now, so are both Ted and Jack.'

Just then, Alma appeared, 'Happy Christmas, Missus, and please say it from us to you all. I don't think we will come up as Jack has now got the bug, so it's something pretty catching, and we don't want to spread it.'

'Well, no. Oh, I'm so sorry, Alma, have you got everything you need? Please let me know if I can do anything. The kids will be so disappointed.'

'Us too.'

'If you feel up to it by then, we are going out to the gathering at Wagtail Dam tomorrow, so please come along. I will pack enough food for you all, so just come. The kids will love it.'

The rest of the day flew by. The children had eaten a huge early dinner, and Caleb's eyes kept drooping, so Rachel packed them all off to bed early. Snuggling up to Mike on the sofa later, she speculated whether Ted and his family would be up to coming out to the dam the next day.

'It just might rain. I wish it would.' Mike looked thoughtful. 'It's months since we had decent rain, and though we are alright at present, it's worrying. Dad is worried too. They've had less than us.'

'I know. I noticed when we were up last, the trouble is when we do, we'll have heaps all at once and everywhere will flood.'

'Better that than none. By the way, are you all set for visiting my folk next month? I wonder what Caleb will think of it all.'

The next morning it was a beautiful day, though it was going to be a hot one. Rachel could tell as she was packing the food. Ted came to the kitchen door. 'You sure about us coming out to the Dam with you today? Alma said you'd pack food for us too?'

'Of course, I'm sure, Ted. Caleb has yet to meet Lenny and Lena, and the others don't know them either. We'll have plenty of food. You didn't help us eat any last night, remember?'

'Alma and Tilly escaped being ill, and I only had a touch of it. Jack was pretty bad though, twins were alright after a bit. You sure? We don't want to give it to you folks.'

'We'll all be out in the fresh air Ted. Don't worry, we are looking forward to you being there. It will do Caleb good too, I'm sure.'

It was good. Caleb was rather shy of the twins to start with, especially Lenny, who seemed to talk more than ever, but before long, the three smaller ones were playing happily, and Ben and Emma took on the role of minders which amused the grown-ups but pleased them too.

It was the one day of the year when the whole area came together. Gazebos were set up, barbeques lit, beer, wine and food abounded. Kids played tag, French cricket, rounders and many other games. Dogs barked, friends caught up with each other. It was glorious organised mayhem, and by the time they all got back that night, they were all shattered. 'I think that was the second-best Boxing Day I've had.' Rachel remarked as she clambered into bed.

'What was the best then?' Mike felt unaccountably worried and rather sad.

'The Boxing Day you turned up here pretending you needed me at the station, and Norma and Jane and all were here getting a party ready under my nose. It was the most wonderful surprise, and you gave me a brief kiss on the lips when you left. I relived that kiss for months after.'

'Come here, you. I'll give you more kisses to remember right now.'

Chapter 49

On the 29th of December, it was arranged that Clarrie would meet Mike in Miles to collect Emma and Ben as she was taking them to Perth to spend New Year's Eve and have more of the holiday over there before they went back to school. Emma was tearful, saying goodbye, and Caleb looked sad and even gave Emma a hug when they parted. Jack and Tilly were still staying with Ted and Alma, so he would still have some other children around. Emma was still very vulnerable, and it didn't take much to upset her, but Ben though horribly shocked at what had happened, was bouncing back well.

'Thank goodness he wasn't targeted in it too', Mike said. It seemed that Keith, bitterly ashamed at what had happened, was going to plead guilty to all charges. He had come clean about everything he had done. It would spare the family being dragged through a trial and all that went with it. Clarrie had put the house on the market just before Christmas and was busy house hunting; that was on hold while she was away, though.

Mike and Rachel were going to visit the Grimshaw's in the New Year, then were planning on spending as much time at home as they could. They felt the last year had been such an upheaval and also an emotional roller-coaster. They were hoping that things would settle down and get back to some sort of normality. It wouldn't be the same as before; they had Caleb now.

On New Year's Eve, they had several invitations to go out. One from Sid and Norma, one from Jane in town, and the Pub was putting on a party too, but they decided to stay at home and take it quietly. Caleb had lots of excitement over the last few weeks, and as they were off again in a few days, they felt it was better to stay home.

As it turned out, it was a blessing in disguise as just on dark an old ute drove up to the house. 'Who the hell is that?' Mike exclaimed, having just got out of the shower. Rachel was in the kitchen preparing dinner. Caleb was in his room playing. They were later than normal as they had sat on the verandah for a long time, just chatting and enjoying the cooler temperature of the early evening. It had been a hot day.

Mike went out onto the verandah, prepared to grumble at whoever it was as he didn't recognise the ute and wasn't in the mood for unknown visitors. He gasped with surprise as David emerged, followed by John and Christine. 'David! What in God's name is this?'

As David came up to him, Mike was shocked at how thin, and haggard David was. The two kids weren't much better. They looked grubby and pale. Christine looked tearful.

David stopped just as he got in front of Mike, his face screwed up, then his eyes filled with tears. Mike opened his arms and clasped his brother in his arms. 'It's okay, mate, it's okay.'

By this time, Rachel had come out and, seeing David and Mike, took Christine's hand and led the two children into the kitchen.

Neither of them said anything to start with, even though Rachel said, 'Are you both alright? Your Dad seems upset. What's happened?' Even as she said these words, Rachel was guessing the answer.

Christine burst into tears, and Rachel took her in her arms. John slumped at the table, his bottom lip trembling. Rachel sat with Christine and let her cry, just making comforting noises. A movement in the corner of her eye made her look round, and there stood Caleb, his eyes like saucers and a look of fear or horror; Rachel wasn't sure which was on his face. As she looked at him, he turned and fled back to his room.

Rachel disentangled herself gently from Christine. 'Won't be a moment, poppet. I'll be back in a jiffy.'

She raced through to Caleb's room. He wasn't there, or so she thought, then looking under the bed she found him. He was curled up in a foetal position and had his hands over his face. 'It's alright, darling, it's nothing to worry about. Come on, come out, and I will explain.'

Caleb peeked at her through his fingers, and Rachel could see the tears streaking down his little face. He shook his head. She tried again, but he refused to move, so she got up and went out to Mike, who was now sitting on the verandah with David, who seemed to have recovered a little. He was talking in a low voice when Rachel interrupted him. 'Mike, please can you come? Caleb is upset and frightened.'

'Sorry Dave, back in a minute.' Mike, seeing the distress on Rachel's face, wasted no time in following her back into the house.

Kneeling down, he peered under the bed. There wasn't enough room for either of them to get under it, and Caleb was too far under for them to reach him. 'Come on, mate, you know Granny and I will look after you. There is nothing to be afraid of. If there was, we'd come under the bed too, then we'd get stuck, and we'd all be in a big muddle then.'

Caleb, looking through his fingers, had a sudden glimmer of a smile and very, very slowly crept out. He held his arms out to Mike, who picked him up and, fishing his hankie out of his pocket, dried Caleb's tears.

'Now sunshine, do you want to go with Granny and meet Christine and John or do you want to come with me and meet their dad David, your Uncle?'

Caleb patted Mike's chest, so Mike, smiling at Rachel and giving her a wink, carried him through to the verandah. Rachel watched them go and felt strangely left out and jealous. She shook her head. That was very silly; after all, she'd asked Mike to help.

John and Christine were still sitting at the table, and both seemed much calmer now. 'Who was that just now, Rachel?' John asked.

'My Grandson, he has come to live with us.' Rachel then told them all she thought they needed to know about Caleb. She emphasized that he couldn't or wouldn't talk and what a hard time he'd had at the start of his young life. She was desperately worried they wouldn't understand, and she had no idea as to what would happen next; if they were staying, even if only for a few days, she didn't want any upsets with Caleb

'I'm guessing your Mum and Dad have split up, is that right?'

'Yes, and I hate her.' Christine sounded very angry. 'Poor Dad, she has taken the car and all his money, and she didn't even WANT us.'

'Sssh, I'm sure that isn't true. I expect it's all been very difficult for you, and your Dad and Mum will have done what they think is best for the both of you.'

'Not true, Rachel. Mum only had eyes for Craig. He is her favourite, she told us to come with Dad.' John said.

Appalled, Rachel sat still for a moment, nonplussed as to what to say to these two children who, it was obvious, had the rug pulled out from under their feet.

Just then, Mike and David came into the kitchen. Mike was still carrying Caleb, who, on seeing the other two, hid his face again.

'I've said they can all stay, Rach. I'll help you get beds made and stuff and….' Mike trailed off as Rachel put her hand up.

'It goes without saying you are all staying, and if we all muck in together, we'll soon have some food ready, and the beds can wait 'till later.'

Much to her embarrassment David hugged her. He had never done that before, and the two children got up and followed suit. 'After the last time, I wasn't sure how you'd take us coming here. Thank you so much, Rachel. Mike was one lucky guy when he met you.'

Caleb had watched the whole episode with a frown on his face, now he wriggled out of Mike's arms and ran to Rachel, arms up. Rachel talked quietly to him for a few minutes, explaining to him that the children's mother wanted a little break from them and David, so they had come to stay for a bit until she felt better.

Caleb nodded gravely. Rachel wasn't sure he understood, but he got down and disappeared to his bedroom. A few minutes later, he was back with a small Lego toy in each hand which he held out first to Christine then John. 'I think he is trying to make you guys feel better,' Rachel said, 'it's all he can think of.'

John and Christine both looked rather bemused but accepted them, saying thank you to Caleb.

Rachel set about making a salad and told Mike to get some sausages out of the freezer to supplement the steak she had got for them to have. It was getting quite late before they all sat down to eat, and David's children looked exhausted by the time supper was over. It was warm enough for them to sleep out on the verandah in their swags, which is what they had been doing anyway, as it was nearly a week since David and Wendy had split. They all agreed it was great to have a proper shower, as they really had been roughing it. David had taken his time, 'plucking up courage', as he put it to come to them. He had been so ashamed of what had gone on before it took him a while to come, and then it was only because of the children. He knew they were hurting too. Before they settled down to sleep, Mike told them as briefly as he could about Caleb not realising what Rachel had said. Though in actual fact, he told them more than she had. Neither of them said anything; they just accepted it, or so it seemed.

It took some time before Caleb settled down, and Rachel worried, but there wasn't much she could do.' I expect he'll wet the bed tonight for sure', she remarked to Mike as she clambered into bed. Caleb had wet the bed every night to start with but hardly ever did now. Rachel worried it would start again.

Chapter 50

During the night, Rachel woke and lay listening. Then she heard it again, a muffled sob, and it was coming from Caleb's room, not from David's kids as she had first thought. Getting out of bed carefully, not wanting to wake Mike, she went through to Caleb. She could just make out his crouched form by the bed. She knelt down beside him. He was trembling violently, big tears coursing down his face. Rachel reached out and turned his bedside lamp on, carefully angling it away from him. She gathered him into her arms and rocked him gently, crooning to him softly. 'Did you have a bad dream, darling? Sssh, it's gone now, you're safe, sssh.'

It was quite a time before Caleb stopped crying so much. Mike had put his head in, having woken up. Rachel saw him but shook her head, and Mike retreated. Once Caleb's sobs had diminished, Rachel picked him up and laid him down on the bed. He clung to her, and she realised he didn't want her to go, so she settled herself beside him, and after a while, his breathing calmed down, and he was asleep. She started to extricate herself, but just as she stood up, his eyes flew open and immediately, he held his arms up. She got back beside him and eventually fell asleep herself.

She woke up feeling very stiff and sore. She had put her dressing gown on, as she slept in the nude normally, and it was gaping open and tangled around her legs. She was very uncomfortable. Turning her head, she found Caleb regarding her with his big blue eyes, then he gave her a huge smile and kissed her cheek. It was the first time he had actually kissed her. He would hug and embrace, but he had never kissed either herself or Mike. It brought tears to her eyes. Seeing this, Caleb stroked her face and made ssshing noises which made Rachel even more tearful. Then Mike appeared, and Rachel told him all that had gone on.

'You okay now, buddy?' Mike asked the little boy. Caleb nodded furiously and got out of bed, and started to get his clothes on, seemingly unfazed by the events of the night before.

Breakfast was a bit chaotic, and in the midst of it all, they suddenly realised it was New Year's Day, somehow with everything else they had all forgotten.

'David, we need to talk.' Mike said bluntly. 'You've got to sort yourself out. Are you going home or what?'

Rachel glanced at David's two children, 'Maybe you and David should go and talk privately, or better still, why don't you take John and Christine out to see the ponies, Caleb?'

All three children looked reluctant, but Christine got to her feet and held out her hand to Caleb. He looked at her hand, then at her, then looking very serious, took her hand, and the three of them departed. 'Please let the chooks out', Rachel called after them.

Rachel poured them some coffee and, with a signal from Mike, sat down. She had been going to leave the men to it but picked up that Mike wanted her to stay.

'So David, what are you thinking you'll do now? Is this what you want? A complete break from Wendy? What about Craig?

'Craig and I don't get on. I know he's my son, but in name only. Wendy has spoilt him so much I don't want to own him as mine. He's a horrid little kid. Yes, I do want to break away from Wendy permanently. She has made my life a misery. I realise now she only married me for what she could get out of the family and me. When things don't go her way, she is very nasty, and I have had enough. I'd like to go back home, but I don't know if I can. Maybe they won't want me!' At this point, David's eyes filled with tears, and he shook his head, unable to say more.

'Of course, they'll welcome you back, mate, of course, they will. The only thing is, what has happened to the money you had? You won't be a partner or have any stake in the place now you know, you've been bought out, don't forget.'

'I know all this, and I don't care, I'll just be an ordinary ringer or do whatever they want me to do. I'll just go and work. It's home. It's where I belong. I don't care about any money so long as I can support the kids. Wendy has all the money. I gave it to her with an agreement she'd leave me alone from now on.'

'Good God, man, that was quick. These things usually take months and months to sort out. How did you manage that?'

'I think Wendy was so taken aback when I turned on her that she didn't argue, and by the time I had got legal papers drawn up, and she had signed it, it was too late. I had never really stood up to her in all the years we've been together. For a start, it was sex, I admit that; she withheld it if I didn't do as she said, she would nag and nag and nag until I gave in. That day we left here was the day I finally woke up to how horrible she was; a couple of days later, I snapped. It was as if a switch had been thrown. I worry about the kids, though.'

Rachel spoke up now. 'David, the atmosphere was toxic around Wendy. They are better off away from her. I am sure seeing their father so beaten and harassed can't be good for them. Back home, you'll have help and support, and so will they. What about Craig though, will you see him sometimes?'

'Rachel, I really don't know how it will all work out. The agreement didn't include the children, and for now, I will let it ride. John and Chris are nearly old enough to decide for themselves anyway. I am pleased to have made the break, and you guys have been marvellous.' David's eyes filled with tears again.

Just then, the three children barrelled into the kitchen. 'Please, can we ride? I've missed it so much', Christine said.

'So have I,' said John, 'and we guess from his actions Caleb can ride too. We saw his pony. It's awesome.'

Rachel and Mike exchanged looks, Caleb hadn't ridden without one of them near him, but he should be safe, surely. Rachel spoke first. 'Okay, but you'll have to help him saddle up, and he is to wear a proper helmet. Also, take it easy, no mad galloping and being silly'.

The two older children had beaming smiles on their faces by this time, and Caleb danced about clapping his hands.

'Off you go and remember what I said.'

David told the children to mind what Rachel had said, and the three of them disappeared. Mike got to his feet. 'Now, mate, do you want me to ring Dad or will you?'

'Maybe you speak to him first. If he doesn't want me back, I'd rather he told you.'

'Yes, David's right in as much as it might be a shock for Henry, and you can pave the way gently, Mike', Rachel said.

Mike was on the phone some time. He had shut the door, so all they could hear was his muffled voice, and Rachel could see the tension rising in David the longer Mike was talking. She tried to distract him, but it was impossible, and she breathed a sigh of relief when Mike at last reappeared. 'Dad's waiting to speak to you, mate. It's all good.'

David got to his feet. He looked relieved but wary as he went into the passageway to speak to his father.

'Dad', they heard him croak as he picked up the receiver. Mike shut the door behind him. 'Let's go and check on the kids shall we love?' he said to Rachel.

The children were riding in the round yard, all trotting round very sedately. They pulled up when Rachel and Mike appeared.

They chatted for a few minutes. John and Christine liked Dusty and Danny and seemed to be getting on with them well. 'So long as you are sensible and watch out for Caleb, you can ride in the home paddock. Once you are through the gate, keep to the fence line and then you will have about an hours ride if you take it at a reasonable pace.' Rachel said, watching the joy spread on the children's faces.

'I think Caleb has bonded with those two quite well, considering', Mike observed as they watched the children ride away.

'Seems so. I have to admit to being a little worried about his reaction when we go to see the family as this little episode seems to have upset him rather.'

'Umm, well, we'll have to see and hope for the best, I guess. He has to meet them sometime, and in a way, this might be more of a help than a hindrance.'

It certainly seemed that way when the children came back. Christine and John were full of it, and Caleb sat nodding and looking happy. David had spoken to his father at length and was set to leave for home the next day with Mike, Rachel and Caleb following a few days later.

Chapter 51

Mike was worried about leaving as it was hot and dry. One of the bores had dried up, it seemed, and though there was still feed, some paddocks were beginning to look sparse. Summer rain hadn't happened, and the year before hadn't been much better. However, the creek was still reasonably full though there wasn't really any water flow. The big pools were getting low, though their favourite swimming hole still had plenty of water in it. They moved the cattle, so most of them were in the creek paddock. They also moved the horses near the yards as Mike thought they would need supplement feed, and he was trying to make it as easy for Ted as he could. Finally, they decided that was the best they could do to make life as easy for Ted while they were away and set off to visit the Grimshaws. Though it was unspoken, they were also worried about Caleb's reaction to the family. It was a lot of people to get used to at once. Rachel had spoken at length to the psychologist, Jenny, over the phone that was in charge of Caleb and told her about the nightmares which were now recurring. Some nights he would go back to sleep, but the last one or two, he had again clung to Rachel and not let her go back to bed. Jenny had said there was good and bad in Caleb's dreams as maybe it meant he was remembering more and would speak soon, but also, the bad memories were surfacing. Repressing them wasn't good, but bringing them out could be traumatic.

When they got there, Caleb clung to Rachel, burying his head and refusing to even look up. Nancy had put a small bed in Mike and Rachel's room for him.

However, everyone was full of the fact David had returned, and Rachel said, just ignore Caleb; he will come round in his own time, so that is what they did. Towards evening John and Christine turned up with David, and Caleb stopped hiding his face and was pleased to see them, though still shy.

'Why don't you take Caleb and show him the poddy calves you've been feeding these last few days, Chris', Henry said. Christine held out her hand, and after a few minutes' hesitation, Caleb took it and looked at Rachel. 'It's fine, Caleb. Chris will look after you, so will John.'

Once they had left, Henry started to ask twenty questions. Of course, he knew about Caleb, but this was the first time they had met. Henry looked much better already, they thought. David returning had given him a much-needed boost. 'Just wonderful Rachel, the first Great Grandson!' Henry beamed.

Rachel smiled, *not technically,* she thought but was pleased to see Henry more like his old self.

Over the next few days, Henry worked very hard to gain Caleb's confidence, and before long, the two of them were off doing things together. They seemed to have formed a special bond as the very young and very old can sometimes. Caleb was still waking every night, though, and Rachel was getting exhausted, so was Mike; all being in together meant they all three woke up.

Early one morning, Rachel was up sleepily pouring herself a coffee when Caleb appeared in the doorway. She'd left both him and Mike asleep, or so she'd thought. Caleb gave her a beaming smile and disappeared out onto the verandah. Ruby, who slept out there, got up and greeted him. Then to Rachel's surprise, Caleb knocked on Henry's verandah door. Rachel moved quietly to see what was going on. Henry then came out, and Rachel heard him say, 'Ready Little Mate, off we go then before everyone wakes up.'

Caleb shook his head and pointed to the kitchen. Rachel withdrew hurriedly, but seconds later, Henry put his head in. 'Caleb and I are off to check out the baby wombat that is down in the front paddock before he goes to sleep for the day. Sorry I was going to let you know last night but forgot. Better go, or else we'll miss all the early morning fun.'

Rachel stood and watched as a big man, a very small boy, and a dog walked away in the sharp light of the rising sun. She would always remember the tall man and small boy, both wearing Akubras, Caleb trying to take as long as stride as possible, Henry taking short strides, holding Caleb's hand, Ruby trotting importantly at their heels. It made her feel very emotional, and Mike found her sitting at the table, drying her eyes.

'What's up love, where's Caleb?'

When Rachel told him, he grinned broadly. 'David coming home minus Wendy and Caleb hitting it off with Dad has certainly given Dad a new lease on life.'

'I just wish Caleb would start talking. Do you think he ever will?'

'I've heard him whispering to Ruby. I think he was using words, and Ted has heard him muttering softly to Puzzle. The psychologist said it may take some time. Some of the trouble is he is making it very easy for us to understand him without words. But it will come right in the end, sweetheart. Now there is no one up yet apart from those two, and I'm missing having a cuddle, sharing a room. How about we go back to bed for a bit?'

'Going back to bed, didn't you sleep well?' Nancy had come in unnoticed.

Mike winked at Rachel and gave a wry smile. 'Having a third person who wakes in the night isn't very conducive to sleep or anything else come to that.'

Nancy seemed not to have picked up on Mike's remark; she was frowning. 'Caleb still asleep? If not, where is he?'

Rachel relayed the story again.

'Oh, how lovely. Henry used to do that with our two. Take them off early, before it's too hot to see the birds and animals who later will be snoozing in the shade. I think that is partly what made Shawn want to be a vet and Julia a ranger. They've always loved the early mornings in summer and reminisce about their grandad taking them out to see things. You never know Caleb might be a vet or some such one day.'

'Well, as you know, I am supposed to be homeschooling him, but it's so hard. Like with reading when he has no speech. He has not been taught anything as far as I can tell, so he is very behind for his age.'

'You'll get there, you'll get him there, Rachel, if anyone can, you can. He's lucky to have you both as grandparents.'

'Maybe. We'll see, a long way to go yet.'

A while later, when Caleb and Henry returned, Caleb's eyes were shining, and when Rachel asked him what he had seen and done for a few seconds, she thought he would speak, but then he grabbed hold of the pencil and paper Rachel always kept handy and started to draw like mad. They could make out birds and animals and asked him questions. Mostly he nodded like mad or pointed and smiled, but he didn't speak, though several times it seemed as if he was on the point of doing so.

For the rest of their stay, it became a ritual. The old man, the little boy and the dog would set off in the predawn light in search of night creatures and early morning birds. Henry told them to start with Caleb would clap his hands in delight, which of course, scared some of the creatures away. He soon learnt to keep quiet and would look up at Henry with shining eyes. Those moments became special to them all, and everyone was so pleased to see Henry transformed into something like his old self.

Chapter 52

When it was time to leave, they decided to stay on for a few days, not wanting to break the spell Henry seemed to have cast. Caleb had stopped having nightmares as suddenly as they had started, and all shyness had disappeared. Finally, though, they had to leave, and Rachel took some time explaining to Caleb about going home. They needn't have worried; Caleb was sad they could see but excited too. He had a bit of a wobble when Henry kissed him goodbye, and Henry looked sad too, but it was arranged that Nancy and Tom would bring Henry to see them soon.

'It was good to be home.' Rachel reflected a few days later as she loaded Caleb and Ruby into the car to drive into town. The psychologist Caleb was under came out from Roma once a month to see him. Up until just before Christmas, it had been once a fortnight, but they were dropping it back as on every level except speech, Caleb was thriving. Many times, Rachel had been tempted to ask Caleb to speak but knew it wasn't a good idea. She had been told it would happen in his own time.

The sun blazed down, and looking around as she drove, Rachel felt quite despairing of the sunburnt land and the relentless heat they were experiencing this summer. Would it ever rain? Some farmers were buying fodder, and lots of people were having to buy tankers of water just for their own use, never mind animals. There was a harsh beauty in the land. The light was so bright that it seemed as if everything was defined with a very sharp pencil, from the trees to the rocky outcrops, to the cattle who were dotted about seeking what little feed there was. All lit up in the blinding light of the sun. *God, I hope there isn't a bushfire. The whole countryside is a tinder box,* she thought. The last fire had been six years ago, and the day after Mike had returned into her life, the wind had changed at the last minute just as it got to her boundary. She shivered at the memory.

She parked in the shade of a big old Moreton Bay fig that stood by the little park and let Ruby out and tied her up; otherwise, she would follow them, 'It's too hot for dogs anywhere but here, Rubes', she said giving her a bowl of water she had brought. Just then, a powerful motorbike came up the main street. Rachel shivered involuntarily. It always made her think of Johnny. Caleb, who was standing beside her, tugged her arm and pointed. He was smiling. It was plain a motorbike wasn't anything he was scared of.

Gathering her emotions, Rachel took his hand and started across the road to the doctor's surgery, where she was to meet Linda, the psychologist. Halfway across, she stopped short. The motorcyclist had taken off his helmet and was looking straight at her; it was Zak. He got off his bike and walked up to them, a look of astonishment on his face.

'Bloody hell, Rachel, this kid!'

Caleb hid behind Rachel at this point. 'It's alright, Caleb, it's alright. Zak, you've scared him!'

'Is he who I think he is? Is he Johnny's kid? How come he's here, what—'

'Zak! Stop! We have an appointment. I'll explain later. We'll meet you in the bakery in half an hour.'

'Sorry. Yep, sure.' Zak watched them go with a bemused expression on his face. Thoughts barrelled through his head about the little boy and Johnny. One thing was obvious, the child was so like Johnny to look at. The same blue eyes and blonde curly hair, but then like Rachel too. He'd find out soon enough.

Half an hour or so later, Rachel and Caleb joined Zak in the bakery. Zak had been waiting for them and Jane, Rachel's friend who owned the bakery, was very intrigued as to what was going on. This time as she approached the table, Zak got to his feet and hugged Rachel. He was a big man, and he nearly squeezed the breath out of her. It took her entirely by surprise, as previously, she had not even had a handshake. 'You called me a pussycat the last time, remember?' he said. Then he turned to Caleb and, bending down, held out his hand. 'How are you, mate? What's your name?'

Caleb stood looking at Zak for a few moments, seizing him up, then looked up at Rachel. She nodded, so he put his little hand in Zak's and smiled as Zac shook it very gently.

'Zak, this is Caleb, and he doesn't speak, at least not at the moment. I will tell you why at some point, but not just now', Rachel inclined her head towards Caleb.

Zak looked somewhat bewildered but sat down again just as Jane brought Caleb a chocolate milkshake and Rachel an iced coffee. She was back a few seconds later, bringing a plate with scones and cream. 'I was hoping for a good catch-up, Rach, but I can see it will have to wait!' she winked at Zak as she said this; she had guessed who he was.

'How's my mate Mike these days? I hear you got your horse back. Was it uninjured and healthy?'

'You know something about all that, don't you, Zak?'

Zak grinned at her and helped himself to a big dollop of cream on his scone. 'Wondered if I could come out and catch up with you guys this arvo. On my way when I saw you tying up your dog.'

'Mike will be stoked to see you, Zak, and we can have a proper chat then.'

They talked some more about everyday things, then Zak took his leave, saying he'd see them later. He ruffled Caleb's hair as he got up, and Caleb gave him a small smile, then hid his face.

Rachel watched him stride across the street, thinking about the first time she had seen him. Jane interrupted her thoughts. 'Scary looking bloke that one with his black leather and beard, he's such a big bastard too. I'm guessing you know him though, not like you to hug strange men, especially big bruisers like him!'

'He's an old mate of Mike's, and he was in Johnny's gang, undercover.' Rachel glanced at Caleb. 'No more talk of that just now, Jane.'

'Oh no, of course not. Now, tell me all about your trip to see Mike's folks and what of his brother David and his family?'

Rachel caught Jane up to speed on all she thought she needed to know, and then, having got some supplies from the supermarket, she loaded Caleb and Ruby into the car for the drive home.

Mike was both surprised and pleased when Rachel told him Zak was on his way, and hardly were the words out of her mouth than they heard the throaty roar of his bike. Caleb stood and watched the huge man get off his bike and embrace Mike. Then they were clapping each other on the back and laughing and talking all at once. Caleb crept over to look closely at the bike. He'd seen bikes, of course, and somewhere deep in his memory, there was a bike, but he couldn't quite recall where it was or what it was to do with him. Then he had an idea. He'd love to have a ride on it, but he knew he'd need a helmet. He glanced across at the adults who were now on the verandah talking.

Minutes later, Rachel felt Caleb tugging at the back of her shirt; she looked around. Caleb stood there with his riding helmet on. Rachel insisted he wore one. She didn't want him to end up as his father had. 'You want help to get Puzzle saddled, do you? We're not going riding just now, Caleb… Rachel trailed off as the little boy shook his head then pointed to the bike.

'I think young Caleb wants a ride on my bike.' said Zak.

Mike and Rachel were amazed it was the first time Caleb had really initiated anything, and he looked very determined. In the end, after a little debate, Zak took him for a very slow ride around the yards near the house. Rather than riding pillion, Zak held him in front of himself with his arm around him. He was too small, they felt, to be safe behind.

Caleb was grinning ear to ear when Zak brought him back to the verandah steps, and after Zak had set him down and got off his bike, Caleb got hold of his hand and did his version of a handshake. Rachel found her eyes were flooded with tears; Caleb was making huge progress!

Zak said he would stay as he had last time. Again, he came with wine and beer. Rachel left the men on the verandah and went to get dinner ready. Caleb hovered near her. 'Do you want to help, darling?' Rachel asked. Occasionally Caleb would lay the table, but so far, that was all he had done, and both Rachel and Mike hadn't pushed it. It was better he did things in his own time.

'Put the knives and forks around then, sweetheart, like you've done before, spoons too. Zak likes his food, and I have a passionfruit tart I've got out of the freezer.' Rachel carried on talking then was aware that Caleb, who had laid the table, was standing beside her, looking at her intently.

'What's up, buddy?'

For an answer, Caleb dragged a chair over and climbed onto it. At this point, Rachel realised he wanted to help prepare the vegetables. She got a small knife out and gave it to him, along with some carrots. 'Just be very careful, it's sharp', she said but again, the tears were threatening. It was almost like having her little boy Johnny back. He had loved to do exactly what Caleb was doing now.

Rachel looked at him, comparing him to his father. Johnny had been an attractive little boy, but Caleb was more so. His hair was blonder, his eyes were bigger and bluer, and he had an air of serenity about him that Johnny had never had. Given his start in life, Rachel found it quite amazing that there was a happy aura around Caleb, which Rachel fervently hoped he'd never lose.

When the men appeared ready to eat, Rachel could see Mike had told Zak all about Caleb. Zak talked to him but didn't expect a verbal answer.

'I take it you've never been married, Zak?' Rachel asked.

Zak looked taken aback, then shook his head. 'There was someone once but my lifestyle, well any relationship was out of the question really.'

'That's a shame; I think you'd have made a lovely Dad', said Rachel softly.

Zak looked hurriedly down at his plate, but Rachel caught the pain on his face, 'Sorry, I didn't mean to upset you.'

Keeping his head down, Zak muttered that she hadn't, but Rachel felt bad as she knew she had touched maybe the only chink in his armour. The evening progressed, and then after Caleb had gone to bed, Mike said, 'Rach, Zak has more to tell us about Smokey and Keith and all that nonsense.'

'Well, we uncovered a bigger can of worms, it seems than we realised, and yes, I was still working when I called in here last time. Anyway, the gang that stole your horse were just the tip of the iceberg, part of an international crime ring. They were into nearly every crime you can think of. Gambling, thieving, paedophilia, pornography, drugs, you name it, they were masterminds of it. Not sure what they had on Keith, but it seems he was the one who tipped them off about your horse, and somehow that artist bloke got drawn in too. They were certainly going to do the racing industry a great disservice had they had their way.'

'We knew most of this already, Zak, but thanks for spelling it out.' Rachel said.

'We didn't know how widespread it was, though, did we, Rachel? From what Zak has told me, we were lucky we got away from Scone without serious problems. They were a pretty ruthless lot.'

Rachel shivered. She suddenly had the thought that the men weren't telling her how bad it was and decided she really didn't want to know. She had enough of violence as it was; whatever it was, they weren't telling her could remain buried.

Chapter 53

It turned out that Zak really was retiring now, and consequently, he hung around for a few days. He went and helped Mike do a few odd jobs, played with Caleb and generally made himself useful. After four days, though, he announced he was leaving. 'Where are you going, and what are you going to do?' Rachel asked him.

'Well, I thought, for now, I might be a modern-day swaggie. I can travel around, see things and enjoy things I couldn't before. It's a big country out there, and I intend to see as much of it as I can.'

Rachel was surprised to find she missed him after he had gone, and so it seemed did Caleb, who had followed Zak and his grandfather around while they did various jobs. He came into the kitchen to Rachel, looking very lost, when Zak roared away on his bike.

Life settled into something of a routine then. It was still boiling hot, and the summer rains hadn't come. Mike was worried about feed, something which had never happened before as Sam, Rachel's first husband, had always been careful about overstocking, and it had never been this dry.

Rachel was busy homeschooling Caleb as much as she could, though, as he still refused to speak, she wasn't sure how much of what she taught got through. However, he could do simple sums without any trouble, so she was hopeful.

Then they had an unexpected visit from Clarrie, who turned up unannounced one Saturday morning. She had both Emma and Ben with her.

'Goodness Clarrie, what a surprise!' Rachel said, coming out onto the verandah upon hearing a car. 'Come in, all of you. Why didn't you let us know? We might not have been here, and in any case, I need to make up beds if you're staying, which I assume you are.'

'It's fine Rachel, this is just a quick visit. I wanted to tell you both face to face, and I did check with Mike when I spoke to him the other day that you would both be about.'

'Tell us what?'

Rachel could see the children were rather het up too. Whatever it was seemed likely to be big news.

Just then, Mike appeared, having seen the car. After the greetings were over, Mike said, 'What's all this about Clarrie?'

'We're moving. We're moving to W.A.' Ben almost shouted.

There was a moments' stunned silence then everyone spoke at once. Mike thumped on the table, which scared Caleb, who had just come into the room. He hid his face against Rachel.

'Clarrie?'

'I've sold the house, and Dad and Mum suggested we move over to be nearer them. The kids and I have talked about it, and I've made the arrangements to have all our stuff moved over and sorted out with the schools and....'Clarrie stopped speaking as she saw the thunderous expression on Mike's face.

'You didn't think to consult me? I'm their father, after all, but it doesn't seem to count for much. How could you decide to do this, Clarrie, without one word?'

'I'm sorry Mike, I—'

'Don't be cross with Mum, Dad. Ben and I both want this. It's horrible living in Brisbane when everybody knows about Keith and what he tried to do to me. The kids at school are kind to my face, but I know they are sniggering behind my back.'

'It's the same for me too, Dad', Ben said, 'It's been pretty rough at times, we all need to get right away, and Mum has had it tough too.'

'I only had the offer on the house yesterday, and I didn't want to tell you until then. Of course, it may not be sold even then, though I think there is a good chance. I could have told you over the phone, but I thought you deserved to be told face to face.'

Caleb had stood looking from one to another, then he went and put his little hand in Emma's and looked at her pleadingly. Emma bent down to him. 'What is it Caleb, don't you want us to go away?'

Caleb shook his head violently and opened his mouth as if to speak, then seeing everyone was looking at him, he shut his mouth again, but his eyes filled with tears. Emma crouched down beside him and put her arms around him. 'We'll still come and stay here in the holidays, and perhaps Dad and Rachel will bring you to see us one day. Would you like that?'

Caleb nodded, then tugging at Emma's hand and at the same time getting hold of Ben's, he dragged them to the door. 'I guess we need to go with him, Emma said over her shoulder, and she went with the boys.

'That's fine.' Rachel and Clarrie spoke at the same time, then exchanged a wry smile.

Mike was still frowning but seemed to accept what the children had said. 'I can see that life has been difficult for the kids, Clarrie, and for you too, I'm guessing.'

'You can say that again. You certainly find out who your friends are! To start with, everybody seemed very supportive, but then someone said I should have known or guessed what was going on, and then the sniping started, and most of my so-called friends won't even acknowledge me if I meet them anywhere. It is rather a toxic place to be for me just now, my part of Brisbane anyway, and I just want to get right away, the kids too.'

'Oh, Clarrie, poor you.' Rachel hugged Clarrie, who promptly burst into tears.

After a few minutes, she gently extracted herself from Rachel. 'Rachel, I have a lot to thank you for. It was you that opened my eyes to what was going on under my nose. I was blind, though I think looking back, I was in denial about Keith. Now I'm paying the price of my foolishness, and so are the kids.'

Mike stood looking at the two of them as Rachel was feeling emotional too, he could see. 'Time to get some lunch, I think', he said. Practicalities helped, and by the time lunch was ready, both women were feeling better.

Clarrie had never really seen Caleb before, and she couldn't believe what an attractive little boy he was. His cute smile and big blue eyes charmed her, and even though he just smiled and used his hands to communicate, she was bowled over by him.

They stayed the night but left early the next morning for the long drive back. 'Don't know if we will see you before we leave, but please come over to see us as soon as you can', Clarrie said. They all ended up being rather tearful, but all knew it was for the best. They could start a new life in W.A., though Clarrie had worried about the children's schooling, she knew the children were very bright and in the pro and cons of it all; it was worth the gamble.

Chapter 54

The dry weather continued; several times, clouds rolled in from the west, but nothing happened. They moved all the cows and calves and some of the young stock they were keeping down to the creek paddock. There was more grazing there, and it was the biggest paddock on the property. Long and narrow, it followed the contours of the creek from the public road to the forestry boundary at the far end, about 5 kilometres. In dry times like now, there were many places the cattle could cross the creek, but in normal times there was only one real crossing point. The banks down to the creek there were shallow, but everywhere else, they were steep and quite high. The land on the far side rose steeply to Sid's boundary, the land their side was quite flat, though the paddock on the homestead side was a few metres higher as the ground gradually sloped all the way back to the house and buildings, not much but enough in times of excessive rain that there was no danger of flooding.

It was hot and humid. Caleb seemed out of sorts, but Rachel put it down to the weather. *Not that long until Henry comes to stay*, she thought. She was really looking forward to it, and she hoped it would finally break Caleb's silence. They were both sure they had heard him whispering to Ruby but as soon as he thought they were near, he was silent. 'It might just be him humming, Rach,' Mike cautioned, 'We know he does that.'

'I'm sure I could hear actual words, though, Mike. I suppose time will tell, though I expected him to speak after all this time. He's been with us over six months now!'

'Hell! So he has. Time goes far too quickly for my liking. I just wish it would rain, we're more or less into autumn, and it's not looking good.'

'It wouldn't be so bad if it wasn't so hot and windy. These drying winds make it even worse. My roses and veggies are all looking sick in spite of my watering them. The only good thing is that we use the water from the house else I'd lose them too.'

'My worry is if there is a bushfire, because everything is like a tinder box, and with a wind like this, a fire would be unstoppable.'

Rachel agreed, remembering the last time the farm was threatened just before Mike reappeared in her life. It had been scary then, but it was even drier now if that were possible.

A few days later, Mike said, 'They say there is a cyclone forming in the coral sea and heading towards the coast. Maybe it will dump some rain on us if we're lucky!'

However, their hopes were dashed a few days later when the storm was downgraded and tracked down the coast. 'No rain for us,' Rachel said despairingly.

Ted, who was nearby, overheard her. 'We'll have a big storm soon, Missus Rachel, too much I be thinking.'

Rachel looked up at the great blue dome above them. No clouds, just relentless glaring blue. 'If you say so, Ted.'

The older man looked at her knowingly with his large dark eyes, 'Fair dinkum!' With that, he walked off. Rachel watched him go. *I hope he's right,* she thought to herself.

A few days later, they woke up to distant rumblings and flashes of lightning, though they were a long way away. It was hotter and more humid than ever, and everything was hot to touch. It was extremely uncomfortable. But still, it didn't rain. Caleb lay on his bed. He wasn't coping with the weather at all and was lethargic and miserable. Ruby sat in his room with him. Rachel asked him if he was afraid of the thunder, but he shook his head. 'If only it would rain, then everything would be better', Rachel grumbled, but they went to bed without the thunder coming any closer.

The next day it was the same, though it seemed the storms were a little closer, although Rachel wasn't sure that some of it was wishful thinking.

The young couple they had staying in the old homestead appeared mid-morning and said they were leaving. 'But you're only partway through your stay. What's wrong?' Rachel asked.

'It's just too hot and too dusty. I suppose living in Brisbane, we haven't experienced anything like this before. It's too hot to do anything. We're not expecting a refund. We'll just be glad to be home.'

Rachel watched them drive off. She had the strangest feeling of dread and shivered; the storm clouds were still gathering on the horizon, but no rain.

At lunchtime, Mike remarked that he thought the storm would miss them anyway, as the clouds seemed to be dispersing and drifting away. No sooner than the words were out of his mouth than there was a tremendous crack of thunder almost overhead. It made them all jump, and Caleb ran and hid his face against Mike.

'It's alright, little buddy, just the clouds bumping into each other, they have a steerage problem, I think! Nothing to worry about. Look, Ruby hasn't even woken up!'

Indeed, Ruby was lying flat out on the floor, trying to get some sort of relief from the searing heat. Caleb looked at her, then at Mike. It seemed as if he was no longer worried then as he got back on his chair and resumed eating his lunch.

All afternoon, the storm snapped and crackled away with louder claps of thunder every little while. Looking at the clouds themselves, they didn't look that heavy with rain. Mike and Rachel were both on tenterhooks as a dry storm was the last thing they needed with everything being so dry. Then, at last, in the early evening, the heavens opened, and the rain came out of the sky in a raging torrent, or so it seemed. Caleb looked worried again as the noise on the roof was deafening but realising that no one else was upset by it, he settled down, and when bedtime came, he seemed quite calm.

However, he woke them at just past midnight screaming and sobbing, and they both rushed into his room. He was sitting up in bed, tears pouring down his face, and it was to Mike that he held out his arms, and it was Mike that ended up cramped beside him for the rest of the night. If Mike moved, his eyes flew open, and he would cling onto his grandfather as if his life depended on it.

The rain continued the next morning, great squalls blowing in the wind like some giant had unplugged a huge water tank in the sky, and it was falling relentlessly down, trying to drown everything in its path.

Rachel stayed indoors with Caleb while Mike went out to check the horses and dogs and chooks. Caleb seemed more his normal self now it was daylight, though a very gloomy dank daylight.

''I opened the yard gate and let the horses into the small yard. From there, they can go into the barn for shelter if they wish. They are looking like drowned rats just now', Mike said as he came back in.

'It seems one extreme or another. I can't recall it ever raining with this intensity before. I expect it has but not for a long time,' Rachel commented.

Late morning Mike, who had been doing some paperwork, came into the kitchen frowning. 'The creek will be well up by now. Do you think we should go down and open the gate? If they are our side, the cattle will be trapped against the fence.'

'I imagine they will be Sid's side, there was more feed over there before all this, but you've got a point. It's the cows and calves I worry about.'

Just then the phone went, and Mike went to answer it. Rachel was busy cooking, so she could stock the freezer for when they were busy and cooking time was short. Caleb, who was sitting at the table, had listened to their exchange about the cattle and the creek. There was one particular calf he had made a pet of. He felt really worried, and Gran and Pops weren't doing anything. They should be going NOW BEFORE SOMETHING BAD HAPPENED!

Caleb slithered off his chair, and going out to the back verandah, he pulled on his boots and his raincoat that he had only worn once when he first had it and had wanted to try wearing it. It was a hot day, and he had been very pleased to take it off. The cold rain and wind nearly had him retreating back to the safety of the house, but he sloshed across to the barn where the horses were sheltering and managed to get Puzzles bridle on. He had to stand on the rail to get the gate open, and the wind took it out of his grasp, and it crashed back, but having got a reluctant Puzzle through and heaving and pushing, he managed to shut it again. The other horses stood watching, not at all inclined to follow. It was wet and horrible out there.

Without a saddle, it was quite hard getting on Puzzle, but after several attempts, he made it, and they set off in the driving rain and wind, which luckily was behind them, so it was almost pushing them along.

They had three big paddocks to cross to get to the creek paddock, and sitting on Puzzle, Caleb managed to open the gates but left them open, thinking he would shut them on his return. A number of times, Puzzle wanted to turn back, but Caleb was determined, and Puzzle loved his wee master, so he complied. Caleb was focused on his mission and didn't give much thought to anything else except for staying on Puzzle's back as he had no saddle. By the time he got to the creek paddock, he was very, very wet and cold and shivering violently. It was raining so hard he couldn't see if the cattle were there or not, but he managed to open the gate and decided to see if he could see them. He hadn't gone very far when he met a wall of water rushing across in front of him. It was too much for Puzzle, who stopped so suddenly Caleb went over his head straight into the floodwaters.

Chapter 55

Rachel looked round to speak to Caleb, but he wasn't there. *Must have gone to his room,* she thought. Just then, Mike finished his telephone conversation and came back into the kitchen. 'I'll go and open the gate then shall I like we said?'

Rachel nodded, 'I'll stay here with Caleb and Ruby. They must be in the bedroom. Are you going on Jock? You don't want to get bogged.'

'That was my thinking.' Mike kissed her cheek absently as he walked past to go and put his wet weather gear on. A second later, he was back in the kitchen. 'Caleb's not in his room, and nor is Ruby.'

'Where are they then?'

A quick search of the house realised their worst fears, and pulling on their boots and coats as quickly as they could, they ran across to the horses. Mike found Ruby shut in the shed where they kept the horses' tack. She was frantically trying to get out. 'Oh God, Mike, Puzzles missing. Where can they have gone in this? OhGodohGod.' Rachel, usually so calm, was panicking and nearly hysterical.

'I think he will have gone to the creek paddock. He was in the kitchen when we were saying about the water trapping the cattle.' As he spoke, Mike was busy saddling Jock, and Rachel automatically started to try to put Smokey's bridle on. She was shaking so much that she could hardly do it and

Smokey, picking up her mistress's distress, started to play up. Being highly strung herself, she didn't like the fear Rachel was giving off.

Mike swung into the saddle, 'Don't worry. I'll catch up with him. He won't have gone far in this.' He opened the gate and took off as quickly as he could on Jock. Ruby, having been let out of the shed, had disappeared into the rain that was still coming down hard.

Rachel gave up trying to put Smokey's bridle on and, hanging the bridle on the fence, ran out to the ute. If she was careful, she'd be alright, she reasoned. Just as she was about to set off, Ted appeared through the gloom by the passenger door. He opened the door and got in. 'I saw Ruby then the Boss go by. Is young Caleb in trouble or something else?'

'He overheard us talking about opening the creek paddock gate and think he must have gone to do it. In this weather, anything could happen.'

'He'll be fine. He's a sensible lad even though he's small. You'll see. I expect we'll meet them on the way back!'

Rachel felt slightly comforted by Ted's words but still had a sick feeling deep inside her, and the 'what if's' kept going round and round in her head. She drove very carefully and, knowing where the boggy patches were likely to be, managed to go across the ground quite well. There were a few hairy moments, but at last, the gate into the creek paddock came into view through the rain, which was now easing off a little.

Relief at getting there soon turned into horror, though. Jock and Puzzle were both standing almost side by side with their reins dangling, then as they got closer, they could see Ruby standing by a small form lying half in, half out of the floodwater, which was getting higher and higher even as they watched. Both scrambled out and ran across, the tears already running down Rachel's face. As they got to him, Caleb coughed and started to struggle to sit up. Ted picked him up and started to carry him away from the wall of water. 'MIKE MIKE, WHERE ARE YOU?' Rachel was screaming, looking around desperately.

'POP'S IN THE WATER SAVE HIM PLEASE SAVE HIM' Caleb started to scream.

Part of Rachel's brain was telling her she had what she was longing for. Caleb was speaking, but she was too distraught to fully take it on board.

Setting Caleb onto his feet, Ted took hold of Jocks reins. 'I'll ride down by the waters and find him you take young'un home and call for help.'

Rachel opened her mouth to argue, but Ted was already in the saddle and seconds later, he was trotting away, watching the water as he went. Rachel grabbed hold of Puzzle's reins tying him to the back of the ute.

Caleb sank back onto the ground. He was sobbing. 'Pops. Pops.'

'Come on, sweetheart, we have to get help.' His distress had the effect of making Rachel calmer. She had him to look out for as well. Soon they were slithering and splashing their way back. As they got to the house, Alma appeared and took in the situation at a glance. 'I'll look after this little one, Missus.' Getting him onto the verandah, she started to strip his clothes off. His teeth were chattering, and between sobs, he kept saying, 'Pops, in the water. Pops.'

Running to the phone, she rang Sid, who answered straight away. He would organise the S.E.S.; he was in charge of them in their area.

Going back outside, she was going to drive back, but Ted appeared on Jock. 'I'm sorry I had to turn back, or else I'd have been trapped too. The water was rising so quickly, it'll be through the fence line by now. I got Ruby to come with me. She knew the boss is out there somewhere she wanted to stay.'

Rachel almost fell backwards onto the verandah steps, tears pouring down her face. 'OH God. What shall I do? I can't bear this.'

Ted was at a loss as to what to say, so he silently untied Puzzle and led the horse and pony away to put them back with the others.

Rachel heaved herself to her feet, then collapsed onto the verandah cane sofa and buried her head in her hands, great racking sobs shaking her body. She didn't know how long she stayed there, but then she felt little arms around her and raising her head, she found herself looking into Caleb's big blue eyes. There were tears in them, but he seemed to be quite calm. Alma had showered him, and he was wrapped up warmly. 'Please don't cry, Granny. I love you. Please don't cry.'

This brought fresh tears, the first real sentence Caleb had spoken and all the emotion that went into those few precious words and their meaning.

Making a huge effort, Rachel asked him what had happened. 'I fell off Puzzle into the water. It was very cold, but Pops appeared just as I fell and got into the water to pull me out. I think he slipped as he put me down. Then there was a branch, or something hit his back and he—he—' At this point, the tears and sobs returned.

Alma came outside. 'I think you need to get out of those wet things, Missus and I've made you tea. Come inside now. It won't help Mike if you make yourself ill now, will it?'

Alma put her arm around Rachel's waist, and Rachel stumbled to her feet. She knew Alma was right, and there was Caleb to think of too. She realised she was shivering too, partly with distress and partly with cold. After she had sat numbly at the table and had her steaming cup of tea, she muttered to Alma she would have a shower, and off she went.

The shower warmed her, and she was just getting dressed again when Caleb, who had stayed with Alma in the kitchen, appeared. He looked at her, his big eyes brimming with tears. 'Granny!'

Rachel scooped him up and laid on the bed, cuddling him. He, in turn, burrowed up against her. She stroked his head and found solace in his little body clinging to her. Then her mind wandered. Mike with his warm brown eyes and broad smile. His strong arms holding her, loving her, protecting her. Sometimes teasing, always seeming to know what she was thinking; her soul mate! How could she even think of functioning without him? He was the whole world. The tears ran again, unchecked. No sobs, just like the rain outside, a constant, unstoppable stream.

Chapter 56

Rachel woke with a start. It was dark, but she could hear low voices in the kitchen. How could she have fallen asleep? Caleb, still in her arms, woke too. 'Granny?'

'Ssh, it's alright, sweetie. We'll go and see what's happening, shall we?'

'Have they found Pops?'

'I don't know, we'll go and see, maybe.' But even as she said this, Rachel knew they would have come and told her immediately, and it was just on dark now. Making a huge effort, she squared her shoulders, and together they went into the kitchen. Sid, Norma, Ted, Alma and Josh were all there, all looking very serious. Ruby came across and licked Rachel's hand.

'Rachel', Sid spoke before anyone had a chance to say anything first. 'It's too dark to continue now, but we'll start again at first light. I've organised a helicopter to come from Roma, and they will be here at first light. We'll find him.'

Rachel nodded, 'Will you find him alive, though?' she croaked.

'Mike is a tough cookie, Rach', Josh said.

Norma bent down to Caleb, 'Hello Caleb, I made some chocolate cake earlier. Would you like some?'

Caleb looked up at Rachel, and seeing she wasn't going to answer, he nodded his head then remembered he was speaking now. 'Yeth Please', he whispered.

Norma had made Rachel coffee and had laced it with some whisky she had found in the cupboard. 'Drink ', she commanded Rachel.

'You must have come the road way to get here. Is it bad everywhere?'

'It actually stopped raining quite a while ago. So hopefully, the floodwaters will start to recede soon or at least by midday tomorrow. It's a bit sticky out there, but the folks managed to get here from town, as you can see.'

'Thanks for coming, Josh' the tears welled in Rachel's eyes again, but she swallowed them down. Norma was bustling about, 'Sid is going back soon, Rach, he has things to see to, and we don't want to worry Barry, he's not been so good lately, but I am staying with you tonight and no argument. Ted and Alma will see to the animals, so you just relax and look after this little one, yes?'

Rachel inclined her head. Her throat was too closed up to speak. Caleb finished his cake and came and stood by Rachel's chair. She pulled him onto her lap. 'I look after you too', he said quietly.

That undid Rachel, and the tears started again, but she brushed them away angrily. She had to stop crying. It wasn't helping anyone. Getting to her feet, she told Norma she'd get out sheets for the bed in the spare room, and so for the next little while, she busied herself. The others had dispersed, and soon it was the two women, and Caleb left in the kitchen. Rachel had made some soup earlier that day, and as she prepared to reheat it, she felt as if it was a lifetime ago. If only she could put the clock back to that morning when everything was as it should be and Mike was there with her. Caleb speaking was the only good thing that had happened, and she rather thought he would have done it soon, anyway. She wished it hadn't happened as it had.

The evening turned to night, Rachel carried Caleb through and put him to bed. It was late, and he had fallen asleep at the table. She laid him on his bed, not worrying that he was fully clothed. He stirred. 'Pops?' he muttered sleepily.

'Ssssh' Rachel stroked his hair back, and he settled again.

Norma was sitting at the kitchen table with her eyes closed, nearly asleep too.

'Go to bed, Norma. It's late. We talked ourselves round in circles. It's sleep time.'

Norma yawned; they had indeed talked of everything, and everybody and Rachel had shared her fears. Now was time to rest.

'What about you Rach, will you be alright? Are you going to bed yet?'

'I don't know. I may sit here on the old sofa. When I was scared of Johnny, I used to sleep here in the kitchen mostly fully clothed—Oh God, Norma, you don't think because I have Caleb now that Mike is taken away from me, do you? That somehow, there's been a swap. I can't live without him, I can't.'

Norma got to her feet and led Rachel to the sofa sitting them both down. 'Of course not, silly. You're overwrought and exhausted, and your brain is making things up. That is nonsense. Do you think God or fate or anything else would play that sort of trick? You need to sleep, then you will think more clearly.'

Rachel let Norma enfold her in her arms and cried quietly for a few minutes, then pulled herself together. 'I am being pathetic, aren't I. Was I like this when Sam died?'

'No, my dear, you were much stronger emotionally, but then you knew what was happening and expecting it. Also, I think though you loved Sam, you love Mike even more, and there have been other things working against you both lately. Shocks too what with Caleb, Emma, Keith, Catherine, Smokey stolen, Mike's accident, the list goes on. All in a short time, really. it's been a rough ride.'

'You're right, thanks, Norma. Now go and sleep. None of us is getting any younger!'

Later, when she was alone, Rachel reflected on what Norma had said. Tomorrow they would have to ring the Grimshaw's, but so far, they had held off, not wanting to upset them unless necessary. Now it seemed inevitable.

Chapter 57

Rachel didn't think she had been asleep, but she must have dozed off as just after first light, the drone of an engine woke her then she heard the vibrations of helicopter blades. The search was resuming!

She rushed out onto the verandah just as Sid appeared in his old ute. 'Sid, I'm coming with you.'

'No, Rachel, you stay here with young Caleb. He needs you, and we will tell you straight away if we find him, or rather when we find him.' Just then, Rachel felt Caleb's arms encircling her leg, so she reluctantly gave in and watched Sid drive away, followed by some other S.E.S. vehicles.

Norma came out onto the verandah, and then Alma appeared, and Rachel could see Ted tending to the horses who were still baled up in the yards.

On the one hand, the time dragged. On the other, it flew by. Three-quarters of an hour passed when they heard the helicopter fly over. What did that mean? Had they found him or given up, Rachel rushed onto the verandah to watch for Sid or any of the others returning. Minutes that felt like hours passed, then Rachel said, 'I see them!' She had bare feet, but she rushed headlong through the muddy ground to meet Josh, who was in the lead vehicle.

He stopped when she got to him. She had half expected Mike to be sitting beside him, even though she knew that was silly. Of course, he wasn't, and Josh looked grave. 'We've found him, Rachel, and he is still alive but in a bad way. They've flown him straight to the hospital. It's touch and go.'

'Oh, thank God you found him, but it's not good?' Rachel was having trouble processing Josh's words.

'Why didn't they stop? I could have gone with him.'

'There is nowhere here to land. It's too wet still, and besides, they didn't want to waste time, Rachel. Mike's in a bad way. He may not make it. I'm sorry.'

Rachel thought her legs would give way then. She stood swaying until Sid, who had come up behind, got out and supported her. 'Come on, old girl. He's a fighter, come on, I'll take you to see him. But I could murder a drink first.'

An hour later, Sid set off with Rachel and Caleb. Rachel insisted Caleb came with her, although Norma and Alma had both said they'd look after him. Rachel just didn't want to be parted from him. She was afraid Mike wouldn't make it, though she told no one else her fears.

The drive to the hospital took a long time as the road was damaged in quite a lot of places and there were still floods about. Sid told her it seemed all her cattle were his side of the creek and, as far as he could tell, were in one piece. He also told her that Mike was in a tree near where the swimming hole was. He was unconscious when they spotted him from the helicopter, and if it hadn't been for the fact his clothing was caught in the branches, they doubt he would have survived. He would have fallen into the floodwaters, and that would have been that. It took the winchman several minutes to cut him free, at the same time securing him so he didn't fall back into the water, which was still flowing fast beneath them. His pulse was weak, and he hadn't regained consciousness when they flew off. They had radioed in to Sid, who was the search coordinator.

It seemed to take a lifetime to get to the hospital in Roma. The storm had caused washouts, and there were still flooded areas. It felt strange as it was now a beautiful day, clear blue skies, and the humidity had gone with the storm.

When eventually they got to the hospital, they then had to wait as they were told a doctor wanted to speak to them first. A nurse appeared and took Caleb gently away with the promise of a chocolate milkshake and cookies. 'Can I come too?' Sid winked at Rachel. Caleb then went happily, as he wasn't keen on the idea until then. 'Now, Mrs Grimshaw, I wanted to explain to you firstly that your husband's heart actually stopped in the helicopter though they managed to bring him back. We have to warm him up very slowly, he has advanced hypothermia, and it's critical that we take great care as there are many things that can go wrong. Not least, his heartbeat may become irregular, or he may suffer pneumonia. He is still semiconscious, which is a good thing and, of course, very weak. But he is physically a strong man, and I think if all goes well, he should make a good recovery.

Mike had an oxygen mask on, and his eyes were shut, so Rachel tiptoed into the room and sat by his bed. She could hardly see him for all the coverings he had on him, even around his head. His hands even had gloves on, but she gently took hold of one. She could feel it was icy cold, even through the woollen gloves. After a while, Caleb slipped into the room, the nurse behind him. Caleb's eyes were round and fearful, but Rachel lifted him onto her lap, and he whispered, 'Poppa.' Mike's eyelids fluttered open, and a ghost of a smile touched his lips.

'He will be fine, Caleb. He'll want to hear you talking, won't he? That means he'll have to be up and about soon.'

Rachel had brought an overnight bag for herself and Caleb. Sid was going home, and it was arranged someone would collect them when Mike was discharged.

It turned out not to be as Rachel hoped. Mike developed pneumonia and ended up in intensive care. Rachel was beside herself. Norma came and stayed with her for a few days, partly so she could take care of Caleb, who was also getting cranky. He was scared and upset and knew if he hadn't gone off on Puzzle, none of this would have happened. Rachel was so focused on Mike she hardly took in Caleb's needs. She spent her days sitting by his bed. He knew she was there and sometimes whispered a few words asking after her and Caleb, but mostly he just slept.

Finally, Norma took charge of Rachel. 'Look, Rachel, you've got to get a grip. Caleb needs you, too, more than you realise. Look at the state of you; you're a mess, you're not eating properly, you're not sleeping, and you are letting both Caleb and Mike down being this way. No good Mike getting better only to find both you are Caleb are in some sort of bad state, is it? Caleb's not talking again now, do you realise?'

They had rented a small apartment near the hospital, and Caleb was in the small room where he slept.

Horror-struck by Norma's words, Rachel went in to him. 'Caleb, Norma tells me you aren't talking to her, is this right?'

Caleb nodded. 'But you'll speak to me, yes?'

The big blue eyes filled with tears, and he shook his head.

'Is it because you think we blame you for Poppa being ill?'

The tears overflowed, 'Yes', he whispered.

Rachel gathered him in her arms and rocked him gently. 'I am so sorry, darling, I have been so busy watching Poppa and not looking after you. Of course, we don't blame you. You were helping as best you could. Now you and I will go back to the hospital and see how he's doing, shall we? He was still asleep when I was there a little while ago.'

Norma watched them go, Rachel, so thin and desperate; Caleb's small hand clamped in his Grannie's hand, so fearful that it was all down to him. His eyes looked dull, and even his lovely blonde curls didn't seem to bounce like they normally did.

When they got to Mike's room, there was a surprise waiting for them. Mike was at last feeling better. 'Hello, you two', he managed to say before coughing. Shortly afterwards, having been reassured that Mike was really on the mend, at last, Rachel sat Caleb on the side of Mike's bed. 'Poppa, Caleb needs to hear from you that you're not cross with him for falling in the water.'

'Aw, mate, of course not. You were checking the stock like a proper stud farmer. Why would I be cross?'

Caleb sat taking this in for a minute, then reached out to Mike, who hugged him close. Then he looked at Rachel, 'Is Puzzle alright and Ruby?'

'They sure are, mate, and we'll be home soon to look after them.'

Chapter 58

Caleb was struggling down the verandah step, carrying a bag nearly as big as he was, though he had grown considerably during the last year. Rachel, coming away from the big new motorhome that was parked outside, stopped him at the bottom of the steps. 'What have you got in there, sweetheart? It looks heavy.'

Caleb looked a little guilty,' just a few things I might need.'

'Can I see? I might be able to help you decide what you do need because we've packed the kitchen sink as it is!'

Sure enough, Caleb seemed to have nearly the whole contents of his bedroom in the bag but let Rachel go through and sort out what he really needed.

It was just over a year since Mike had nearly lost his life in the floods, and it had made himself and Rachel think hard about what they wanted. Rachel had never really been out of Queensland except for the trip to Scone looking for Smokey. Then, six months after Mike's recovery, Jack and Tilly turned up with the twins. Jack had enough working at the mines and wondered if Mike would give him a job. Mike was delighted, and it didn't take them long to build an extension onto Alma and Ted's cottage; Caleb and the twins were great mates, and Jack and Tilly fitted in well. It meant that Mike and Rachel could go travelling if they wanted to. Rachel was still homeschooling Caleb anyway, and she could do that from anywhere.

The accident had taken a heavy toll on Mike. Though he didn't like to admit it, his lungs were still feeling the effects of the pneumonia, and he still had a hacking cough, though it was getting better. So they had decided to go and, having bought a big new motorhome, were off the next day via the Grimshaw's place. They were staying there a few days, and Henry was looking forward to spending time with Caleb. The two of them had a special bond. Then across to the N.T., and on to W.A., and seeing Clarrie and Emma and Ben. Then they would work their way home again and no doubt, after a rest, set off once more.

Mike came across to where Rachel and Caleb were. Ruby was sitting watching, wagging her tail. 'Bed early tonight, young man, big day tomorrow.'

'Many big days to come too, I think', said Rachel reaching up and kissing Mike. 'I am one lucky woman to be going travelling with the two best men in the world.'

Shawline Publishing Group Pty Ltd

www.shawlinepublishing.com.au

SHAWLINE PUBLISHING GROUP

CPSIA information can be obtained
at www.ICGtesting.com
Printed in the USA
LVHW030913061121
702610LV00016B/817

9 781922 594587